BIRDING

Also by Rose Ruane

This is Yesterday

BIRDING
ROSE RUANE

corsair

CORSAIR

First published in Great Britain in 2024 by Corsair

1 3 5 7 9 10 8 6 4 2

A CIP catalogue record for this book
is available from the British Library.

HB ISBN: 978-1-4721-5800-0

Typeset in Bembo by M Rules
Printed and bound in Great Britain by
Clays Ltd, Elcograf S.p.A.

Papers used by Corsair are from well-managed forests
and other responsible sources.

Corsair
An imprint of
Little, Brown Book Group
Carmelite House
50 Victoria Embankment
London EC4Y 0DZ

An Hachette UK Company
www.hachette.co.uk

www.littlebrown.co.uk

For all my sisters and siblings in this world: no matter how you have been made to feel in the past, you are beautiful, you are loved, you are enough, and you are perfect exactly as you are.

'You become responsible, forever,
for what you have tamed.'

ANTOINE DE SAINT-EXUPÉRY,
The Little Prince

Prologue

In a small seaside town, autumn is winnowing into winter and two women – strangers – are as yet unaware their lives are about to collide.

This town is a sentence of buildings scribbled along the deckled edge of an estuary, where the ribcages of old boats jut from the mud at low tide.

It's not on the way to anywhere else. It is the final stop on the railway line; a place of last years and lost souls.

People come here because they've run out of time or money, imagination or hope.

Some come here because they're running away. Others have lived in this town so long they can't imagine home meaning any place but this one.

People come here to see the edges and endings of things.

Here, hours pass sluggishly. The short days feel long; drowsed out in boredom, frustration and comfort. Rain mutters against windows and lamps are lit long before the evening news begins.

Here, cold leaches into every corner and bone.

Steel sea and cement sky meet in a bleak, flat Rothko. Gulls skid across its face, shrieks like sleet.

Turnstones and sanderlings hunch on the groynes, muffle into their plumpness, waiting for the sea to recede as squalls shove oily waves towards the perfunctory beach. Cans and carrier bags, sweet wrappers and nylon rope compact into the shingle. Litter collects on the steps up to the wide promenade, where pound shops, pubs and shabby attractions punctuate strips of empty units, creating a half-shut, hardscrabble atmosphere.

Beyond the beach, streets lined with terraces and bungalows crouch behind Victorian buildings with mid-century interiors; carved up into bedsits and B&Bs, their pastel facades crumble like stale cake after a party.

At one end of town, there are docks where cranes lift containers off ships the size of islands. Lorries whisk them away to huge distribution centres that hulk facelessly among flat fields inland.

On the quayside, stern-faced herring gulls rove, scavenging through mounds of trawler net with lethal yellow beaks. Ducks paddle aimlessly between boxy fishing vessels in the harbour.

Industrial noise and fishy smells leak from black huts and metal-sided buildings. People wearing wellingtons and rubber aprons heft polystyrene cases packed with ice and seafood onto trucks.

At the other end of town is a pier. It looks like a creature in its death throes; wounded and skeletal.

Seabirds roost in the helter-skelter, crusting the sides with stalactites of guano.

The plastic Astroglide is streaky and cracked. At the foot of its buckled stairs, coconut mats are littered like junk mail in an empty house.

The building at the entrance still contains a flashing, deafening arcade, a rowdy bar and snooker hall. The decades have slowly turned its name sarcastic.

The Palace.

Once, it was *the* place to go: three floors of dining and entertainment, grandly decorated and luxuriously carpeted.

Once, people dressed up in their Sunday best to eat Steak Diane by candlelight, foxtrot to live music in the ballroom, applaud magic shows and comedians in the theatre.

Now the carpet is sticky and threadbare, traipsed by people in leisurewear on their way to neck pints and feed coins into fruit machines. They stumble out hours later with light pockets, looking seasick.

Over the last few decades, cheap foreign holidays have demoted this resort to a day-trip destination.

For half the year, the beach is populated by plovers and curlews mooching the tideline, but from late April to early October, people *do* visit.

On bank holidays and sunny Saturdays, visitors stream from the station carrying bags of swimwear and sandwiches. They meander through sweet shops and amusements, potter and paddle on the beach, before boarding the last train home with sunburnt shoulders and stomachs full of chips.

Coaches bring dwindling groups of pensioners to holiday in hotels where the food remains unacquainted with garlic or spices and a glass of fruit juice can still be ordered as a starter.

Then, after autumn half-term, bitter gales deport the summer scent of hot fat and sugar, leaving brine and chill in their wake.

Hotels empty. Behind darkened dining-room windows, fanned napkins sit in wineglasses, gathering dust.

Snack bars and bucket shops shut. Each spring, fewer re-open.

Over at Funland, the fairground, colourful lights are extinguished, the rides are tarpaulined and the shutter is pulled down over the entrance, revealing a large graffitied penis, mid-ejaculation. Last week, somebody daubed on an even bigger swastika.

Above all this, knife-thin light makes it impossible to discern early morning from late afternoon.

This ashen gloom falls across a statue that squats at the centre of an unloved and unlovely flowerbed. It depicts a smiling, swimsuit-clad woman, sitting astride a beachball, gesturing towards the sea with her raised right arm.

Everyone calls her the 'Come On In Girl', this anonymous white-bread bathing belle whose parted thighs and placid smile have become as familiar as McDonald's golden arches or a stop sign.

She was created to advertise train trips to this town. During the summer of '53, from station billboards the length of the land, the Come On In Girl waved heedlessly as horns and Hitler moustaches were scrawled all over her face. She continued simpering, though speech bubbles forced obscenities into her mouth and anatomical details of varying accuracy accumulated on top of her modest red one-piece.

All through the autumn of 2004, she beckoned from posters in the London Underground, as thousands of commuters drifted past her emptily encouraging smile, repeated and repeated up the length of the escalators, this time publicising an exhibition about the history of the British seaside.

Since then, she's been printed on T-shirts, tea towels, tote bags and mugs. From fridge magnets, fascist gifs captioned 'Fuck Off Out' and the hand-painted signage of a queer feminist book shop called Come On In, Girl!, she goes on

4

waving and smiling; fiercely wholesome, blandly blonde and unthreateningly pretty.

In 2009, a grimacing, ham-fisted statue of her was erected on the promenade to commemorate the centenary of her male creator's birth.

For all these years, she has sat in her litter-strewn flowerbed, straddling a beach-ball, emblazoned now with a Tippex swastika, hair highlighted with streaks of bird shit, bronze breasts rubbed shiny as bomb casings by all the hands that have groped them.

The platonic ideal of a fun girl who never minds or moans, never farts or ages.

Her smile never falters. She never says no.

All she ever does is issue the same invitation, to everyone who passes by: Come. On. In.

Chapter 1

Maybe it started eleven months ago, in the coffee shop, when Henry finally said sorry to Lydia.

Maybe it started years previously, in poky flats and rented rooms where Henry did . . . well, whatever Henry did.

When he inflicted whatever harms his abstruse, equivocating apology invited Lydia to absolve him of.

Lydia still can't fit a name to them.

Maybe it started almost three decades before, on the day Lydia stood surrounded by pigeons in Leicester Square, hugging her best friend and bandmate Pandora, looking up at a reproduction of their album cover – a mugshot-style photo of them under the words *The Lollies Are Legal*, wearing nothing but knickers and cheesecake expressions and holding identity placards over their bare breasts – displayed on a billboard the size of a double-decker bus.

Maybe it started the day that photo was taken, when Lydia and Pandora, all of nineteen, overheard the photographer telling the make-up artist to, 'Get some slap on those eyebags; they're meant to be jailbait and they look fucking ancient.' Or when he sighed, lowered his camera, and told them to, 'Lez it up a bit, look like you're enjoying yourselves,' and they did.

Maybe it even started the first time no one said, 'You don't have to,' or 'It's not your fault.'

Or maybe, it simply starts the day you're born and all the becoming begins right then.

Lydia is contemplating this, staring at the statue which always looks to her like a drowning woman trying to catch the attention of a lifeguard, when a restive sparrow lands on the Come On In Girl's gesturing hand.

Lydia lifts her phone, zooms in, frames; catches the shot just as the tiny bird takes flight.

She looks at the photo and is pleased. The dun fans of the bird's wings are spread, scratchy wire feet not yet quite tucked, almost drawn into its body like the wheels of an ascending jet, the distance from bird to bronze in perfect golden ratio, a sliver of sky inside the gap.

Look to the beauty: that's Lydia's mantra, though it's becoming harder to heed and sounding hollower and more fragile every day. Increasingly, the world appears to her all shell: a Kinder egg containing no toy. But she knows if only she can force herself to dwell in the minute poetries and pathos of the everyday, then she can better bear the agony she's been in for almost a year now.

She posts the picture on Twitter and Insta, annotated with some trite but appealing observation about escape and freedom. The comments from her substantial number of followers begin to climb right away:

Love this Lydia *heart emoji* *bird emoji*

Great shot *camera emoji*

Gorgeous, needed this today, thank you x

Trio of heart-eyed smiley emojis

Pleasure sparks, falters and fades within seconds, like a cheap light-up novelty with spent batteries. Her photo ceases to symbolise hope, becoming content more than communication. And once again, she's wondering what the fuck she is doing in this town.

She's been here nearly two months; an unplanned weekend break that slouched into a permanent state of temporariness. As if that couldn't be said to describe her entire life up to the late August day when Pandora called out of the blue.

Pandora was the last person Lydia had wanted to talk to, but some animal impulse to survive made her answer the phone. She had recognised it as her only chance.

For days, death had been ranging round her head.

She'd stopped imagining afterwards, stopped caring who might be sorry, wasn't envisioning the uneasy collision of her parents and friends around her lily-topped coffin, had ceased compiling the soundtrack of exit songs.

Lying by a sealed envelope without a name on it and a litre of vodka, Lydia simply wanted to unhappen and un-be. She imagined only the relief of thinking and feeling nothing after months suffocating in hell's own Matryoshka of doubt, recursively dismantling and restacking the nested questions Henry had crammed into her head in that coffee shop months ago.

But then the phone rang.

Lydia knows she accepted the call and made a noise. Maybe she tried to say 'Hi' or 'Pan', but what came out was as much spasm as sound.

She hardly remembers anything else. Just vivid, disjointed

flashes: throwing clothes into a bag; the train pulling out of London through the suburbs as a low gold sun unravelled bolts of navy shadow across the pavements; thinking, *It's beginning to be autumn, and maybe I'll feel the first cold day of it after all.*

But she does recall watching the city's outermost edgelands spool by, the train's fluorescent interior superimposed on the retail parks and playing fields, each abstracting the other, as an imagined cold elided with a remembered one.

The brumous January morning, creeping towards a year ago, when Lydia walked into a coffee shop near London Bridge to meet Henry and walked out almost two hours later, feeling like a shell of the person who entered.

So much easier to conjure the irrelevant details of the place: the way the seating was unabashedly designed to discourage lingering; the contrived, brittle friendliness of the barista that made Lydia feel more of a nuisance than if he'd been openly rude; the raucous laughter of a stranger – joyous while Lydia was waiting for Henry to arrive, violent as a plate being smashed by the time he'd embarked on his quibbling, self-interested monologue.

Henry took a deep breath, as though knocking back a shot of Dutch courage, and said, 'So listen, mate, I've been thinking and I reckon we need to talk.'

Lydia thought, *Shit.* Felt the word as a gut clench or the nasty sweaty sparkle preceding a faint.

Everything fatal and slow, the way time extends for the occupants of a crashing car. Lydia had an almost leisurely capacity to observe minute details: pastries arranged on artisanal wooden boards on the counter, a woman fumbling in her bag for her purse and disgorging a wad of sanitary towels instead.

Lydia knew, she just *knew*, what was about to happen, as soon as Henry – the most assiduously avoidant human she'd ever encountered – said, 'We need to talk.'

The subject had been everywhere: opinion pieces, hashtags, news reports. Everyone Lydia knew had been discussing men like Henry who had done things to women like her.

In the months prior, no matter how it sickened her, Lydia had felt compelled to guzzle down all the hot-and cold-running horror in the papers, on the internet, and everywhere. And the whole time, she'd wished her only thought was, *Great, they're getting these bastards*.

But that had not been Lydia's only thought.

To her shame, she'd found herself hoping it wouldn't happen to Henry.

For various reasons, she'd been increasingly sure for years that she's not the only one he has . . . *done things to*.

And yet, she'd prayed it wouldn't happen to him.

In fact, Lydia had already decided that what happened between them in the past deserved to remain there, even though it could be news.

It really *could be* news.

Because one of the ways in which Henry could be considered *one of those men* is that almost everyone Lydia knows probably knows who Henry is.

He's famous.

Albeit in an artsy, niche way.

But he *is* famous.

Lydia clung to her coffee cup, which at that moment felt like the only solid thing in the world, wishing she was thinking, *Finally,* finally, *he is acknowledging that what he did was wrong*.

But she wasn't.

She was thinking *shit, shit, shit, shit, shit, shit* ... freefalling through the sibilants as if her head was a Word document filling with hundreds upon hundreds of italicised *shits*, watching a brown frill of bubbles shrink from the edge of her undrunk coffee as Henry flourished his tepid semi of contrition like it was a generous gift.

In reality, he was handing her Pandora's box with the lid half-off and it was inevitable that all the rage and humiliation Lydia had stashed inside herself would come marauding out.

So, months before she entered the coffee shop, and certainly since she left it, Lydia's been mired in making and remaking the decision not to count Henry as one of *those* men. Not quite, not really. Or at least believing that even if he had been once, he was not any more.

Even now, guiltily, grudgingly, she admires him for realising on his own, without being told, that he *could* be thought of as *one of those men*.

And yet, when she thinks about what Henry said that day about her possible perceptions of his past behaviour, Lydia is still not sure she's capable of distinguishing realisation from revelation.

She *is* sure the distinction is important. She thinks, maybe, one's *engaged in*, the other *inflicted upon*, so it matters how reluctantly the participant became willing.

She's still not sure if she was willing. She only knows that when Henry apologised, she couldn't tell him there was nothing to apologise for.

Lydia remembers that, as the train finally pulled into the seaside station two months ago, she'd been picturing the hurt, astonished look on Henry's face when Lydia did not, *could not*, tell him that he was unlike those other men.

As she stepped onto the platform, she'd performed a dazed,

cartoonish head shake to disperse the tormenting mirage, smelling the unmistakable salty briskness of the coast; sharp cold delivering itself to her cheeks, smart as a soap-opera slap.

Only two other people disembarked, both in business wear, faces sallow with fatigue and moving with unmistakable homegoing hurry. Lydia futzed about with Google Maps, watching the pulsing beacon onscreen face the opposite direction from the one she needed to walk in, and turned back.

Under a street lamp's amber shower, a swirl of wind strewed a crisp confetti of yellow leaves through the light. Lydia reorientated herself, finding her way down a shuttered shopping street towards the promenade, where the warm orange glow of Pandora's new home had been visible. The freshly built glass box burned like a beacon on top of The Hotel Duchesse Royale – a run-down Victorian building on the seafront that Pan was planning to renovate and relaunch as a chichi boutique destination.

Blundering into the reception, Lydia found Pan perched on an eczematic Chesterfield, scrolling her phone.

Lydia had barely noticed the drabness, the dispiriting atmosphere or damp; she'd simply crumpled into Pan's arms and begun to sob.

'Tell me everything,' Pan had said, with her lips against Lydia's unwashed hair.

And Lydia hadn't, because as soon as Henry admitted fault, she understood that confiding could mean what happened would become another smouldering garbage bag on the unchecked trash fire everyone knows about, leaving Lydia holding the match.

Trash fire: she hates that that ugly internet-ism is the phrase she defaults to. Apt enough until she parses it, with its false equivalency between abuser and abused – flames aren't fussy, consuming Argos catalogues and albums full of family photos just the same. Everything's indiscernible once it's ash.

But, that's how it would be: the conflagration would consume Lydia as well as Henry, and it would burn through Henry's family and hers, Henry's friends and hers. And Henry's fans, who find solace and enjoyment in his work, would have that taken away from them.

Lydia would be doing all those things to all those people if she spoke to the wrong person. Or maybe anyone at all.

Sharing a secret is like coughing on the Tube: once those microbes are out of your mouth, they're out of your control, infectious and unstoppable, no matter how you might wish you could suck them back in.

Then there's every chance Lydia would have to read about herself being discussed as if she is an argument, an abstract idea, a story and probably a liar, a bandwagon jumper, a publicity seeker and a filthy whore who was asking for it.

So she'd just described her suffering to Pan in terms of loneliness and lostness; some nebulous, middle-aged mental-health crisis reaching terminal velocity that seemed to reflect Pan's perception of how shitty Lydia's life was anyway.

'Tracks,' Pan had said, with a down-mouthed clown face. 'That tracks, Lydie, love.'

And Lydia had noticed nothing happened behind Pan's eyes as she topped up Lydia's wine glass, just a hollow sort of 'sucks to be you'.

And that sharky blankness confirmed Lydia's suspicion that telling her would be setting Pan up to fail and herself up to be failed; it would add to the unspoken between them. The old avoidance of addressing the past, tiptoeing round each other, on the edge of a hole, shying from sharing confidences that might threaten to nudge them in.

Now Lydia's loneliness is even more pronounced by Pan's proximity. The terrible friendless feeling follows Lydia everywhere and it seems like she'll never stop being angry with everyone for not relieving her of a burden she has shared with no one.

Enough, she thinks. *Enough.*

Enough: the word she wields like scissors, trying to sever the threads that hold her in these sticky webs of rumination. She imagines it as a full stop to her thoughts: ink black, final and freeing. But it always sprouts a comma's curved tail, and the miserable meditation mithers on.

She stands and gazes disconsolately down the promenade, taking in empty shops and intimidating pubs, the scrawl of rollercoaster track at Funland, the narrow smear of beach.

Litter mooches along the pavement and the sheer nothingness of it all makes Lydia's heart feel like a dead fist clenched in her chest. She begins to walk back towards the bleak betwixt of The Hotel Duchesse Royale, wishing she'd picked up her headphones so she could at least make this kind of funny by listening to 'Every Day Is Like Sunday'.

But right now, Lydia feels like she will never find anything funny ever again.

Right now, Lydia feels resentment and hurt blooming inside her like mould.

Right now, she's convinced she'll never recover the ability to enjoy a split-second's unawareness of the fact that she is someone to whom *things have happened.* To whom things have been *done.*

Beset by a pain and rage so visceral, dramatic and bodily that she wants to drop onto all fours and howl like a wolf at the moon, Lydia looks back over her shoulder at the Come On In Girl.

The statue grows smaller, further away with each step, still manically waving, grit-toothed grin fixed even as the gull swaggering about on her head releases a long, thick money shot of shit.

How satisfying it would be to bulldoze it over. Flattening her would feel like doing her a favour. Putting the poor bitch out of her misery.

Trauma scrawls itself all over everything, Lydia thinks. And it is loyal as an old dog; humiliation twice as faithful. She understands the kindest thing that can be done for an old dog at the end. Walk into a room with a pet, exit holding a collar.

She's not sure who the dog is in this metaphor.

Henry?

Herself?

The situation?

All she's sure of is that months ago, in a coffee shop, Henry strapped Lydia into a suicide vest, condemning her to wear its threatening heft as privately as an undergarment.

Although, Lydia does know where the detonator is.

Finger on the fuck-it button, she grasps the phone in her pocket. Thirty-five thousand followers. One tweet.

Withdrawing her hand, the frost-sharp air bites.

She's nowhere close to sending the message she's written and deleted at least ten times a day for months.

Or at least not yet.

Anyway, how could Lydia possibly do that?

In spite of everything, Henry is still her friend.

Chapter 2

'Not nice behaviour, Joyce. Don't be greedy,' says Betty, Joyce's mother. 'Start with a Rich Tea and work up.'

'Sorry, Mum.' Joyce's apology comes instinctively as throat clearing. 'I just fancied a little taste of chocolate.'

Joyce doesn't know what's got into her. Chocolate Digestives aren't a starter biscuit. Nice people have a plain biscuit first – it displays restraint and shows that you're decent.

Niceness, decency and each other are all Joyce and Betty have.

Once, they had another life in a big villa up on the cliffs above town, filled with chic new fashions, furniture and party guests. They lived there with Daddy, who disappeared; whose unexplained absence of two-and-a-half decades Betty refuses to discuss.

Joyce's memories of who Daddy was, who they all were back then, are as stilled and unseeable as koi under thick ice on a frozen pond.

They did have koi, they did have a pond, gnome-ringed with crazy-paved sides.

They had flowerbeds and a sun terrace where Joyce and her mother used to drowse each summer, tanning on a pair of patterned loungers as the distant whoops from Funland floated up, reminding Joyce that people her own age were down in town, doing things she was forbidden to; roaming in packs, drinking on the beach, lying down together under the pier after dark.

Joyce must avoid the sticky flypaper of these recollections. She must merge placidly with the rote existence she shares with her mother. They live as best they can, moving through the hours with the stolid thoughtlessness of clock hands.

They live in a one-bedroomed flat in a bland brick block, four streets back from the promenade. Big, old furniture salvaged from the villa crowds the narrow rooms. Side by side, their twin beds idle under flouncy satin counterpanes.

Days pass, one at a time, like candles methodically snuffed. Weeks and months and years appear and disappear over the horizon like container ships and cruise liners. And Joyce tries hard not to count them or wonder where they go.

Just like Daddy.

On the few occasions Joyce does try to reminisce about him, Betty contradicts her on every minor detail. 'You can't keep things right in your head, Joycey,' she says.

And it's true.

Maybe truer than ever.

That's why she and Mum need their routine. Shopping, home hairdressing, skincare and housework, their meals and programmes; activities that keep life proper, in spite of their diminished circumstances.

Every day, when Betty and Joyce return home from the shops, they shroud their matching dresses in plastic wrappers, inter them in the wardrobe and put their mules and housecoats on. With *circumstances* being as they are, Betty deems it best to protect their out-and-about things, riddled already with mends, from excessive laundering. The repairs are deftly done, cleverly concealed, but nonetheless dismaying.

Afterwards, in their tiny kitchen, Betty and Joyce lay the tea tray.

While the kettle boils, they put milk in the pretty jug and biscuits on a bone china plate, then place those on a doily.

There being only the two of them is no excuse for slovenliness.

Someone could come to the door at any time.

If a person was to discover Betty and Joyce pouring milk from the plastic container and eating biscuits directly from the packet, they'd think: *These people are not nice.*

These people have let themselves go.

These people must have nothing to live for.

Joyce puts the biscuit back on the plate. A thumbprint in the chocolate, chocolate on her thumb.

Joey, Betty's budgie, *scrat-scrats* in his cage, beak worrying the bars.

Betty is still going, very cross this morning: 'Chocolate makes you porky, Joyce. You know you've a tendency to get thick-waisted. Not attractive, being a porky pig.'

She makes some oinking noises.

'Have a Rich Tea. Now, as I was saying, before you rudely interrupted, wasn't she a nasty little thing? Common. Anyway, she had that gorgeous doll in her fist, and she was shouting . . . Do it, Joyce, you be the girl.'

They are going over the terrible palaver in the shop this morning. Step by step, replaying the scene in order to identify what went wrong. How *Joyce* caused the situation to go awry.

Joyce tells Betty, 'Sorry.'

She asks if they can't just leave it.

'Absolutely not.'

Betty speaks with the solemnity of a judge handing down a tough-but-fair sentence. 'We have to be clear about your mistake.'

Joyce tells her mother that she does feel clear. Very clear and very sorry.

She doesn't tell her that she also feels as if wasps are blundering around behind her face. That lately, without understanding why, Joyce feels this way every time Betty opens her mouth.

But Betty says *she* is not clear. 'Not at all, and I won't be until we go through the events as they happened. So now you be the girl and say the things I told you to say so we can see where you went wrong. Joyce? *Joyce.*'

'Look at the dolly, Daddy, look at her dress,' Joyce sighs.

Betty tuts. Having dispatched her Rich Tea, she advances to a Custard Cream and carries on. 'The father – unshaven, naturally, and I'm sure I caught the smell of drink – said, "She's nice," and the girl . . . '

Betty clears her throat.

Joyce fills her mouth with tea and holds it there.

'You be the girl again, Joyce, and say, *Can I get her?*'

Joyce swallows her tea. 'May we buy her?'

'Not like that, Joyce. Like a peasant.'

'Can I get her, please?'

'No "please", Joyce. You're the girl and you're not nice.'

'Can I get her?'

'"How much?" he said, and I said, because by this point, I could not hold my peace any longer, I said, perfectly pleasantly, "Careful now, sweetie, she's not really a dolly." And he said, "You what?" And now it's your turn, Joyce. Do it properly. Like I told you.'

Betty is talking in her crystal voice: clear and classy, with sharp edges that forbid careless handling.

Joyce asks, as her mother informed her the child had, 'How is she not a dolly, Daddy?' And turns to Betty: 'You're silly. She *is* a dolly.'

Betty smiles tightly. 'The sauce! Honestly, would you believe it? So, I said: "That's not the way we speak to grown-ups, poppet. She's an ornament, she's china. For looking at, not for little girls to play with." This is no good, Joyce. Go and get one of the girls, I'll have to show you.'

The girls eye Joyce. Their girls, their collection.

China dolls fill the living room. Shelves upon shelves lining every wall, neat rows of white porcelain faces, glass eyes in watchful lines, pouty-painted mouths. Fussy Victorian dresses, matching hats and coats. Lace and velvet and frills and ringlets. Small cold hands, tiny plastic shoes.

Back when Joyce and Betty and Daddy lived in the villa, Betty kept Persian cats and yappy pedigree dogs. Fussy, irascible trip-hazards with names like Mitzi and Lulu. But since the move, the ... downturn in fortunes, Joey the budgie and the ever-expanding crèche of china children have had to suffice.

Betty scans the ranks, 'One of the lesser girls, I think. Maybe Petra.'

Joyce reaches up for Petra.

'No, Joyce, actually, bring me Dorothy. She's more servant class with the mob cap.'

Lifting Dorothy from her stand, Joyce smooths the doll's apron and touches its chestnut curls. Supporting its head as carefully as a real child's, she hands the doll to Betty.

As her mother takes the doll, a sinking, sunset sensation yawns in Joyce's heart.

Betty weighs Dorothy in her hands, looking her over with the mean, idle scrutiny of a tyre-kicker. '"Seems like a doll to me, missus," he said – the father this was. *Missus* said with a very unpleasant edge. But I stayed very calm, extremely good-natured, of course, and told him, "Well, of course it's a doll. Not a doll to play with though; it's an ornament, a collector's item. I collect them myself." "Worth something is it? Antique?" he sniffed, and I could just see the pound signs in his eyes.'

Betty snorts derisively and carries on, '"No," I told him, "it's not worth a lot, but to a connoisseur like myself it's worth having." I told him I would buy it for my daughter. That's you, Joyce.'

Betty points to Joyce as though she might need to be reminded of the fact, and rattles on.

'"Your daughter?" said the beast. "You said it wasn't a toy. Kayleigh?" That's what the girl was called. *Kayleigh*. What sort of a name is that, Joyce? Sounds like being sick. He said, "Kayleigh, do you want the dolly? Daddy will buy you the dolly."

'"They like all the Sindys and the Barbies these days," I told him. "It's not a toy," I said. "She'll break it and it will be ruined and, and, besides, it's not safe for a little girl." I said, "It's not safe, you see. It's china, it could break. If *Kayleigh* was running with the doll and she fell, it could smash, and, if she fell onto the smashed parts she'd be hurt, then this lovely doll would be ruined—" and he cut me off.'

Betty pantomimes the man's laugh.

'"You what?" he said. "You just want this doll, you mad old—"' Betty tosses her dyed black mane, 'Mad, Joyce, *old*? I said, "How dare you?" I said, "People these days," and that's when you came in, Joyce. Pay close attention to your conduct here, it's the most important part.'

While this was beginning in the charity shop, Joyce had been taking her time. Walking along the prom as slowly as she could, stockpiling solitude, watching her breath gather in frosty clouds.

A tanker had been hulking along the horizon line. On the scrappy beach, a lone dog-walker hunched against the wind, throwing a tennis ball for a collie.

In the bandstand, gaunt people in tracksuits passed a bottle around, smoking.

Joyce had been glad her mother wasn't there to see them. They would have set her off; they only just avoided a scene in the Post Office.

It was the group of young men. Shabby shoes and cigarette smells. Loud voices, speaking another language. Betty had been making the noise that denoted she was gestating remarks. A hen cluck, informing Joyce she was about to start.

She'd said, breezily – Joyce knows she always has to go in *breezily* – 'The queue's awfully long, Mum. Why don't you pop along to our nice shops and I'll wait here.'

Betty had done sucky mouth, which meant she was swilling her thoughts around like a wine taster, then agreed the queue was unbearably long, nowhere has the staff these days, and clicked off in her patent court shoes.

While prolonging the cold and quiet, Joyce had noticed two middle-aged women walking with their arms linked, laughing.

Look at the state of them, Joyce had thought. *They've let themselves go*. Frumpy anoraks, training shoes and mannish

22

haircuts, raucous laughter. *They are not* nice. And yet the sight of them had incited a malnourished feeling in her guts.

Joyce had still been chewing over the thought, like gum that had long lost its flavour, when she'd wandered into the charity shop, unprepared to find Betty in the thick of one of her little contretemps.

When Joyce entered, she saw the man and the girl do the double-take she's used to. 'Jealous,' Betty always says. 'Inferior people stare because they resent how poorly our attention to detail reflects on their own slack habits.'

But Joyce knows people stare because she and her mother wear identical outfits and hairstyles, attired as if they are twins.

Dresses, always dresses, never trousers; their coats and bags and court shoes; long hair home-permed, dyed jet-black; their make-up, like two doll masks painted in the same factory. Very nice, very decent, seamlessly matched. A lifetime's habit of exactitude Joyce never used to question.

But it has begun to feel stuffy and constricting, as if Joyce is outgrowing all her clothes. Now a circus sensation of freak-show foolishness tails her everywhere, and when her mother isn't looking, she lingers in shops by the racks of denim and runs her fingers over the soft fabric of casual sweaters.

The gas fire putters and whines.

The bars of the birdcage vibrate as Joey gnaws them.

'So, he said . . . Joyce! Joyce?'

'Yes?'

'This awful man said – and you *allowed him* – said, "Your mum's mental, love." And I was still charming, Joyce. I rose above the insult. I said to you: "Darling, this gentleman and I were just discussing this doll." And he said, "Excuse me, missus, but I'm about to buy that." And very gently, Joyce, as

I'm sure you'll agree, I took the doll from him and told him it's not a toy.'

Betty slips Dorothy from one hand to the other. '"It's not a toy, it's a collector's item, which my daughter and I collect, and *I* am going to buy it." Now Joyce, get ready here, just let's examine what you do.' Betty turns to Joyce, 'I say, "What do you think, Joyce? Shall we buy her?" And you say . . .'

'Well, she's . . .'

'"Yes, she *is* lovely, Joyce." And that man snatches – ' Betty strangles Dorothy ' – he snatches her and says, "I'm buying this for my daughter, you effing—" Oh my goodness, Joyce, the language! And you say . . .'

A meaty beat of silence.

'Tell me what you said, Joyce Wilson.'

'I said, "Let's just go, Mum. Let's go home and I'll make you a nice cup of tea."'

'There we are, Joyce. Do you see? *Unbelievable.* Letting that awful man speak to me like that. All that commotion. The doll wasn't even anything special. Joyce Susan Elizabeth Wilson, I am cross with you. Put the television on, we've missed the start of *Escape to the Country.*'

Joyce switches the television on: colour and light flood the screen.

A couple, younger than Betty and older than Joyce, are picking out a cottage to retire to. Normally Betty would have plenty to say about the woman's broad bottom and the man's tatty fleece. About the idiocy of their house-buying criteria or the ugliness of the decor. But today she emits thunderous silence.

Tight air squeezes words out of Joyce: 'Look at this one, Mum. It's so pretty. I'd love a little cottage like that.'

Betty glares at the television.

'Isn't the garden gorgeous?' Joyce continues. 'Look at the roses. I'd love to have a garden and grow roses.'

'Oh, would you indeed?'

'Yes, and I'd have pretty flowerbeds, a wishing well and—'

'And who would do the gardening, Joyce?' Betty raises an eyebrow.

'Well, I expect . . . maybe, I—'

'You need a man for gardening. And you haven't got a man.'

'I was only imagining . . . a garden. Like our old one.'

Mistake! Mistake to mention the old garden, the old house, old anything.

Mistake to ever mention life before. An error Joyce keeps committing lately. Memories have started to press against the surface of her thoughts in a way they never used to.

'What a scene you made in that shop, Joyce, and now you're talking all through my programme. About our old garden no less, when you know it makes me ill to dwell on our . . . *circumstances*. Inconsiderate, rude. You are extremely rude to talk over my programme.'

In Joyce, an intense thrumming like a train arriving, like breakers whipped by a storm. She picks up the chocolate biscuit with her thumbprint on it and pushes the whole thing into her mouth. Pushes it and mashes it, fills her cheeks and lets crumbs fall into her lap.

'*Dis*-gusting, Joyce!' says Betty. 'What is wrong with you?'

Sound shoves at the biscuit pulp. There is a sentence that begins with 'I' and Joyce is glad that there is a plug of Chocolate Digestive between whatever the words are and her mother.

'That's it, Joyce,' says Betty. 'Consider yourself sent to Coventry.'

As the sweet mass seals Joyce's mouth, she finds herself wondering what it's like in Coventry.

Or anywhere else at all really.

Joyce stands. She drifts over to the small window in the corner of the living room, where – if she angles herself correctly, side on, teetering on tiptoes – Joyce can just about glimpse a scrap of the sea.

Chapter 3

'Fuck, Lyd, my fanny absolutely stinks. Honestly, it smells like Scampi Fries.'

Pan is sitting on the chicly hovering pill of a toilet while Lydia wallows in the vast bathtub, haloed by designer candles.

Their flames totter as Lydia laughs. 'Classy bitch.'

Lydia had been contemplating a new little flap of sagginess under her breast, pinching and rolling it between her fingers, when Pandora wafted in without knocking.

Sitting upright with a slosh, Lydia had thrown an arm over her breasts, reached for a towel, then wondered, *Why bother?*

Lydia looks over at Pan with her knickers stretched between her knees, perceiving her as a palimpsest: the curvy cutie-pie girl she knew, aged into a harder, handsome beauty. A more compelling and complex attractiveness about her now.

Deft highlights make Pan's hair look glossily sun-kissed rather than bleached, her subtle cosmetic interventions hardly tell; she has gym-toned arms and wears clothes whose cut mutters money and taste despite their lack of ostentation. Yet something of her youthful scrappiness still appears as an edge, creating the impression that Pan could both charm at a society gathering and handle herself in a Wetherspoon's brawl.

Lydia's taste has always tended towards the bright, the garish even, but for the last few months she has worn more muted colours: lots of black, like winter plumage.

Since the whole thing with Henry, she's swapped dresses and skirts for trousers and inflicted an undercut on her once blonde, now mousy hair. It made her feel like an invincible Boudica for the first few weeks, but is now growing back in a way that makes her look as if she's recovering from brain surgery.

A wave of dismay overtakes Lydia. Pan was always the prettier – emitted an unforced erotic air, still does – whereas Lydia has always had to summon something, imagine herself under the desiring gaze of another, to feel sexy.

Now she's deep into her forties, the mirror confirms what Lydia always suspected – her kind of beauty was contingent on youth.

First, ageing downgraded beautiful to pretty, now prettiness has depreciated into a sort of bland pleasantness that's impossible to get excited about.

At parties, people Lydia has met on multiple occasions introduce themselves, leading her to conclude she has one of those inoffensive faces which is hard to summon when she isn't present. A self-deleting face that evaporates from people's consciousness the minute Lydia departs.

Earlier, craving a little vitamin shot of validation, she'd tried to take a selfie to post on Instagram, but no amount of chasing the light and angling the camera produced anything she felt comfortable sharing.

I look like I've been over-inflated then left to leak, she thought: dull skin and deep crow's feet as if she's fallen asleep on a fork. Jowls. Something flaccid and froggy about her chin. The face Lydia once had changing places with the one she'll have in the future. A mixture of mulch and desiccation.

She's pretty sure she's perimenopausal. Her periods have become irregular, ovulation is more painful each month, inciting migraines, fluey fatigue and a blind bodily horn that makes her masturbate twice a day and promises that this is the end of her fertility. It's like that part of a fireworks display where the crescendo of rockets declares that it's almost over.

In bed at night, she cups a little flesh apron at her belly, the one so many of her friends have, but Lydia's lacks any meaning to pack the place under her skin.

She never meant not to have a baby but intention and opportunity always arrived asynchronously: each appeared without the other, like the occupants of a wooden weather house.

And she thinks it's probably fine. Good, actually. Probably, actually good, in fact, that she never became a mother, because when she inventories what she's missed, it's the belonging more than the baby. She feels fatuous and ephemeral as a balloon when she is around her friends who have children, lacking the solemn gravity parenthood seems to lend their existence.

Not that Lydia dwells on her childlessness that much – it's just one component of a greater loneliness – but listening to the erratic tinkle of Pan's piss hitting the water, Lydia is engulfed by affection for her. Cherishing the sibling familiarity accrued through adolescence, deepened by their two years on tour together as The Lollies.

Hard to conjure the brief period when that name meant a band – music and magical possibility, stardom not scandal. So difficult to remember the flight preceding the fall, before shame and pain overwrote whatever joys there had been.

But while all else has hazed away and turned foggy with

unspeaking, this ease around the physically intimate has remained, an enduring laxity that strikes Lydia as touching.

Pan twangs her gusset and vamps fascinated horror, 'I'm surprised the stink hasn't knocked you out. I think I need a vet, Lyd.'

'Can't smell it over the million quid's worth of scented wax on fire over here,' Lydia smiles.

Mistake. Mistake to mention money, even in light heart. Pandora talks at tedious length about the price of things but recoils from acknowledging their cost.

Pan pulls her pants up and stands abruptly, something open in her slamming like a door in a draft.

Affluence can't abide contrast, which arrives as accusation.

After the brief bright burn of the band and its prolonged dissolution, Pan had made a conventional success of her life while Lydia sank like a stone, tearing another hole in the fabric of their friendship. They'd pretended not to notice, until maintaining a veneer of equality became increasingly untenable, initiating their unremarked avoidance of one another.

Before Lydia's arrival at the hotel, her last meeting with Pan had been at least eighteen months prior, in a private member's club on Dean Street.

The concierge made Lydia wait just inside the door while someone summoned Pan down to vouch for her. The whole time, his eyes had browsed the blades of grass on Lydia's skirt, accumulated from lying in Soho square, drinking Polish lager, commiserating with a flat-broke writer friend who'd just been dumped by his boyfriend and dropped by his literary agent within the preceding forty-eight hours.

Lydia had breezed up to the club – first soft surf of tipsiness lapping her brain – feeling uncommonly warm towards her life, enjoying herself as someone who could switch seamlessly between cans in the park and celebrity haunts, experiencing the juxtaposition as a richness until the concierge deflated her with his high-handed treatment.

When Pan arrived after an age, Lydia had noticed the Snoopy smile she exchanged with the concierge, as if apologising for lowering the tone by signing Lydia in.

'We're up here,' she'd said while planting smackers in the air on either side of Lydia's face.

We had turned out to be the singer from a band who'd been on the up as The Lollies were on the down and his wife, who ran a Fortune 500 company.

'That Gucci?' She'd pinched a corner of Lydia's skirt.

'Primark.'

'Oh. Nice dupe.'

She'd brushed at the grass on Lydia's skirt, asking if she'd been mowing her lawn.

'Don't have one,' Lydia had replied, with much more truculence than she'd intended. The whole night had gone downhill from there, ending with Pan pushing Lydia's bank card back to her when the bill arrived, looking at it like she was trying to settle a real tab with toy money.

'Oh,' Pan had said, slipping her Coutts card into a calfskin wallet, 'that wine we've been drinking, our favourite, it's . . .' she left an eggy ellipsis ' . . . my treat.'

Meaning this little mid-week drinking session costs more than you make in a month.

And after that night, as if by mutual assent, Pan and Lydia's names moved further and further down the lists of messages on their phone screens, until they were no longer visible at all.

Then Pan rang Lydia out of the blue.

Now, halfway out the bathroom door, her features

31

assembled into a grave look of studied vulnerability, Pan says, 'I actually need to chat to you about something, sweets.'

Lydia knows this look. It's the Princess Diana, three-of-us-in-this-marriage face.

Jag in Lydia's heart, anxiety spike.

That calculated expression of frailty always puts Lydia in mind of the day Pan quit the band; triggers the same vertiginous sensation of events entering an earthward spiral.

Lydia starts grasping for the towel.

'No, you relax, enjoy your bath. There's about twenty quid's worth of Diptyque in there anyway. So gorgeous and really *strong* – all those flower essences and delish musks. I guess you totally forget how tiny a drop of it you need if you're normally a Radox gal. Remember how nuts we used to go with the products on the odd occasion we were put up in fancy-schmancy places back in the day? I suppose, when we were babies, we just never imagined we'd have such lush stuff in *our* places.'

Pan smirks pointedly at Lydia as she corrects herself, '*My* place. Anyway, one of my faves. Yours too, judging by the generous quantity of bubbles. Love that stuff. Yum. Heaven. Bliss! I'll fix us some drinks and see you in the lounge.'

She breezes out, leaving Lydia to feel snout-smacked, like a dog that's jumped on a sofa where it's not allowed.

Culpable, too. Pan wouldn't have said that bitchy shit if Lydia hadn't made a crack about the costliness of the candles.

Another undimmed intimacy between them: the knowing knuckle to the heart that easily finds its mark, deniable but definitely intended.

Not good, thinks Lydia. So able to express their understanding of each other in rough emotional horseplay, but not in open communication.

Humiliation always so near at hand nowadays; the soul-chafe invoking Henry.

Simultaneously Lydia asks and answers the question, *What am I doing here?*

When Pan called and discovered Lydia's distress, despite the distance and unease between them she'd simply said, 'Come. Come now.'

And Lydia had started packing.

Pan had always lent some of her apparent invincibility to Lydia. On stage she'd steadied her, even in the band's dying days, on tour supporting a bigger, all-male band. By then they were tarnished by the tabloid scandal over The Lollies' provocative artwork and album title. The audience watched in the spirit of a witch trial or day trip to Bedlam.

Every evening they endured shouts of 'Get your tits out!' and pints of yellow liquid thrown onstage, only some of which were lager.

Backstage, listening to the crowd bay as the backing track began, Lydia would say, 'I want to go home, I don't want to do this.'

While Pan would shrug, 'Fuck 'em. I came here to perform.'

That old energy had drawn Lydia here.

Pandora's attitude to all 'dreariness', everything painful, sad, ugly or unsavoury – from hangovers to her own parents' deaths – has always been: keep going, carry on moving, if you refuse to feel it, it can't be happening.

Even her own family nicknamed her 'Panzer division'.

Lydia has always been carried by Pan's sheer force of will; even when unsure if she's being bullied or beloved, Lydia's always ridden pillion on Pan's survival instinct.

But whereas Pan has perfected the art of utter denial, Lydia has not. It never works.

For a while, the change of scene had made the ... *thing,* the *situation,* the whole *business* with Henry, seem smaller, further away. She'd been able to believe she'd left it in London, that maybe it was not that big a deal after all. But now every time she moves, she can feel it inside her like a tumour or a tapeworm.

Even with Pan for company, the rote denials of Henry's wrongdoing that, over the years, became as instinctive to Lydia as putting her hands down to break a fall, still haven't rematerialised. The preceding months have felt to Lydia like acclimatising to a paralysis, as if she keeps unthinkingly trying to use her immobilised limb.

Lydia begs herself not to think of Henry, but already a Greek chorus of Henries are knee-to-knee with her in the tub.

Henry looking at Lydia with lascivious anticipation.

Henry looking at Lydia like she was a sock he'd just wanked into.

Henry's way of subtly making Lydia crave his approval by implying she was faintly ridiculous and completely expendable.

Henry swatting her skirt up over her thighs, eyes glazed with the furtive greed of someone ripping paper off a stolen gift, while Lydia poured her whole being into watching a cobweb drift back and forth in the stale breath of the air-conditioning.

Henry swiping her skirt back down as if placing his napkin over the remnants of a regrettable meal.

The delightedly naughty look that lit up his face when they were flirting.

The callous, disdainful one when he was pushing her away, making Lydia feel like it was her fault for expecting anything else, making her feel dumped despite the fact they were never going out, not really.

The wounded wonderment on his face in the coffee shop when Lydia assented to his apology instead of dismissing it as unnecessary.

Jesus Christ, his face: Henry had looked like a child in the acute silence that occurs between a fall and a scream.

Henry is not a child, of course.

Yet it had been so hard to suppress the urge to comfort him.

Henry always had a way of framing his most brutal violations as accidents of clumsiness and naivety; always managed to foreground the childlike, defenceless aspects of his character when absolving himself of cruelties. And he continues to have an uncanny knack for making whatever he has inflicted on Lydia seem as if she has done it to herself.

A bait and switch that's left Lydia responsible for protecting Henry from the consequences of his actions, taking ownership of the mess left behind, as he saunters off like an irresponsible owner pretending not to notice that their dog has shat on the pavement.

Disparate versions of Henry accompany Lydia wherever she goes. They are all equally him.

Henry her lover.

Henry her friend.

Henry her abuser.

Henry then and Henry now.

Henry in his twenties: the toddler-ish mixture of confidence and vulnerability that Lydia found at once irritating and arousing when she first met him at a party. Before she'd even got home that night, he'd started carpet-bombing her with texts: hyperbolic compliments, poetic affection and literate filth that made her feel like the smartest, most desirable woman alive.

Henry in his thirties: the successful playwright still curating the combination of loneliness and self-satisfaction that provoked and seduced Lydia back into the cycle of swearing off and seeking out.

Henry in his forties: kinder and more careworn, less bulletproof, yet still possessed of the footloose evasiveness that was so bafflingly addictive, whose adolescent propensity for trying to annoy Lydia into re-engaging often worked. A cheap, convincing trick.

It always reminded her of that time in the early days when she'd been with Pan in the green room at a Saturday morning kid's programme on some PR round. A famous conjuror whose shows Lydia had grown up watching on TV was also waiting backstage and when Pan went to the toilet, Lydia had asked him to do a bit of magic for her.

Taking a greedy suck of his B&H, he'd looked her over with the tiredness of a teacher being asked an inane question for the thousandth time. 'No such thing as magic, love,' he'd replied, dragging on his dogend. 'They're illusions, tricks – they're my professional skills and you can't afford my hourly rate.'

Excruciated, Lydia loosed a laugh that struck her as sounding manic and shrill, then they'd sat there festering in silence.

A runner popped in to say five minutes 'til live and left. Then the taciturn magician said, 'I'll show you a quick trick after all, shall I?'

He'd held his palms out, 'Nothing in my hands, right?'

'Not that I can see.'

Then he'd exclaimed his famous catchphrase, gripped Lydia's tits, given them a crushing squeeze and laughed. 'Just a bit of fun, love. Just a bit of fun.'

And a meagre heartbeat later, Pan was back, a runner was

rushing them down the corridor and Lydia was bopping and miming under hot lights while cameras zoomed and swooped at her mouthing the lyrics to The Lollies' single hit: 'Up for it, up for it, going out and up for it.'

That incident is only one of many that have retrospectively revealed their true nature; like the world's shittiest magic-eye picture, its concealed image snapped sharp by the altered focus of Henry's admission.

With his apology, he has re-drafted Lydia's understanding of almost every facet of her life. Like Luminol and UV light on a crime scene exposing handprints and splashes, the blue glow of secret, innumerable stains that had always been there.

She'd been confronted by her altered feelings immediately.

Happened violence declares itself from everywhere now, so that when Lydia reflects on her life, a smear runs from adolescence to adulthood as though a corpse has been dragged through her history.

All the times Lydia has been ogled, catcalled, needlessly rubbed against, flashed, pawed, unfunnily 'teased', all the inappropriate remarks she ignored, are re-framed as intolerable, as abuses she was complicit in enabling.

And that's before she even begins to contemplate the times when she grudgingly permitted fucks and touches she didn't really want. Out of what?

Politeness. She has called it politeness, as if allowing a man access to her body because she'd kissed him for so long that he'd missed the last train was an obligation demanded by good manners, on a par with offering tea to an unwelcome guest. Automatically accepting responsibility for every hard-on she'd been presented with, like a cashier redeeming a questionable voucher she'd lacked authority to refuse.

The day after Henry's apology, Lydia had been on her way

to the cinema when a bricklayer had wolf-whistled her and lobbed a shout of 'All right, sexy!' down from some scaffolding. She'd screamed up at him to *fuck off and die*, then called him a pervert. And afterwards had cried.

Once she would have muttered *twat* under her breath and thought nothing else of it.

Failing to be outraged.

Failing to imagine another world in which she did not accept such behaviours as frustrating inevitabilities on a par with tax returns, menstrual cramps and long queues for the toilet.

This, Lydia had realised as she'd fled home instead of going to the cinema, was what Henry had done: with a single conversation, he had transformed everything that was never really OK – all the misconduct she had spent her whole life normalising and neutralising in order to function – into things which were, which *are*, actively, excoriatingly, agonisingly *not* OK. And ever since, Lydia's life appears in retrospect to have been one long, emotionally unhealthy game of whack-a-mole that she shouldn't have been playing in the first place.

Enough, she thinks. *Enough.*

She gets out of the bath, slings on a pair of Care Bear pyjamas so discoloured that Funshine looks as if he's dying of liver failure, and goes into the living room, where everything suppurates taste; so white and pristine that Lydia feels like a stain.

Pandora is reclining on the corner sofa in her own sleepwear, mushroom-coloured separates that move like poured cream and probably cost more than most people's monthly rent.

On the sleek cube of a coffee table, something purple waits in martini glasses. Cherries lurk specimen-like in the liquid.

Pan is staring out the window, to the balcony, where gulls patrol, squawking and unleashing oily jets of faeces.

'Cunts,' says Pan. 'Filthy, noisy fuckers. Gonna get some bird spikes put in.'

'Oh Pan,' Lydia sighs, 'don't, they're just . . . it's the seaside, they're seagulls. It's nature; lovely really.'

Lydia walks over to the window. Rainbow bulbs polka-dot the line of the pier. Far out at sea, a big lit-up ship makes stately progress along the horizon and further out, red lights blink atop the wind turbines as they turn their dreamy calisthenics.

'Lydia, you're such a soft heart sometimes. They're pricks. Gross. Look at all the shite on my balcony.'

'That is a lot of poop, Pan. I'll give you that,' Lydia says. She snaps a picture of their drinks, posts it on Instagram captioned *Friday night done right babies*, then takes a slug. It tastes surprisingly cosmetic.

'It's an Aviation, don't you like it?' Pan snaps.

'Love it,' Lydia lies. 'So what's the chat?'

'We need to talk about you staying here,' Pan says, in the light tone she always uses for heavy subjects. 'Laurence is having a nightmare with her dad and so she's going to need yo— *her* room. I'm hopping over to bring her home. Tomorrow, actually. Says she can't hack even one more day with Alain. Tears, the whole shebang, you know? Not that I blame her, obviously. Prick. Fucking prick. She's a perfect pain in the hole, God love her, but Alain is such a wanker.'

'Oh.' Lydia's blood slides into her boots. 'Yes, of course, I completely understand.'

Laurence, Pan's sixteen-year-old daughter, has been living with her father, Alain, in Paris, after some kind of mother–daughter fracture that Pan has mentioned cagily and seldom these last weeks.

A soul-deep sorrow carves Pan's face when she does, inter-cut with anger, so Lydia knows immediately that the situation must be dire for Laurence to return.

That poor girl, Lydia thinks, born into the volcanic land-scape of Pan and Alain's relationship, which from the first flush had seemed needlessly tempestuous and teenage, even to Lydia, who considers herself a complete catastrophe.

After Pan and Alain finally divorced — about a decade after it first became obvious to everyone else it was inevitable — Laurence had been alternately prized and rejected, shuttled back and forth between parents in some poisonous, punitive pass-the-parcel. Treated less like a child and more like some-thing between a bargaining chip and a bomb. None of it can have been any good for her.

Not that Lydia knows how she's been impacted — it's been so long since she saw Laurence last. Years and years, a queasy quantity to contemplate.

Lydia is Laurence's godmother and is, anyway, the adult and interloper in this. She is shamed by how speedily her con-cern accelerates away from Laurence, reflexively returning to herself, wondering what the fuck she's going to do, where the hell she's going to go.

Of course, the hotel is not home, and yet the thought of leaving makes her feel unhoused.

That too makes Lydia despicable to herself: conflating her privileged situation with that of people who sleep on the street.

Nowhere Lydia's lived as an adult has earned the word home, no place has been sufficiently safe and stifling. But there *is* a room in Catford that she's still paying rent on. Her latest address, one in a long series of temporary rooms where Lydia's fiscally expedient presence has been begrudged by a homeowner who wants to live alone but can't afford it.

Places where the closest Lydia comes to ownership is the scent of her perfume hanging in the air, a pillow moulded to the shape of her head and her clothes puddled half-in, half-out of her suitcases.

In two years' time, Lydia will be fifty and likely still leading the loser life of a drifter decades younger. Blundering blindly from one temporary situation and convenient choice to another with no greater sense of purpose or direction than she had in those first lost years after The Lollies crashed and burned.

Even less sense of identity: there are only so many times, Lydia thinks uneasily, that you can wonder who you are and what exactly it is you're *for* before it becomes a sort of semantic satiation of self: like trying to spell the same word so many times that its meaning devolves and dissipates completely.

Her thoughts lately are all just pulverising noise – psychological death-metal, punctuated by shouts and falls which wake her in the night. Bad days and bad dreams inextricable from one another.

'You understand, don't you, Lydie,' Pan says.

It isn't a question, just like it wasn't a question when, barely a full minute off stage after playing the opening slot at a muddy outdoor festival to an audience of ten people, one of whom had lobbed a burger directly at Lydia's tit, Pan had said, 'Right, that was shit, don't you think it's time to call it quits?'

Lydia said the same thing then as she does now: ''Course.' Feeling, as she so often does, as though she lacks a solid core, a discernible personality.

She worries that's why she makes friends so effortlessly and drifts away from them just as easily – there's nothing about her to cause offence and even less to miss. She's just *so nice*. Like a Digestive biscuit.

People have always told Lydia that she's *so nice*. Especially while making her redundant or dumping her or cancelling their plans with her or asking for unreasonable favours. Sometimes simultaneously.

So nice, said like niceness was a terminal illness they were not prepared to watch Lydia die of, uninterestingly.

And although Lydia understands Pan can't know what a perfect clean shank to the kidneys it is, it still feels deliberately designed when Pan smiles – a sort of administrative, ending things upturn of the mouth corners, like a bureaucrat rubber-stamping a document – and says, 'Aw, course you do, Lyd. I knew you would. You really are *so nice*.'

Chapter 4

'I've got the nicest feeling about tonight, Joycey,' says Betty, snapping her powder compact shut. 'Don't you?'

Just like every Saturday evening, Betty and Joyce are applying their face, getting ready to go to the social club. Side by side, in lace slips, they sit at their vanity unit; cream and gold, somewhat chipped, skirted in floral chintz.

'It's always nice at the club,' Joyce applies mascara.

'Yes, but I've got one of my special feelings, Joycey. I think tonight might be the night to meet a man.' Betty bounce-squirms on her stool.

She's lovely on club nights, thinks Joyce; like a best friend. A lunge of guilt follows the thought. The past keeps itching in Joyce, springing up like hives. The inflamed sensation makes her mother's little ways grate.

This winter, their seaside home seems scabby to Joyce; bleak and intolerably small, so that their old life appears to have been an endless summer whose sunny seductions keep ambushing her.

Once the season ends and winter arrives, only the old, the frail, the broke and broken remain. Those who depend on walkers and scooters, stumbling people with eyes made vacant by substances Joyce has no concept of. People who live in B&Bs. The ones Joyce can't see any harm in, but who make her mother start mouthing off.

Or Joyce *used* to think those people made her mother start, but recently, she can't help thinking that her mother goes looking for them, actively seeking reasons to rant. And the stupid paper makes her worse.

Joyce and Betty used to have such a lovely time together reading about the royals, admiring Her Majesty's outfits, seeing what William, Kate and Harry were up to. But now Mum takes a dim view of Meghan. Pushy she says, hard-faced. Joyce suspects that's not Betty's only problem with her, and it's not one Joyce shares, so now even the royals are fraught.

Joyce prefers the days when they pass the newsagents and Betty puts a hand to her brow and says, 'I couldn't possibly take a paper, Joyce. I couldn't bear any more ugliness. We have enough troubles of our own.'

Weeks shuffle by until Fridays. Fish Friday lunches at The Golden Sands cafe. The £4.99 special with bread and butter and a nice pot of tea. One Knickerbocker Glory and two spoons. Joyce was always fond of a banana split. Betty finds them uncouth.

There's something smutty about bananas, she says. She simply cannot see the need for them.

Before he disappeared, Joyce's father used to buy her banana splits. Or anything she wanted on the scarce, magical occasions it was just the two of them.

He'd say, don't tell your mother and buy Joyce bubblegum (*common*), hotdogs (*common, obscene*); he'd let her eat chips from a paper cone with her fingers while walking along the prom (*no better than a pig at a trough*).

There weren't the usual rules with Daddy. Or if there were, he and Joyce enjoyed the cosy furtiveness of breaking them together.

Daddy didn't tell on Joyce for eating gobstoppers or riding the carousel horses in a skirt. And she didn't tell on her daddy for having a whisky or a cigarillo or a flutter.

For so long she didn't think of him. She didn't let herself. It hurt. And, besides, Joyce used to think Betty would know, that it would be physically visible. Betty had led her to believe that lying stained her tongue black.

Lately, though, it's as if there is a window open in Joyce's stuffy head and her father is the wind that blows through it, throwing everything into the air.

It reminds Joyce of the time their villa was burgled, back when Daddy was still around. He didn't phone the police – it turned out nothing had been taken, just emptied out into heaps on the floor.

The moments in which Joyce wonders why Daddy left, where he went, whether he's alive or dead, create the same feeling in her that she experienced on walking into the house, discovering their cupboards' contents strewn everywhere.

Her mother's refusal to talk about Daddy, unless it is to rail about his responsibility for their diminished circumstances, somehow akin to Betty's uncharacteristic silence that day, as she set grim-faced to tidying it all away.

Joyce wishes she understood, wishes she could see Daddy again or at least understand what happened to him, but her wishing feels so disloyal.

Joyce makes herself count the nice times with her mother, as if doing so repays embezzled funds.

We are going to the club, she tells herself, this is our special Saturday.

'Cat got your tongue, madam? I am talking to you. Joyce? Honestly, cloth ears, dolly daydream, I don't know where your brain goes. I said I've got one of my special feelings, I really think we might meet a man.'

'Well, it's more men your age, Mum, but I suppose there might be someone.'

'Don't be sour, Joyce. You've always got to be so sour. Anyway, I meant for me as much as for you. Come here.'

Betty thumbs at a smudge in Joyce's lipstick.

'That's better. I have that special feeling I get. I always know. I had it on the day I won Miss Halcyon Holidays and I've got it now. I think we're going to meet a nice man.'

'That would be nice, if you met a man and I could ... '

'Oh, Joyce,' tuts Betty. 'Self, self, self. We might *both* meet a man. Oh, imagine, Joyce! Imagine if we met a nice father and son and I liked the father and you liked the son and we'd go on outings to French restaurants ... and, Joyce! A double wedding – imagine us being brides together!'

Stupid, careless curiosity. Joyce asks, 'What was your wedding like?'

Mistake.

'*Joyce.*'

Betty stands and starts to brush Joyce's hair, roughly. 'The wedding was lovely, I was stunning. Why must you bring him up, Joyce? Really not nice, snide to ask. Your hair is a bird's nest, Joyce.'

Betty scoops the bristles firmly into her daughter's hair and carries on. 'They were saying, everyone was, that I was the most beautiful bride they had ever seen. A total stranger, an *absolute stranger* to me, Joyce, asked me to wait outside the church just a moment longer so he could get his camera, so that he could take a picture of me because he said ... '

The brushing softens and slows. In the mirrors, Joyce sees a triptych of Bettys smiling at her own reflection over the top of her daughter's head.

'This was a stranger, remember, Joyce. He said he had to have a picture of me because I really was *the* most beautiful bride he'd *ever* seen. And, of course, your father could not believe his luck. Oh, Joyce, why do you always have to bring up horrible things? You can do your own hair. It's a rat's nest, I can't begin.'

Betty lets go of the brush, sits, applies lipstick furiously, watches Joyce try to extricate her tangled hair from the bristles.

Joyce's scalp hurts, 'What do you think my wedding will be like?'

'I don't know, Joyce. It's very hard to imagine since you haven't got a man.'

Joyce teases strands from the brush, still attached to her head.

Betty goes to the wardrobe and starts to pull out dresses. They whisper in their plastic.

'I'm so used to you being a spinster. Shall we wear our peaches and cream or pinkie-flowery? Joyce?'

Betty holds up dresses against herself, switches them back and forward like she is administering an eye test.

'Peaches and cream or pinkie-flowery?'

'I don't mind.'

'Pinkie-flowery then. Peaches and cream does your hips no favours. Too many chocolate biscuits,' Betty snort-laughs. 'But I'm sure if you controlled your appetite, you could make a beautiful bride.'

She drifts around with pinkie-flowery ghost-dancing in its wrapper in her arms.

'I've always known the day would come, always known you were dying to get away from me.'

'I'm not dying to get away from you. How are we having our hair?'

'Chignon. No one wants you to be happy more than I do. Don't you dare accuse me, Joyce. The sacrifices I've made for you.'

Pinching kirby-grips out of the heart-shaped pin box, Joyce starts to twist up her curls. 'Tell me about when you won Miss Halcyon Holidays.'

With this magic, Betty can always be diverted.

'Oh gosh, Joycey, not again. You just love this story, don't you?'

And she does. She really does.

'Well, it was the most beautiful day. Such a wonderful summer. Perfect sun, every single day. The days were so long, so warm.'

Joyce always feels as if the lighting in the room changes when Betty starts to tell the story. She can almost see reflected swimming pool ripples strobing on the bedroom ceiling.

'Mummy and Daddy and I were staying at the old Halcyon Holiday Camp, the one just down the coast. Long gone, of course.'

Joyce has noticed Betty's flow always snags on mention of her own parents – dead long before Joyce was born, before Joyce's mother and father got married.

'And . . . and . . . All the boys were like dogs in heat, flies round a honeypot, Joyce, just mad about me. Daddy was run ragged turning them away when they came calling with flowers. And my daddy was such a smart man, such a rugged man, a real, proper man, you don't get men like my daddy any more. Ties. Hats. Decent. Always wore ties

48

and hats, my daddy. He used to terrorise those boys, such a big man.'

Another small trouble flits across Betty's expression. She bumps against the vanity. Pots of cold cream, bottles of scent and setting lotion chink and wobble. Pinkie-flowery slumps in Betty's arms.

'Where was I? A lovely summer and of course they had a Miss Halcyon Holidays competition. And, well, from the moment we arrived practically, they were begging me to enter, the people that worked there, the host and so on, and, of course, they don't have those things any more since the bra burners. What was wrong with it? It was just a bit of fun. All that bra burning, it's just an excuse for ugly women to take revenge on beautiful women. Jealous, Joyce, they're just jealous. That's why we've never had any women friends. Why *you've* never had any women friends . . .'

Betty places her hand on Joyce's shoulder. Joyce can smell her. All the usual scents. But underneath something recently arrived: a small animal smell. Straw, dampness. A hutch.

'You could win Miss Halcyon, Joycey. Any day of the week. If they still had it.'

She kisses Joyce on the top of her head.

A dusty, light peck. Hot. Joyce finds herself thinking of a moth skittering against a lampshade. Breath catches in her throat.

'Is there anything you want to say to me?' Betty asks. 'When someone compliments you, it's considered good manners to give a compliment in return.'

'Oh, you're beautiful, Mum. You're lovely.'

'Blood out of a stone. Honestly, Joyce, you can be so ungrateful.'

'I think you're lovely, Mum. We look the same.'

That was true-ish, for a handful of years, around the time Joyce was in her twenties and Betty in her late forties. Betty *had* aged well, and at that point, Joyce was *a little tired*. That was how they referred to it. But that was over twenty years ago.

Now, no matter how soft and forgiving their lighting arrangements are, no matter how identically they are styled, Joyce and Betty are like two plates from the same dinner service – one which has been in daily circulation and one which has been kept for best in the china cabinet.

'*You* think *you're* lovely then, do you? Prideful, Joyce. Not an attractive quality, self-regard.'

Betty's smell is very strong in Joyce's nostrils. 'God, I can't win with you,' Joyce snaps.

'Don't swear. Don't be truculent. How will we ever find you a man? There isn't a man on God's green earth who would tolerate this kind of sauce.'

A flare, a streaking firework inside Joyce's skull.

'Why haven't I seen photos? When you won Miss Halcyon. Or your wedding? I've never seen your wedding pictures.'

'Well, you must have, Joyce ... *stupid* ... of course, natu-rally, in the past, at some point, when you were younger, you must have. You know how forgetful you can be, Joyce. Scatty madam. I mean, *of course*, there *are* pictures, whole albums actually, honestly ... *rude* ... can't keep things right in your head. But they've been misplaced ... lost in the move. Yet more things *I* lost in *the move.*'

Betty looks to Joyce like a child caught in some pri-vate activity.

The ambushed quality of her expression shames Joyce, who softly, brightly says, 'Shall we finish getting ready, Mum? Shall we finish getting ready and go to the club?'

'And meet some nice men?' Betty asks in a cringing way that makes Joyce want to hold her mother, tell her she is sorry.

'And meet some nice men,' Joyce replies, resigned to the certainty that there will be no one at the club that she and her mother haven't met a thousand times before.

Chapter 5

The cursor blinks sceptically at Lydia as she slumps on the scabby chesterfield in the hotel foyer, trying to work; wheezy old laptop open on her stomach, waistline thickened by the two cashmere jumpers she helped herself to from Pan's wardrobe after she left to bring Laurence home.

Dustsheets drift in the draught and the white glare of low sun prying through plate glass makes a mirror of the computer screen, confronting Lydia with a version of her face so Shrek-like and hideous that it rivals every front-camera selfie she's ever accidentally taken.

Angling the lid to banish her reflection, she types: *The cold weather's here to stay, so whether you're going out or staying in, here are our top picks of this winter's budget buys for fashion fabulousness and cosy comfort.*

After the band burned out and her attempt at a solo career tanked, Lydia had picked up some writing work through a hot idiot with a fashion magazine and a crush on Pandora, looking for ways to ingratiate himself. She found she was adequate at it and has just about scratched out a living – albeit an uncertain one – ever since, augmented by the spits and occasionally gluts of cash from 'Up For It'.

Never enough to make her rich, sometimes enough to lessen her precarity, even occasionally enough to provide a calendar year of near comfort – like when 'Up For It' had been used in a car commercial and on the soundtrack of *Bibby's Big Movie*, an animated toy tie-in about a magic pink-haired pixie.

'Style journalist' is what it says on Lydia's social-media profiles, but that seems to her a gross overstatement of what she actually does: she writes articles so insignificant that their large number adds up to nothing.

Lots of snacky little irrelevances with Lydia's name on them: cruddy crumbs and scrapings. The occasional think-piece; half-arsed, middle-brow versions of smarter, more original ones written by smarter, more original writers.

Younger writers.

Much younger writers.

A style column in a free magazine shoved in the faces of commuters who don't want to read about Lydia's hot take on this autumn's remix of the classic trench any more than they want a pamphlet imploring them to accept Christ into their lives.

Sometimes Lydia googles herself and trudges through the tinselly trash of by-lines: This Summer's Hottest Holiday Buys, columns on internet dating for a glossy that folded, pieces from a Sunday lifestyle supplement. *I tried Beyoncé's pre-tour diet and workout regime and here's what I discovered! I've started keeping a bullet journal and here's why you should too!*

Until recently, Lydia had always trusted that there was more life left to live. A whole other one, even, if she's honest with herself; some second sitting where her plate would be refilled with a more appetising version of the flavourless years she has chewed down to the bone.

But here she is, with nothing to hold on to, none of the things her friends have: not a baby or a book, not even a Boston Terrier.

Treading water this whole time, thinks Lydia. *I have been treading water this whole time. Just a shipwreck survivor, still clinging to the flotsam I grabbed when everything solid shattered and first I started to drown.*

And the realisation reduces Lydia's entire existence to Kate Winslet's wardrobe door: just a smashed plank, a flotation aid she's relied on so long that she can no longer remember the boat it used to be part of, let alone where it was heading; treading water so frenetically that she failed to notice that her life raft has been breaking up beneath her.

Cracking her knuckles, Lydia types: *This winter you can be hot or hygge or maybe even both with our pick of cute cosy looks that won't cost the earth!*

'What a load of absolute bollocks.' She holds down the delete key and watches the cursor reverse, gobbling up letters.

The deadline isn't for another few days and she feels the familiar skating away of attention, concentration skidding off in opposite directions like Bambi's hooves on the ice. She repeats the same impossible level on Candy Crush until she feels migrainous and certifiable, then grazes guiltily on Twitter and Instagram and Facebook.

Facebook congratulates Lydia on a friend anniversary. Katy Pugh. The last time she'd seen her in person, Lydia had been holding Katy's hair out the way while she vomited Archers and orange onto the school playing field after their sixth-form leaver's disco three decades ago.

Facebook has co-opted their images into a celebratory video: Lydia's profile picture revolves in a cloud of balloons, taunting her with a youthfulness that seems horribly remote even though it was only taken a couple of years ago, while Katy's shows a nice suburban mum brandishing some novelty knobject on a hen night.

'Fucking desolate,' Lydia calls into the emptiness. Speaking aloud, alone, makes her voice sound deranged.

And it is.

She is.

Actually, *fucking desolate*.

She asks herself why she can't just be glad. After all, Pan was not evicting her, as she had assumed. She was simply being demoted to lesser quarters.

'Ta-da! The Flamingo Suite!' Pan had said, unlocking the door to one of the empty rooms on the floor below. 'Sorry, Lyd, I know it's not the best, but it's yours if you want it.'

Not the best was an understatement on a par with describing terminal cancer as 'being a bit under the weather': the dim room looked and smelled like a place where bad, sad sex had happened regularly since last it had decorated. Which, judging by the peeling Pepto-Bismol paint and stained satin, was the 1980s.

The floors below Pan's apartment are like an underworld. Even the Flamingo Suite, on the third floor with a big window looking over the sea, feels subterranean: the Bosch bowel of the building in dizzying contrast to Pan's sleek cube perched above like a deluxe crow's nest.

It is punishingly cold: some central pipe burst after the first frost and the hotel's heating failed, so that despite myriad buckets cluttering the corridors, the carpets are marshy, the ornate cornices are stained with brown dribbles, and where the flocked wallpaper had already been peeling, now it bubbles and sloughs like a nasty skin complaint.

Builders carrying out renovation work come and go all

day, every day, leaving piles of planks and rubble, generating dust that descends gradually through the evenings, leaving everything gritty, making Lydia's sheets and mouth feel sandy.

The atmosphere in the hotel is relentlessly chilly and dank.

Mouldering smells submerged under the exorbitant miasma from reed diffusers and scented candles in the apartment above become claggy and clinging down here. As much flavour as funk.

'Sorry, Lydie, thanks for being such a brick,' Pan had said last night, once they'd drained their drinks and moved Lydia's laughable belongings downstairs.

'No, thanks for letting me stay on, it's so kind of you.'

Halfway out of the door, Pan peered back in as if checking on a child.

Tearful with a conflicting mix of gratitude and self-pity, Lydia had avoided Pan's eye and, looking away, had noticed a book on the dressing table: a copy of the Qur'an.

The night Lydia arrived, as Pan recounted her shrewd, impulsive purchase of the hotel, Lydia asked had it been empty.

'Oh, well, no, there were resi— guests. Just a few. A handful. Off-season, you know, Lyd? People who . . . the previous owner had a different . . . clientele, a very different business model. And there's others, plenty here which accept . . . which operate that . . . business model, so . . .'

The flail and squirm of her had made Lydia want to say, *You mean asylum seekers? You mean people on bail and benefits?* But gratitude's an indentured state and Lydia had felt unable to do anything but relinquish her distaste and end Pan's disquiet before she freed herself from it by expelling Lydia from her life.

'Well, you know what you want for the place,' Lydia had pulled the hook out of Pan's cheek.

Lydia is the champion of letting go: a practised escape artist. She's squirmed free of all sorts of principles and aspirations, rather than wrestle in the chains of wanting something or believing anything. Much easier to let values and dreams slip their strings and speed out of sight like carelessly carried balloons.

Last night, just before Pan had gone upstairs, she'd said, 'I do like this, Lydie, you being here. I really feel like we're reconnecting.'

Reconnecting or repeating? Lydia had wondered.

'And Laurence will be happy to see you, you know? She dotes on you.'

Flush of shame, Lydia feels it leap to her cheeks: the picture of Laurence in Lydia's head is at least five or six years out of date. Prepubescent and irrelevant. Some godmother. What a piece of shit.

'I might sort my stuff out and hit the hay, if that's all right, Pan,' she'd mumbled, throat sour with incipient sobs.

'N'night, Lyd,' Pan had hovered in the doorway, cheek leaning against the frame, looking as if, perhaps, she wanted to hear something. But Lydia let Pan walk away.

Lydia has walked away from, and let others walk out of, every version of her life.

She's worn three different engagement rings but only got as far as planning one wedding.

Eight years ago, she'd been in a relationship with someone she was going to marry. Harriet.

Lydia's other two fiancés had been men, as were all her previous partners, and although she'd always entertained curiosities and crushes – wanking over lesbian porn sometimes – a handful of inebriated nightclub snogs had comprised the sum of Lydia's sapphic experiences. Each was imbued with an uneasy element of display, taking place in public places and leaving Lydia suspecting she'd performed queer desire for straight men in a manner barely distinguishable from The Lollies' corporately calculated faux-lesbianism.

So it had surprised Lydia as much as everyone around her when she'd started dating Harriet, a sleek, chic art dealer with a Mary Quant bob, a voice like hot-buttered fuck and enough money for both of them. Not just enough money: an excess so enormous, Lydia felt fruitless self-rebuke each time she walked through the nearby housing estate on her way to the Tube.

Harriet used a fraction of it to buy a vast run-down house in an up-and-coming area and together, they spent two years making it so immaculate that *Homes & Gardens* magazine did a feature on it. Then, just after they'd started visiting wedding venues, Lydia had been checking Harriet's trouser pockets before taking them to the dry cleaners and found a receipt for a weekend for two in an extortionate Mayfair hotel, stamped with a date when she'd supposedly been schmoozing collectors in New York.

That night, once Harriet returned from her gallery, Lydia confronted her. Having felt eerily flat all day, Lydia relished the fierce aliveness of screaming at Harriet, who, although apologetic, seemed sorrier for being caught than she was for cheating, especially when offering in mitigation that, 'It's not like she meant anything to me, it was only because she's a lesbian too, Lydia, and sometimes you're just so . . . *straight.*'

Instead of the incandescent anger Lydia anticipated, a feeling of hollow deliberateness crept up on her as she continued shouting the sorts of things anyone uncovering unfaithfulness might be expected to.

The embodied activity familiar; a sensation she hadn't experienced since the band. Lydia realised she was performing, miming even: just opening and closing her mouth round words she didn't mean.

Immediately, she stopped shouting and stood very still in the surgical perfection of a kitchen that cost more than entire houses elsewhere, understanding that she was staging a distress she ought to be feeling but wasn't. Because although Harriet was extremely rich and sexy, everything else about her was patronising and suffocating and no matter how hard she racked her brain, Lydia couldn't think of one thing she would miss about her apart from the orgasms.

Plus: Harriet had displayed a wary unease around Pandora that Lydia found kind of sinister, as if she imagined Pandora's success made hers seem less exceptional and feared that Pan's bolshiness might give Lydia *ideas*. Harriet had loved being the alpha in their relationship, treating Lydia like something between a 1950s housewife and a dim but adorable pet.

As an art dealer, Harriet understood the high value of scarce resources. When Lydia withdrew with icy dignity, demanding nothing but money for a few months of rent on a studio flat, she'd unimaginatively tried to win Lydia back with jewellery and bouquets, which might have been flattering if Lydia had given a shit.

Remembering how little she had cared then infuses her with unease now. Sometimes she wonders if she actually cares about anything.

Lydia feels bummed and tweaky; like she wants to go somewhere or do something or eat something calorific or have a glass of wine or put make-up on and post a selfie or call somebody or do a bit of online shopping she can't afford, or maybe go back to bed for a wank and a nap.

She sits up and puts her laptop on the couch beside her, sighing.

Maybe I'm just having a hard time accepting that I'm normal, she thinks. But Lydia knows her ability to access relative material comfort for so little effort isn't really normal, that the way she can dip in and out of the different parts of her life, visiting them like a zoo – fancy parties she can still get herself invited to if she's inclined – is not most people's normal, and that festering purposelessly in this hotel to hide from the past and avoid making decisions about the future isn't normal.

And she's pretty sure being this preoccupied with adolescent questions about what to do with her life, at the age of forty-eight, is also not normal.

All her life, Lydia has been asking herself what she wants to do with the rest of it. Every time she thinks she's finally found the answer, something goes wrong, someone throws it back into doubt, making Lydia feel as if *she* is a question in the world instead of a fact. And not a particularly thought-provoking one.

Especially since the encounter with Henry in the coffee shop.

Panicky tears are prickling Lydia's eyes when her phone buzzes.

She picks it up and a Pavlovian jag of adrenaline yelps through every cell and synapse at the sight of his name on her phone screen: Henry.

It is Henry.

And to Lydia's horror, humiliation and shame, she's extremely glad that it is.

Chapter 6

In cold cream and curlers, Betty doles out Joyce's night vitamins and they climb into their twin beds. A goodnight whisper, as blush satin eiderdowns slide up to the necks of their nighties.

Outside, streets away, boy racers roar muscle cars up and down the prom with the bass thumping. A siren. The white noise of the sea. And somewhere, someone is singing. Their Saturday night had begun the way it always did, with two gin and tonics on the hammered copper tabletop – catching reflections of the club's pine panelling and peach light in its divots – as they sat surrounded by old people listening to old music. Sentimental sing-along songs about chaste romances that relieve the elderly of their age; lyrics clear and timeless in their heads as a recipe for roast chicken.

Widows in sparkly Saturday tops, shoulder shimmying in their seats. Cheap drinks and peanuts. Bingo and a raffle. A maximum of three drinks then home. That was how it always went.

But this night had not been the same.

Betty, after deigning to engage in some brief small talk

with old acquaintances at the bar, remarked on how Fat June (*the beast*) had got even fatter (*how is that even possible?*) and Edith (*poor soul*) apparently has her cancer back (*curtains this time, you mark my words*).

Betty had tapped Joyce's glass. 'You're making light work of that, madam.'

Joyce, giddy from the first few sips, had said, 'I think there must be a little dog under the table, drinking it when we're not looking.'

And Betty had laughed, 'Oh Joyce, you're such a card. You make me laugh, a little dog under the table . . . ' She had taken a big drink from her glass, 'Look, Joyce, the little dog's drinking mine too!'

The club had been packed and happy. Joyce's heart was quite tender, very buoyant inside her chest. She'd taken another slurp.

Betty had her club face on, effervescent and amused, 'Naughty dog! He'll be awfully tipsy.'

Joyce had swigged back the last of her drink. 'Woof woof!'

Too far!

'Joyce! What's got into you? You're behaving like a hod carrier. You always get too silly, Joyce. That's always been your problem, I remember when you were six and—'

'Betty Wilson!' A dapper old gent had approached the table. One of those perjink, moustachioed Rotary-club types. Brass-buttoned blazer. Signet ring on a finger like a hairy chipolata. Tie from some old-bores' society. Matching pocket handkerchief.

'Angus Stirrup, as I live and breathe! I haven't seen you in years!'

Betty had done her face. The one she models for the mirror before they leave the flat on Saturdays.

'Too many years, Betty. I see you've brought your sister.'

The man winked and a sourness had flooded Joyce as Betty grinned and simpered.

'Angus, you rogue! You *must* know this is my daughter.'

'Forgive me. I forgot this lovely lady had a daughter because she simply doesn't look old enough. You simply *don't* look old enough, Betty.'

Betty giggled, 'Angus. You're such an awful man. Isn't he an awful man, Joyce?'

'Definitely.'

'I see she's a firecracker like her mother, this one.'

'She gives me hell, Angus. Hell. Joyce, get us another little drinkie.'

'Gladly.'

'No ladies, allow me.' Angus had composed his features into a Lancelot look, suggesting that to him, a woman buying her own drink was tantamount to letting one take a shit on the round table. It had moved Joyce to rise to her feet.

'Do sit down, dear,' he'd said, motioning Joyce to sit back down.

'Honestly, you and Mum catch up. I'll get us a drink.'

As Joyce walked to the bar, she'd looked back, amused by the obvious offence she'd clearly caused Angus by countermanding his order; disgusted by Betty's coquettish giggle, flapping a hand before her face like a duchess' fan; overcome by a visceral, vertiginous sense of her mother's smallness. *Cheap*, she'd thought. *That's what you'd say to me, if you saw me behaving that way.*

Joyce had had her jagged feeling – the one she gets after a breakage, if one of the dolls is knocked off during dusting. Breathless and calamitous, hoping the damage isn't too bad, oddly hungry to see what else might shatter once the breaking has begun.

Joyce asked the barmaid for two gin and tonics. Ice and a slice, please.

Then Joyce experienced that prickly, invaded sense of being looked at; scrutinized, not unkindly, by a man with a friendly, eager expression.

'Are they both for you?' he'd asked her.

Joyce is no good at estimating ages. People are either much younger, much older or about her age. About her age means anything from thirty to sixty. This man was about her age with the pillow-middle of someone who spends too much time sitting in cars or in front of computers. Dun hair thinning at the temples. A plain suet pudding of a face but so kind; something about his grey eyes that was consoling.

'Are they both for you? The drinks?'

'No! One's for my mum. One's for me.'

'Sorry, just joking, I just meant, I wouldn't blame you, I mean this, it's all a bit, not our thing, is it? I brought my gran, she's ninety, she likes to come here.'

'I came with·my mum.'

'It's nice for them and everything. Like it's good to get them out, isn't it? God that sounded rude.'

'Rude?'

'Nothing, look, sorry, it was clumsy of me. Can we start again? What's your name?'

'My name is Joyce.'

Joyce could not remember the last time she'd been in a situation that required her to introduce herself.

'Martin. Pleased to meet you, Joyce.'

He'd shaken her hand. His was big and warm. It had engulfed Joyce's and she'd felt scooped up from the inside.

Under the blankets, Joyce takes her right hand in her left. Her smile feels so bright in the dark bedroom that she peers at Betty to see if it has woken her up like a light switched on suddenly. But the old woman's mouth is slack, emitting congested snores.

'So, you come with your mum,' Martin had said. 'That's really nice of you. It's not that great for us though, is it? Except, well, I mean it is great knowing that they like it. Mum and Gran. Your mum and my gran. That made it sound like we're related, and I've only just met you. Look sorry, Joyce – I'm not very good at this. You must think I'm a total plonker.'

'No. It's. Nice. This is nice. I'm not very good at this either. I don't get out much, I don't talk to people much.'

'Tell me about it! Work! It sometimes feels like you're never away from work, doesn't it?'

'Actually, I don't work. At the moment.'

'Sorry, I just assumed. That's a shame, the economy, what with politics, the economy and ... such ... it's hard. What *did* you do?'

Joyce had her mistake feeling, like she was saying all the wrong things.

'I haven't actually, I've never, Mum always needs me.'

'Wow. You're amazing, putting your mum first like that. I mean it must be hard, caring for someone sick.'

'Well, she's not really, we both ... I can't explain. She just needs me. To be there. She needs me to stay with her and ... sometimes it's hard. Sorry. Now I feel like an idiot, telling you all this private stuff. Mum wouldn't like it. I've got her drink anyway. I'd better take it over.'

'No, it's great. Not that ... I don't mean ... I mean – your mum – it's hard, that's awful. I mean it's great to talk to you, Joyce. Please don't go. I'm really enjoying talking to you.'

'It's nice, but Mum's drink.'

'Why don't I come over with you and say hello?'

'Oh, no, I don't think it would be a good idea. She can be ... she might be ... '

'No. OK. Listen, Joyce, look, God, I can't believe I'm saying this, forgive me, it's going to sound forward, and I wouldn't normally be so forward or ... Joyce. You seem nice. You seem lovely. And good-hearted. You obviously do a lot for your mum. And I just wonder if, good grief, I can't *believe* I'm being so forward, but it seems like maybe you deserve a nice night out.'

'This is a nice night out.'

'Oh,' Martin looked at his shoes. Smart shoes, once, but not any longer. Plain – almost like school shoes. 'I was more trying to suggest, I suppose, in a round-about way, I was trying to see if maybe you wouldn't come on a night out with me sometime.'

Crestfallen, Joyce had been overwhelmed by the desire for something unaffordable – a coat out of her price range or something unacceptable, like denims or white stilettoes. She didn't know what to say.

'No, of course. It's fine. I shouldn't have asked.'

'No! It's not that! I'd like to. It has been so nice. This talking. But what about Mum?'

'Surely you can leave her on her own sometimes?'

'Yes. I can leave her alone sometimes. And she *is* always going on about how she'd like me to meet a man.'

'I'm a man! You've met me!'

'Yes, you are, Martin. And I would like to go out with you some night.'

'Are you on Facebook or can I get your number or give you mine?'

It was as if Joyce was one of the plastic wrappers they keep their dresses in; flimsy and transparent, empty and surplus.

'I could see you here next Saturday, would that be OK?'

Martin looked at Joyce as if he was trying to measure something or do a sum. All the ice in the drinks had melted.

'I'm sure Gran would like me to bring her down again next week. She was in hospital, see? That's why I've moved here. She's just got out. There's only us, but if she stays in decent fettle, I'm sure we could come again.'

Martin and Joyce had shared a smile, childishly shy and pleased.

Joyce floated through bingo, and raffle hour, and when she and Betty were putting on their coats, Martin had caught Joyce's eye and smiled again. It felt like passing a note at school.

The wind was biting on the walk home as Betty regaled Joyce with Angus' witticisms and explained how normally he spent Saturdays at the crown-green bowling club near the caravan park on the cliffs, but it was closed for refurbishment over the winter, and his wife had dementia and was in a home, and she never was the sharpest knife in the drawer anyway, and she drank too much besides.

And Joyce, not feeling the cold, had been half-happy for her mother, who seemed so pleased, and half-inclined to ask her why she always had to talk about every bad fate that befell others as if it was all their own fault, their just deserts.

Instead, she'd thought of Martin. She and her mother had both put their dresses away and applied cold cream while humming lightly.

Cosying down in bed, Joyce thought about Martin's smile

and felt her body melt with a boozy warmth and sweet indulgence like liqueur chocolates at Christmas. Then the feeling sobered. Because when Joyce told Martin that she could leave Betty alone sometimes, she had told him – and herself – a lie.

Chapter 7

At 8.30 in the evening, Lydia watches Henry leave the hotel.

'Fuck,' she mutters, whole body quaking. 'Shit.'

She feels vaporous and faint – as if she's falling, or perhaps as if the ground underneath her is subsiding.

From her vantage point at the big window of the grandiosely named 'Ballroom', which is really just a function suite with a chandelier in it, Lydia sees Henry descend the steps, cross the road and drop his keys in the gutter.

As Lydia observes him bending to retrieve them, fumbling to unlock the car door, he appears to her as someone she's never seen before. The street seems to telescope out until Henry is light-years away.

She strafes the empty room with curses.

Under the orange streetlight, Henry stands by the open door of his Volkswagen. His long, warped shadow spills across the pavement; one foot planted on the road, the other in the car, like a film still. He looks up at the hotel.

Lydia is sure the darkness conceals her, yet nothing seems safe. She shrinks behind the musty velvet curtain and its folds close around her: heavy, eager fabric like a human embrace.

Outside, Henry lifts his glasses and rubs one eye with his fist like a tired child. An impossibly familiar gesture.

It makes Lydia wish Henry would walk back across the road, come inside, say or do something to change the last hour or at least make sense of it. Equally, she wishes he would hurry up and get in his car, piss off and never come back so she can start the work of trying to forget she ever knew him. Again.

Without beginning to understand what has just happened to her, Lydia already knows that she will always wish tonight had unfolded differently, will always wish that *she* had done things differently. Will yet again wish she had been able to find her voice.

It was the coffee shop all over again; an event which should have been unrepeatable, only this time it was even worse.

While Henry was talking, it was as if he had taken Lydia's voice from her throat and replaced it with a stone. She had watched him drawing shapes in the air with his fingers as he spoke, the way he always did, observing that on this occasion, the gestures appeared imbued with the creepy quality of someone performing a hypnosis – one that had worked.

Lydia longs for a cosmic delete key. One she could press to erase her own existence. She notices that it is her life, not Henry's, that she has the instinct to obliterate and is sickened by what it exposes about how much more indelible she assumes Henry to be than herself.

Henry gets into his car.

The curtain enclosing Lydia is permeated with a mildew stink that reminds her of school: PE changing rooms, old sites of humiliation, early experiences of ignominy. Where the fabric touches exposed skin, it feels like being pawed by sweaty hands and it drags her back into her body where her throat, heart and stomach wrestle so aggressively she thinks she might throw up. But she must watch Henry leave. She cannot begin to comprehend what has happened tonight until she is certain she's alone with what he's done to her.

A bubble of blue light materialises through the car door, revealing Henry in silhouette. His thumb twitches across the phone screen.

She wonders who he's texting.

It could be anyone.

Lydia has never met Henry's friends.

He has never met hers.

Short, loose chains of acquaintances connect them, but Lydia only knows this from bleak, pissed, small hours internet sleuthing after his ghostings.

Lydia has known Henry for sixteen years, for all that time living a handful of miles apart on opposite sides of the river, tantamount to distant continents in London terms. Their intimacy has always been intermittent, lapsing into silences that last for months – years even – while enmeshed in other relationships, then emerging from stasis at a breakneck pace. One well-timed 'Hey, you awake?' the single spore that sends the number of messages mushrooming. Flocks and flurries of words zipping back and forth from breakfast to bedtime – sexual, supportive, funny, friendly, bitter and downright nasty – with in-person encounters occurring infrequently, three or four times a year. For every warm and joyful meeting, at least one that starts smooth and curdles quickly or is awry from the outset, instigating a retreat into the virtual. Their relationship conducted, once more, through the texts and sexts which have allowed their affiliation to float untethered from the rest of their lives, so divorced from rules and norms that the inexcusable has always felt reasonable.

The boundary between the remote but real and the purely fantastical so blurred that slowly but surely, Lydia has heedlessly collaborated with Henry to draw up, in increments, a perfect gaslighter's charter. One so effective that after Henry's admission in the coffee shop, Lydia had felt it was somehow incumbent on her to be conciliatory, to try to redraft something meaningful from the ugly chaos. She'd convinced herself that the bad things Henry did were interleaved with enough good ones to conclude that one could not exist without the other, the way both words and blank spaces bring a poem into being.

Henry had tried so hard, at least at first, to ensure they remained friends, which assured Lydia that there *had* been a point to all that misery.

But he'd grown lazier and more complacent, slower to reply to her messages if he replied at all. Rather than getting angry, Lydia had prostrated herself, sent a message saying she realised her hurt was too hard for Henry to cope with, putting herself out like a bin on his behalf. Hoping he'd say 'no', say 'sorry', make himself available again. But instead, he'd said, 'Thanks so much, you're always so nice and I really appreciate it.'

Instead of hating Henry, Lydia had felt small and spineless as a mollusc: hating herself for relinquishing the only power over Henry she'd ever possessed.

Although she'd also been relieved; glad, on some level, of that power that had made her even more despicable to herself.

The interior of the car darkens for a beat before the headlights come on. The engine clears its throat, roars, then carries Henry away.

A fox crosses the promenade. Its eyes flash green, its sharp, vigilant face caught for a moment in the receding taillights which abandon it quickly to the dark. Then Lydia's phone emits a ghostly glow through the fabric of her trouser pocket. She pulls it out.

Lydia. Hi, look ...

Great, Lydia thinks, *the old Hugh Grant, mumble-bumble routine.*
Henry's contrived awkwardness ignites her rage immediately.

... I don't really know what to say, or know how
you must be feeling after my slip up ...

Typical, trying to make another abuse into some cartoonish slip on a banana skin.

... I just ...

'Just'. The favourite word of manipulators, the magic shrinking spell of those four controlling letters that make the sender benign, the recipient unreasonable.

... wanted to ...

Henry's wants yet again triumphing over Lydia's needs.
Her hands shake so hard she drops her phone and she doesn't pick it back up.
Lydia doesn't care to know what the rest of Henry's message says.
A first. For years the zero-sum game of Henry's affection and attraction towards Lydia ruled her world remotely; his

replies to her messages, or lack of them, able to make or break her day. A fact he'd 'joked' about once, during one of their rare face-to-face meetings. One of many such 'jokes' that robbed situations of their proper gravity, made froth of their heft and which Lydia had laughed along with, including some which alluded unabashedly to the incidents Henry would, years later, apologise for. For a time, at her most sickly spellbound, Lydia held these incidents in almost affectionate regard, even looked upon them as the avatar of everything sad and dark and careless and damaging that they had overcome in order to still be friends.

All this awareness is fresh to Lydia, raw no matter how rotten the stink of the realisation; she hadn't been thinking any of this when Henry had said she'd been on his mind a lot lately, and since it turned out he'd was nearby, staying with his parents further round the coast, why didn't he pop by for a quick visit?

Nor had she been thinking, as she is now, *pop* and *quick* — textbook Henry. Always arriving with his exit strategy prepared, reminding Lydia that she is a light snack, a pitstop, and *Oh, go and pop off a fucking cliff, Henry*, she thinks.

Even after the coffee shop, after *everything*.

Despising that what she'd focused on in Henry's message was the part where he said he *had* been thinking about her. Detesting that she'd taken his intention to visit as a compliment, one which dazzled her blind to the underlying insult.

More odious now Lydia knows that, in *just popping over*, Henry had in fact been bearing another bombshell, yet again conveyed towards her as lightly as a Post-it note.

Lydia picks up her phone and opens her contacts. She is trying to work out whose friendship she could call upon, trying to work out who she could decently call or text. But her connections with other humans dangle lifelessly like a fistful of torn wires, making her feel like an inept thief trying to hot-wire a stolen car.

Lydia's friends have proper lives; substantial, adult ones filled with stressful jobs and caring responsibilities which reduce Lydia's woes to so much juvenile *sturm und drang*.

And Pandora? In the unlikely event she answered her phone? Well, it wouldn't be fair. Besides, she's dealing with her daughter.

So, Lydia has no one, really; no one whose support she could request without feeling like a crook, a leech, a user and a bitch. There is not one single person she could reach out to without adding to the festering midden of self-rebuke.

She tries to insist to herself that it's not that bad, but then she knows it must be because she wants to call her mother. And Lydia wanting to call her mother means things are desperate.

Already she can imagine exactly how that encounter would go.

The call will be answered, television noise will blare into the phone, then her mother's voice will command her to hang on, then retreat, shouting, 'Derek? *Derek!* Turn it *down*, Derek, the television, Derek, turn it down! Karen's on the phone. Karen. Karen. Derek, damn it – *Karen!* I said it's Karen on the phone, turn the flipping television blooming-well down.'

When she and Pan signed their record deal, Lydia changed her name by deed poll. Her parents refer to it as her stage name as though it's a white coat or branded baseball cap; a uniform she wears to go to work in.

They continue to call her Karen with the same obstinate dismissiveness and insinuation of fatuous whimsy they have always applied to anything Lydia said, did or wanted that existed at odds with their narrow prescription for acceptable human conduct. Hearing herself referred to as Karen will reduce Lydia to the bullied girl whose quiet misery was dismissed as surliness and oversensitivity.

The noisy static of the History Channel will be fleetingly replaced by the particular small quiet of Lydia's childhood home. Recognition will evoke the orderly magnolia null of their bungalow in the small cathedral city's suburbs, making Lydia feel stifled even before her mother's stream of irrelevances begin. News of the church warden's wife's hysterectomy and the neighbour's dog's blocked anal glands; the size of the wasp that flew into the kitchen yesterday and the actual, literal price of mince nowadays.

Lydia will have to suffer through the usual celebration of Barry, her boring bully of a brother, and his tangible Tory successes — businesses, babies and home improvements — freighted with the implication that Lydia's existence is trivial, a failure which demeans the whole family. Pandora isn't even here to laugh as Lydia holds the phone away from her ear and mimes blowing her brains out.

Lydia's phone goes dark in her hand. She slips it back into her pocket.

How could she explain what has happened to her tonight?

What she *let* happen to her tonight.

Tonight, Henry revealed to Lydia that a few months from now, a prestigious London theatre will stage a play that Henry is currently writing, based on a fictionalised version of what happened between the two of them, and she sat there and said it was fine.

She sat there and agreed with Henry that he's an artist, that artists must be free to make their art, that perhaps it was a good thing, really, maybe, perhaps it was a good thing. That yes, it felt painful, but he *is* an artist, that those were his life experiences too, and naturally he has to process them however he sees fit and that she supports him.

But now that Lydia is alone, she feels as manipulated, violated, coerced and invaded as she has all the other times Henry forced himself on her.

The worst part, it seems, is that Henry had apparently not intended to tell Lydia about this play, which is to be a *comedy,* of all things.

Not only was telling her not the express purpose of his visit, but the information simply skipped out in the course of inconsequential chit-chat. In fact, Henry had felt so comfortable, so sure everything was fine, so, so . . . *so free,* he had informed Lydia that her humiliation was being milled into his 'art' in the same casual tone in which he mentioned a jumper he'd bought and the great new brunch spot near his house.

The bastard.

That fucking bastard.

He has done it again.

Inside the curtain, Lydia deflates, crumpling and sagging until she is hunkered in half with her face resting on her knees.

The hotel at night is full of noise: clanks and creaks, whistles and moans from the plumbing that make Lydia glad she doesn't hold supernatural beliefs.

Tonight, there is a strange thin whine; eerie and wounded, vibrating through Lydia's body, pouring out of her mouth as steadily as water through the hotel's pipes.

A piece of her consciousness has parachuted out of the moment and is up on the ceiling watching and wondering why she is howling so pathetically.

The rest of her – crouching bulkily among the drapes with all the absurd violence of a brick in a sock – knows, and is reduced to screaming and screaming and screaming, tears mixing with spit.

This is the moment when tonight really begins to happen. When the coffee shop begins to happen, when last year and all the years leading up to it begin to happen. All the diminutive, distancing details disappear – the lacy scrap of cobweb, drifting balletically in the draft above Lydia's body on the bed; the pastries on wooden boards in the coffee shop beside the woman raking apologetically through her handbag for her purse – so that now, Lydia *is* the body on the bed and the one on the high stool listening to a man admit what he did to that body years before.

All the little observations of absurdities and poetries Lydia hoarded up in horror, jamming them between the self they happened to and the one who'd have to live with them like a modesty screen or a forensics tent – gone.

And she knows – *of course, Lydia knows* – that merging with minutiae in those moments is a trauma response. These last months, she's read relentlessly about the instinctive mechanisms of protection, the kill switch wired into us all, as engines built for survival. Recognising her vivid, indelible sense-impressions of cobwebs and pastries as the air raid shelters she took refuge in.

But tonight has expelled her from them, locking their doors behind her. There's nowhere left to run, nowhere to hide from the fact that ten years ago Henry violated Lydia, then five years ago he violated her again and less than a year ago, with his admission of guilt, he finally made those violations real and hers.

Then tonight, with his announcement that his abuses of her are going to be made into a play, he did it again.

A comedy.

Somehow the most egregious transgression of all.

Now Henry is gone, Pandora is gone, there is no one to call and Lydia is stranded inside the ballroom curtains at The Hotel Duchesse Royale with nothing but her victimhood for company.

Chapter 8

Lydia wakes at lunchtime with tropical-smelling blue sick on her pillow and a miniature cricketer jammed under her tit.

Assailed by spectacular pain in her head, churning in her stomach and a used feeling between her legs, Lydia moans, thanks her lucky stars that she didn't drown in her own vomit and plucks the tiny figure out of her flesh.

Lydia's brain is mush sloshing around inside her skull and the sensation of neurological damage extends all the way to her feet and fingertips. Her blood feels fudgy and sluggish, heart beating double-time to encourage it around her body.

Holding the cricketer up to her eye like a jeweller, Lydia squints at his shoddily painted face; queasy strobes of memory illuminate how he came to be lodged in the crease between her stomach rolls and under-boob.

There were pints. Several. Cheap, gassy lager, chased with shots – burning blue ones tasting of bubble bath. Lydia burps, thinking nothing says 'emotional car crash' like a person in their forties necking shots as if it's fresher's week.

After dropping the buckled figurine on the bedside table, Lydia limps to the en suite and runs the shower. While the water warms, she purges a jet of neon puke into the toilet.

Squatting under the shower, water batters Lydia's back, rinsing blades of grass and mud stains off her legs. She watches them disappear down the plughole, already feeling so much like wildlife that she doesn't bother getting out to pee.

Yesterday, after Henry left, unable to linger at the scene of her humiliation, Lydia had crashed out of the hotel into a crisply cold night. Nothing felt automatic, not even breathing. She'd sat on a bench on the prom with her eyes closed. Gathering in air, holding it, letting it out. Counting, concentrating; leaving no space for thoughts to leak through.

She'd looked at her phone, found the home screen cluttered with messages from Henry and crammed it back into her pocket, wishing she had the wherewithal to throw it into the sea.

Then she barged into the nearest pub, one of several on the prom that still smelled of the 1970s. Dirty deep-fat fryers, beer-saturated nylon carpet, male body odour and bafflingly, over a decade after the smoking ban, stale cigarettes.

Inside, the electric mutter of televised sport had mixed with the bray of a pub bore espousing some Brexit-means-Brexit rhetoric involving Churchill and capital punishment.

When Lydia walked in, there had been a glitch in the atmosphere; a fleeting silence, the prickly charge of scrutiny recognisable to any lone woman walking into a bar.

She'd ordered a pint of lager and sat on a pleather banquette the colour of diseased liver, positioning herself as near to the door as possible.

The bore had continued regaling his hypnotised mates with the same monological mish-mash of misdirected hatred and conspiracy as thousands of other identikit arseholes in bars the length and breadth of Britain.

Sighing heavily, Lydia had considered going over and

demolishing his despicable beliefs with lucidly articulated wrath, imagining the righteous chilly brilliance of the rebuttal she'd mount. But she reads those smug self-reports on Twitter all the time; long threads describing the writer's heroic intervention. *I challenged a racist in a restaurant. I took a misogynist to task on the Tube and everyone around me applauded.* She rarely believes those anecdotes are true, she thinks they're a guilty sort of wish fulfilment – expressing what the person wishes they'd done, imagined they did and hopes they one day might. And, anyway, she'd felt like she might burst into tears if she tried to speak.

She was feeling the sweaty guilt of choice, of privilege – her ability to be a bad ally without being found out; asking if she had any right to consider herself an ally at all, concluding she didn't, despising her worthless white guilt and hoovering up another gobbet of self-loathing – when a man walked over from the bar and sat down.

'Mind if I sit down and say hi?'

He looked like the bass player in a Toploader tribute band. Paunch bifurcated by the waistband of skinny jeans, hair in the product-heavy tousle around the temples that seems to have replaced the old-school, pedal-bin-lid combover as the modern strategy for concealing baldness. Clearly, he'd once been conventionally handsome – he had that look of fruit on the turn: a bit boozy and bloaty but just about edible in a pinch.

'You're already sitting down,' Lydia had shrugged.

'Mick.' He'd held out a hand.

'Karen,' said Lydia and shook it.

A stupid lie at the beginning of a stupid situation that Lydia had already launched herself into by not telling Mick to sod off, or at least being frosty.

Already she'd known what she was going to do; just to see if she still could, after the way Henry had made her feel.

After accepting Mick's pints and blue shots – after he'd been circumspect about why they couldn't go back to his place, after she'd lied about staying with friends so they couldn't go back to the hotel – everything had been hazy, aslant and multiple, so Lydia can't remember exactly how she ended up with Mick thumbing his brewer's droop into her in the middle of the village green of Minitania – *Where the buildings are small but the fun is big!* – but she can remember that she did.

As the shower dribbles over Lydia, she half-recalls climbing a fence, puking over a mock-Tudor pub the size of a cornflake box and collapsing face first onto the inch-high cricketers as Mick pulled up her top so he could, 'Feel those sexy tits of yours while you're getting shagged.'

She'd let Mick mash away arrhythmically at her hind-quarters for a while, with the tedious, performative brutality of someone who watched too much porn, as cold prickled her skin and toy-town streets smeared and swarmed in front of her.

Mick had kept saying, 'Nearly there, nearly there.'

While all the time Lydia was thinking, *Barely here, barely here.*

And in the end, what forced the words 'Stop, can you stop, please?' out of Lydia's mouth was the realisation that she didn't care.

Lydia had realised she didn't care if Mick carried on fucking her or not once he'd started, just like she hadn't cared if Henry carried on brutalising her once he had started, because – the fact was filtering into Lydia's core, with the winter night's chill – so much of the sex with men that she'd consented to, and all of the sex that she had not, felt the same.

Experiences to be endured, no matter how inept, saddening, painful, demeaning, plain shit, unwanted or even violent, because it wasn't really *for* her.

That all her adult life, Lydia's boundaries had been pushed and stretched, erased and re-drawn so many times that she had no idea where to draw them or how to defend them. Perhaps they had simply been obliterated.

Herself was a place that had been invaded so many times she could no longer imagine any way to limit the damage but to surrender. That this sad, wasted, al fresco experiment was just like all the other times when Lydia had been half-in, half-out of her body, like a guest at a bad party keeping their coat on in the hope of leaving. It was the most depressing thought Lydia had ever had.

'Can you stop, please, Mick?'

He'd carried on pumping.

'Get off me,' Lydia had bucked her body out of Mick's grasping hands. 'Fucking get the fuck *off me*!' She'd twisted and reared, crawling forward, so that Mick's dick plopped out of her and they'd collapsed together onto the grass.

Bare breasts studded with tiny cricketers, winter wind smacking her naked arse, Lydia had begun to sniffle. 'I want to go home.'

A zoetrope whirl of Micks loomed in front of her, kneading their floppy cocks.

'Come on, Karen . . . I was nearly there, lemme finish.'

A blur of semis flailed at Lydia's face.

'Fuck *off*.' She'd batted her left hand at them, using her right to start clawing her pants up. 'I don't want this. Get out my way, I'm going home.'

'Come on,' Mick slobbered. 'Lemme just finish myself off over your tits.'

'Oh, fuck *off*, Mick. Just *fuck off*,' Lydia slurred.

'Bitch. Crazy, mad, stupid bitch. Fucking fuck off then if you're going.'

As she'd pulled down her top and taken off, Lydia heard the jangle of Mick trying to buckle his belt, then a crash as he stumbled over nothing and fell sideways onto the miniature cathedral, snapping the spire off.

Sitting in the shower tray, shivering, Lydia laughs.

The laughs turn back into sobs.

Even though the pipes are shrieking and the water is running tepid, Lydia can't imagine getting out.

Can't imagine another day of trying to think her way out of this predicament she's in or trying not to think at all.

She supposes she had better get herself out of the shower, into her clothes, google the address of the nearest STD clinic, and more pressingly get to a chemist to buy the morning-after pill.

The thought of putting anything in her mouth yanks a retch from her.

She gobs blue froth into the drain where it catches in strands of hair like a tiny disgusting jellyfish.

'Right, up, out,' she commands herself and stands.

Her vision swims and her smashed head begs not to be taken anywhere but back to bed. Drying her hair feels like being punched in the skull so she winds a damp bun up into an elastic band, knowing that the cold air outside will make it feel like a snowball balanced on top of her head and not caring.

Her belongings are scattered round the bedroom as if she had detonated her handbag when she got home. She picks up her phone.

One per cent battery.

A message from Henry.

I really appreciate you getting in touch . . .

Shit.

Lydia scrolls up, past the huge wall of text Henry has sent, to four equally extensive and completely illiterate diatribes of bitterness and sentiment she must have sent last night – a cocktail of honey and weedkiller.

She mashes her face to her hands and moos a *fuck* containing a thousand u's into her palms.

Her battery dies before she can read any more.

She plugs her phone in to charge, lurches into yesterday's clothes and leaves the hotel without it.

As she walks towards The Golden Sands cafe to experiment with struggling down some coffee, she passes the window of the paper shop, notices that the board advertising this morning's edition of the local Sunday paper reads: YOBS TRASH MODEL VILLAGE.

Chapter 9

Somehow a whole week goes by in the small seaside town, the weather growing more bitter, dawns coming later, dusk arriving earlier.

The tide turns over and over on itself and on the prom, Christmas lights are strung up between the ornate streetlights that measure out its length. Carols play over shop tannoys.

Since last Saturday, life had felt sparkly and available to Joyce, laid out on trays like rings in a jeweller's window. As though that strange feeling of hers – the hungry, haunted sensation of craving something imperative but inarticulable – had written away to a mail-order catalogue, delivering Martin by return of post. At least, it appeared to Joyce that way as long as she kept moving.

But every time she sat still, she was inundated by doubt, understanding that she was getting ahead of herself. Then Joyce felt like she was a rowing boat with a leak and one oar: taking on water, filling and sinking, flailing in circles.

All week, Betty had a severe case of 'the mentions': Angus this and Angus that. And all week Joyce resented Betty's freedom to speak, the M of Martin's name always stuck between her lips like a kiss with no cheek to plant it on.

Angus Stirrup is already in the club. He has saved them a seat at his table. He showers Betty with compliments and insists on buying their drinks.

As the minutes pass, and pensioners filter into the bar in ones and twos, Joyce's insides feel like a penny-falls machine – a tinny bright teetering shelf of coins clinging to the edge, never tipping over. There is no sign of Martin.

Angus plies Betty with stories in which he puts people straight, sorts things out and is generally a genius surrounded by dimwits.

'So, I said to the chaps, Thai restaurant? No, thank *you*. The only *tie* I'll be having anything to do with is the one around my neck!'

'Isn't that just *too* funny, Joycey?' Betty jabs Joyce in the ribs. 'Didn't you hear what Angus said, wasn't it just *too* funny?'

Horrible, horrible idiot.

'Hilarious.'

Betty hisses, 'Gussy up, Joyce, for heaven's sake.' She complains to Angus that, '*Someone*, not a million miles from here, can be a *real* wet weekend.'

'Well,' smiles Angus munificently, 'she'd probably prefer some company her own age. My niece Shandy's on her way, she's a hoot, she'll cheer this one up in no time.'

'Shandy?' Betty simpers. 'What an *interesting* name.'

'Short for Sharon. Suits her, *very* bubbly, now let me tell you about the time I . . .'

Angus goes on and on, Betty hanging on his every word as Joyce tunes out, a dwindle and whine in her head like a plug being pulled.

Joyce keeps dwelling on yesterday.

Yesterday morning Joyce had burned the toast.

'Careless girl,' Betty scolded. 'Silly, we don't have money to waste.'

Betty had looked peculiarly aged to Joyce, as she chided her. Shrunken and desiccated, like the dead mice they sometimes find in the airing cupboard. They climb in through gaps around the pipework, get trapped and die among the towels and sheets.

On those occasions, Betty bemoans their neighbours' unsanitary habits, muttering darkly about how they never learn *our ways*, about the poor repair of the building and the general dilapidation of their circumstances, while Joyce wraps the tiny stiff body in newspaper and carries it downstairs to the outside bin.

They had taken their tea and toast in front of *Homes Under the Hammer*. Betty had a great deal to say about the man who was renovating a bungalow, the bungalow he was renovating and the deficiencies of both, while Joyce shunted toast around her mouth.

'Quiet this morning, Joycey. Cat got your tongue?' Betty had asked.

'Bit of a headache.'

'You seem rather Maudie Moo-Cow. Someone's Auntie Flo is preparing to visit.'

Maybe, Joyce thought, maybe not. Her monthlies have become unpredictable; shorter, heavier, closer together and further apart. For the first time, she'd suspected with dismay that the foreign humidity of her strange feeling might be connected to that.

The realisation that she *is* old enough for it to be . . . her . . . that *time of life* . . . induced a sensation between Joyce's belly button and her pieces; nervy and hollow, like the feeling she used to get when she rode the big dipper.

She said nothing. Another unspoken. Such a cache of unexpressed feeling building, like a wall sneaking up one brick at a time.

Each other is all they have, and Joyce can't keep things right in her head, she *knows* she can't, understands she *needs* her mother to do it for her. Yet, in some way, secrecy feels as thrilling as it does hazardous: as much like burying treasure as laying landmines.

Betty had pottered over and picked through Joyce's hair like a chimp.

'Oh, dear, thought so: roots,' she'd said, as if diagnosing Joyce with a shameful complaint of her lady's areas.

'This will never do, not with Club Saturday tomorrow.'

Joyce had gone over to the convex living room mirror, gold-framed and circular like a porthole on a genteel ocean liner, where a bulgy funhouse version of herself looked back: roots just beginning to show. Mousy-frosty, unlike her mother's which were completely white, like a turnip-top emerging through soil. Time moves so fast, she thought, and her pulse revved.

After breakfast, they'd gone out.

As they walked along the prom, an efficiently brutal wind bullying in off the sea flapped their coats and skirts up like a pervert trying to glimpse their underthings. Joyce had felt odd – off-balance as they approached the semi-derelict pier where men in hard hats and high-vis were erecting a fence round another hole in the boards.

'I do sometimes wish,' Betty had remarked, 'that it would hurry up and fall into the sea.'

'Me too,' Joyce replied vehemently.

The Palace, at the pier entrance, is like a mausoleum for the life Betty and Joyce once had, a goading reminder of their diminished circumstances.

Joyce's father used to own The Palace. Betty and Joyce were local royalty back when he did, with all the kinds of attention that invited.

The Punch and Judy man, the clown and the magician always singled out Joyce in her nice outfits: velvet dresses with matching tammy hats and Dorothy bags. They picked her from the jostling crowds of children for special treatment. Sweaty men, grinning at her father in the hope of being re-employed the next summer, holding Joyce a bit too tightly, hands brushing over her private places by mistake.

Other children picked Joyce out for special treatment too.

'Fucking pier,' Joyce had shocked herself by exclaiming, as they hurried towards the chemist to buy hair dye.

'I beg your pardon, lady! What on earth did you just say?' Betty clutched her chest, 'I feel sick, I could faint.'

'I said disgusting pier, Mum. The pier is disgusting.'

'Oh, thank heaven, Joyce! For a second there I could have sworn you said something else.'

Joyce had felt a bubble of mischief form under her sternum, 'Really, Mum. What did you *think* I said?'

'Joyce! I wouldn't repeat the word if my life depended on it.'

Joyce had to pretend to blow her nose with her lace-trimmed handkerchief, partly so that Betty wouldn't see her laughing and partly to stop herself from saying anything else.

The swirling, unhinged sensation had tailed Joyce all day. Yesterday evening, side by side in coral velour arm-chairs, whose seats and headrests looked a little fatigued, Betty and Joyce had eaten tinned sardines on toast from their lap trays.

Supper from lap trays was admissible only on very unpleas-ant days or very pleasant ones.

Everything on television that night had been 'fishwives'

91

(soap operas, *EastEnders* especially), 'inane' (situation comedies) or 'I couldn't possibly, why must they invade our living room with such misery?' (almost everything else apart from nature programmes, which must go off at the slightest whiff of death or reproduction).

Instead, Betty had selected a video cassette from the special cases that disguise them as leather-bound literature. They'd watched *The Sound of Music*. Again. Fast-forwarding, as ever, through the Nazi-heavy segments since Betty simply can't, *can-not*, see why you'd put something as horrid as Nazis in a lovely film like that.

And as she'd watched the Von Trapp children prancing around Salzburg, Joyce had felt as though large sections of her life were missing, having been sped through, leaving only the vaguest impression of how it had been to live them. Only humid jumps of colour remained; a hand, a mouth, a kiss or an argument.

Once, when Betty had had to endure a long dental treatment, Joyce, unprecedentedly alone, had eaten an entire pipe of Pringles and a whole four-finger Kit-Kat washed down with a tin of gin, while she watched *The Sound of Music* including the parts she'd never seen.

It was sad, very sad, and not at all nice in places, and yet it was better. More substantial: the romance and songs more beautiful given full context.

And after disposing of her illicit feast's evidence in the outside bin, she'd understood, in some hazy way, that the experience of watching the whole film had something to tell her about all the parts of her life she could not obtain or even fully remember, without being able to craft the understanding into something useful.

She is still incapable.

Hard to believe she had already come to be *forty-six*.

Forty-six and unable to fall asleep in a single bed in the same room as her mother, unable to tell her about the nice man she has met.

Chapter 10

Somehow a whole week goes by in the small seaside town, the weather growing grimmer, sky the colour of unwashed bedsheets, light hours murky and truncated.

The tide turns over and over on itself. It is barely bonfire night but already the shops are full of phallic chocolate Santas and tubs of sweets the size of car tyres. And it makes Lydia feel even more like she's strapped to some Spindizzy; slowing and speeding revolutions. Just turning paralysed circles while the rest of the world rushes on.

Her life in the town and in the hotel has taken on a schizoid split: on Monday evening, Lydia had been drowsing on the couch in Pan's apartment, thrashing in the shallows of a nightmare about Henry with his fingers in her mouth, pushed so far in she was choking, when she heard Pan's voice.

'Lyd!' Pan had sounded surprised to see her. 'You're in here. Fine, of course. I said you could, during the day. It's fine. Anyway, look who's home!'

Dry-mouthed, dream still scuzzy on her, Lydia had sat up to see an unrecognisable person standing with Pan. 'Mum,' they'd said, shucking Pan's arm off their shoulder, 'personal space, please. Ever heard of it?'

'Fuck me pretty, Lyd. Can't even hug my own daughter. Can you see the shite I have been getting all the way back?'

'Laurence!' Lydia yawned, smiling. 'Sleepy, sorry. It is *so* nice to see you! I take it you'd prefer not to hug?'

The big-bodied, adult-appearing person – swamped by a baggy black tracksuit, with cropped, denim-blue hair, a septum ring and shy, lopsided child smile – who was, of course, Laurence, had held her arms out. 'No, it's fine, it's nice to see you, Auntie Lyd.'

Auntie felt like a blanket fort, a snug wrap of belonging.

'Oh, very nice,' Pan groused. 'It's all *get off* when I want a hug, and cuddles for Lydia.'

Pan looked huffy as a toddler told no.

Lydia had put her arms round Laurence, who was taller than her, heavier. Her soft warmth reminded Lydia of how it had been to hold her as a baby. Somehow Lydia feels more responsible and tender towards Laurence now that she is more emphatically a person than when she'd been that unknowable little thing. One of those long, unpretty babies, serious-faced, like a wise Christ-child from a Renaissance painting, but so ridiculously tiny and *unheimlich*: at once animatronic and too real. Breakable, as if her head might fall off.

'I use Lol now, Auntie Lyd.'

'Lovely,' Lydia had replied. 'Lovely Lol.'

She'd kissed the top of Lol's head and noticed her blue hair smelled dirty.

'Lol. What's wrong with Laurence?' Pan used ostentatiously accented French. 'Lol. God, you might as well have an emoji for a name.'

And a look had passed between Lydia and Lol: a trapeze artist's flying catch and release. A sort of wry, in-this-togetherness that added to the cosy sensation of being adopted family.

'Is there anything to eat?' Lol had asked, head nuzzled into Lydia's shoulder.

Pan had paused, looking pointedly at Lol. 'Dinner's in a couple of hours.'

'I'm hungry now.'

'You had lunch and snacks on the ferry. Dinner's in a couple of hours. Go and put your stuff away.'

Lydia had cringed at the way Lol reacted by hanging her head, hugging herself, cupping her hands around her rolls and giving them a squeeze. An action permeated with unconscious self-comforting and painfully conscious humiliation.

As Lol left the room, Lydia had thought of her own mother's attitude to weight, hers and Pan's. Those *Very Hungry Caterpillar* last day lists: you ate this, then you ate that. The unending, repetitive monologues about food and eating, like being fat-shamed by Stewart Lee. Scolded for eating too much and too little; you're not going to scarf all that are you but clear your plate, don't waste food. Loaded adjectives: gobbling and guzzling.

The lifetime of disordered eating. Chowing down on her feelings these last few weeks, living on the smallest, most joyless utility meals these last few days.

Lydia's gullet feels like a knotted sock. Her empty stomach the one clean place inside her.

The practice of starvation comes back so quickly. The surrender and control, the giddy upward drift of refusing her body, the feathery distancing effect of perpetual light-headedness.

And Pan's always juice cleansing and 'clean' eating, forty-eight-hour fasting and low-carbing. Never stints on the wine though. Flogs herself over food and cracks through at least one bottle of rosé every evening.

All these contortions learned from being a body in public. The first time The Lollies' manager told them they wouldn't be playing their own instruments any more, they had meekly assented to the record company drafting in session musicians: bitter indie boys who treated Pan and Lydia as if they'd stolen something that belonged to them, transacted through a snotty, baby-brother combination of flattery, snubs and goads.

Only Pan had had the balls to at least ask their handlers why.

'People want to see you ... they don't want you hidden behind instruments. They want to see your ... you dancing. Moving about.'

Their manager circumspectly scrying their arses like a lookout peering around a corner in case the police were coming. 'Bit of moving about might not be a bad thing. You'll need to be fit, to do these shows, you know? You want to look good, look the best when we shoot the record cover.'

That photo session, and all the other ones for teen magazines and music papers: suck it in and push it out and pull those down and lez it up and they'd been nineteen and green, eager to please, delighted to escape the stultifying suburbs of the small cathedral city. And so they had done it all; made themselves poseable as dolls and pliable as Plasticine. Never once had it occurred to either of them that it was anything other than their job to try harder, accept that there was simultaneously too much and too little of them in the world, and never once did it occur to either of them to say, 'Fuck you' or 'No' or 'Stop', let alone, 'There is exactly the right amount of me in the world, and I'll conceal or reveal as much of it as I choose to.'

Every careful question they raised, no matter how gently,

97

met a reception that implied they were, at best, naïve, ungrateful and humourless; at worst confrontational, difficult to deal with and mental, actually, fucking mental, girls, to be honest. The cancellation clauses in their contract mentioned in minutes.

'Pan,' Lydia had cleared her throat, loud and crass as a revving engine, 'I think Lol's a bit ... you know ... self-conscious about her weight.'

'Oh, *Laurence* is self-conscious about *everything,* it's all identity and angst. Gender and mental health and autism and sexuality. Obsessed. You'll see. This navel-gazing stuff is what's driven a wedge between her and Alain.

'She said she's being traumatised. Traumatised! Can you imagine? The most privileged kid alive, music lessons, ballet, swimming. She had a fucking horse at one point. And the school fees! The holidays we took her on. She's been to more places at sixteen than I'd been by the time I was thirty! Traumatised. Fucking hell.

'She thinks she's bisexual, you know? Or what's the new thing, pansexual. What even is that? And how would she know? She's only just turned sixteen, fuck's sake. Everyone experiments, everyone tries on personalities like hats at that age and—'

'Maybe she's just who she says she is though. You know I really think kids these days, like all the community and access to information online, they're so much more aware of—'

'Don't you dare, Lydia.'

Pan had taken on a piggy-livid look Lydia had learned to fear. Screw-eyed, flush-cheeked and tight-lipped. 'I am *not* taking parenting advice from you. When was the last time you even saw her before today, *Auntie* Lydia?'

'Sorry, Pan,' Lydia had hung her head, just like Lol. From

the first mention of her, she'd been carrying the shame of those derelict years. Two presents biannually, straight from Amazon, becoming vouchers when Lydia realised she no longer had the first clue what Lol's interests were.

All the years, five at least, which had slipped by, thinking of the child with syrupy sentimentality but never seeing her; intention never becoming action. But she thought: *I can do something for her here, now.*

'I know, Pan. I'm sorry I've been shit. I *know* I've been utterly, *utterly* shit, but I'm here now and I want to do better. I'm going to do better and part of that is, I just think, around food and weight, especially with girls, you've got to . . . like, don't you remember the way . . . how they used to speak to us about all that?'

'Oh, no, no, no. That was different. We were older, we were . . . we signed up for that. We knew what we were getting into.'

'Did we though? Pan, really? *Did we?*'

Voice froggy and raw, breath scarce and sharp. Lydia hadn't probed Pan so boldly in years; the first time she'd raised the questions she'd been carrying about The Lollies years.

'Yes. Yes, we did. I mean, *I* did maybe . . . you didn't. And anyway, this isn't about the past, this is about now, Laurence, *my* daughter, so let's not . . . let's just. Not.'

That Lydia had inched out onto a limb with Pan over Lol was something she held Henry responsible for. The past as Lydia had lived it had been humiliating and haunting enough before what she'd reluctantly called his apology. Since last Saturday, she'd wiped it clean of that name, re-christening it as just one more shitty thing Henry had said to invalidate her, one more shitty thing he had done to un-person her. But his re-editing of her history remains irreversible, and

Lydia finds that she can no longer abstain from challenging situations in which silence sufficed before, no matter how uneasy the unspeaking.

All these 'un' entered her vocabulary in the coffee shop, she notices; the ever-ascending amount of impossibilities, another imposition. Even her inner monologue moulded by his selfish so-called sorry.

And although Lydia had loathed it, now it's no longer there, she missed the false equivalency between Henry's behaviour and hers which had meant she wasn't a victim.

In some sick way, it had been tolerable when Lydia had viewed herself as needy and difficult and, on occasion, quite mental. The maelstrom madness of those heartbroken drunk-dials and text arguments and the cooing conciliations and incandescently hot make-up sexting felt like equal parts of a tempestuous affair. So whatever Henry had done, Lydia had done too.

Stripped of the bleak comforts of such an illusion, she has simply been *done to*, which makes her a victim.

She doesn't know if she'd give it a lower-case or capital V, if she had to write it down, unsure if it's an identity, a predicament or both. All she's certain of is that decades of defying the definition have ended, so that things which used to seem inevitable now feel intolerable.

It hurts so much to realise she deserved better.

It hurts so much to realise she was failed.

It hurts so much to accept it wasn't her fault she was harmed.

All the little cuts Lydia refused to let connect at the time arriving as one big eviscerating wound, making it obvious each had deserved to be tended to, where instead she'd scolded herself for being clumsy and careless enough to accrue them.

And Lydia had been unable to bear the thought of a middle-aged Lol having to take her own scalpel to such a scar in a few decades' time; the thought of her having to navigate the same sordid sufferings and retrospective reinterpretations.

Insufferable to imagine an aching, adult version of the teenager trying to caretake the younger one, all the woes trivialised at the time assuming the gravity they always deserved. The grief. The actual grief in that, the too late of it.

'I know, Pan, I do. But it's like, recently I've been looking back, thinking about all the toxic shitty messages that were crammed down our throats on the regular and . . . just, look, I find myself wondering all the time, how we might have been able to feel. Or not. To not have to feel, about ourselves, our bodies, if no one had spoken to us . . . or if they'd spoken to us differently. Like just then, when Lol— She just wanted something to eat, you know, and . . . '

'You don't know. What do you know? You've scarcely seen *Laurence*, can't even keep a pot plant alive, so . . . ' Pan had stopped there, letting her words tail off and curdle in the silence, seeing Lydia deflate under the death blow.

You don't know, can't understand. *You're not a parent.*

Never any room to see how distance might create perspective, no sense that a childless person is still an encyclopedia of experiences, some of which might be useful. Insightful or illuminating.

Not at all.

When the children are small, being treated like you might use their fontanelles as an improvised ashtray and feed them gin off your fingertips; when they're older like you might get them a facial tattoo or a bag of heroin for Christmas.

And there's just no fighting it at the best of times, and this, that, then, the other day, was not the best of times.

While Pan was away, Lydia had blundered from sleepless nights into sleepy days, writing articles. Had spent her evenings tormenting herself on the internet, elliptical public allusions to her agony flocking to the tip of her finger, eternally on the cusp of posting some vague sad status soliciting sympathy. But she couldn't bring herself to go fishing for the *U OK hun?* and *DM me* replies that might pick the lock on her silence.

She'd promised herself she wouldn't drink, then by seven had been meandering through the dank hotel dustsheets to retrieve a bottle from Pan's apartment, where the wine fridge was as well-stocked as any restaurant.

Returning to her room, drinking from a questionable mug and sitting on the bed with her laptop.

She'd googled herself and googled Henry, digging away, mining the social-media accounts of women she suspects Henry has at some point fucked and fucked over, just like her, with or without their consent. Cookie-cutter, semi-successful, completely insecure women of a certain age, on the up or on the down, who Lydia's worked out he might have been toying with, be trifling with still.

Getting drunker and drunker, asking herself what Henry *did* to them, if she really believes he did *it* to her. Acquiesced to if not invited, deserved if not wanted.

Wondering if she would ever have held Henry to account if he hadn't done so himself. Or if she'd have applied *that* word to it, the word that blinks bright inside her mind then disappears, like a fritzing red neon flicking between the feeling that it's too extreme to describe the complexities of what occurred and the only word for what it was.

And when she did call it *that*, overcome with rage and pain, she'd start composing a tweet: the nuclear button, the *fuck it all* one, naming him, using the word. But then she'd remember how rabidly some people had defended Henry in the comments below a rare three-star review of one of his plays, imagine the words rushing out of her grasp, taking her privacy with them, turning her into the public face of victimhood and liars.

She'd delete it, pass out in her clothes, then the next day do it again.

Left to her own devices, she'd have carried on.

But after Pan brought Lol home, after Lydia had defused their incipient fight with an insincere apology, she had felt, for the first time in a very long time, a sense of purpose.

Thus began the fractured existence which had typified this last week.

Spending time with Lol, starting to get to know her, throwing herself between Pan's most careless words and Lol's sensitivities, both of them appearing hellbent on misunderstanding one another. It felt something a little bit like family.

Lol painted Lydia's nails. An earnest, messy bodge that had made Lydia love the hot-pink hot mess, which almost instantly began to chip.

She liked the warmth of her hand in Lol's large, dearly dimple-knuckled paw that made her seem so raw and vulnerable.

The comforting quiet between them. Lol's unselfconscious concentration: tongue peeped between her lips, school-like, small childish, being so careful and messing it up nonetheless.

Pan came in, blonder and bigger-haired than usual, swearing. 'Never again, I'm going to have to go up to London to Mario. Should have known better, lazy really. I mean, state of this *Only Way is Essex* wig. Shouldn't be surprised, she was like a Poundland Gemma Collins, the hairdresser. I mean sweet, total sweetie, couldn't have been lovelier, but no. Not for me. What's going on here? Nail bar? Careful not to get any of the coffee table. Do mine though, darling. You could do mine. Might as well have pink nails to go with my Barbie barnet.'

Looking up, screwing the lid onto the polish, Lol said quietly, 'Oh, I'm not, like, all that amazing.'

'You've done a lush job,' Lydia had fanned out her fingers for Pan, who looked them over and said 'Oh' through a tight smile. 'Nice, maybe I'll just . . . actually. That's not my colour. Tea?'

Lydia told Pan there were plenty of other colours to choose from, but Pan was back at the window, knocking the glass to shoo away the gulls.

'I need to order those bird spikes, stat. Go on. Fuck off, dirty bastards,'

Lol gathered up her stuff and sloped out of the room.

All those little missed moments, Lydia thought: the connections let fall like crumbs, possibilities whose loss goes unmarked, dropped like small coins that could add up to vast sums, if only they were kept and counted.

And how many of her own, she wondered, were lost by posting on Twitter and Instagram, most of all texting Henry, hundreds, thousands of times throughout the years, trying to make him a spectator to her, to make him see her seeing things, perceiving the poetry and beauty of life in a vain attempt to feel lovely to herself.

Fuck.

She could have just, should have just, kept a diary: all those lost thoughts she should have articulated only to herself, moments she should have been present in, hundreds handed to Henry like a cat trying to ingratiate itself to its owner with a chewed shrew and received just as welcomely as one.

The next day, Lol and Lydia had baked cookies, smiling in the chocolate- and vanilla-scented warmth of the kitchen, and had slipped into talking about what they might bake at Christmas.

'Oh, I don't know if I'll still be . . . I should probably go back to London sometime. Sometime soon.'

The crestfallen look on Lol's face had felt like a compliment, one that had dragged at Lydia's heart the weighty way love does, surprising her.

Then Pan came in, commented on how good the cookies smelled and warned Lol not to eat too many: one a day, make them last. Lol had slunk back to her room and Lydia returned to lurking in the Flamingo Suite, feeling even more like a moribund teenager than Lol, whose body Lydia could envision sprawled or curled disconsolately on the bed upstairs. The bed Lydia had occupied, raking over her past, worrying about her future, until Lol arrived – Lol who doesn't have that much of a past yet, but who has a whole huge future ahead, one Lydia wants to take part in making painless; preferably beautiful.

But for the moment she's aware they're both in the not-present-now of the internet, the inert trance of scrolling social media, skimming articles, consuming and consuming.

Lydia so often finds she's unable to stop even though the stories and pictures make her feel even emptier, shrinking her and sinking her, until she's drowned in data and images, other people's fake happiness and real misery, assaulted by fact after fact of such negligible provenance that she doesn't even know what constitutes truth any longer, until eventually not even her own heartbeat, the spit in her mouth, the sensation of her pulse convinces her that she exists in any meaningful way.

Aware of Lol, one floor above, probably swigging from

the same poison bottle; no good, whether it has a sickening effect or a mithridatic one. It feels to Lydia that it seals a Möbius strip around the two of them, travelling its topology in opposite directions, right now meeting in the middle.

And now it is Saturday, a week has passed since Henry was right here.

Lydia sits down on the saggy bed.

Lydia looks around the messy room.

Condensation fogs the windowpanes. Brocade curtains buckle their brass pole, dust collected in the flock.

The tired, impersonal furniture is cluttered with almost-empty jars of expensive creams and cosmetics Lydia can't afford to replace – work freebies, fripperies that used to help delude her that life was better than it is.

Clothes are heaped in open suitcases: dirty and clean mixed; jumpers in Jesus Christ poses, arms flung apart; crumpled knickers and balled-up bras; and in the far corner a cairn of mismatched shoes.

Restlessly, she picks up her phone again to find a notification onscreen: a WhatsApp from Henry which reads only: *Lydia?*

She opens the app, Henry is online.

Then he is not.

Then he is.

She knows the patterns of his chat – he's talking to someone, flirting probably. Trying to manage his personal PR disaster in one run of messages while flirting himself into a future one in the other.

Unscathed, she thinks, unstoppable.

Typical.

Lydia types Henry's name into Google. Fan-love and

five-star reviews appear: blizzards of praise for Henry's plays; Lydia scrolls through them all.

Time and again he is lauded for being a compassionate chronicler of human cruelty. Time and again he is commended for his understanding of regret – an ongoing theme of his work.

Lydia is jagged by the 'G' of genius so many times that she begins to feel like her heart is studded with fishhooks, like a macabre pomander.

Not one of the articles ever questions why Henry might know so much about cruelty, possesses such a profound understanding of regret. And not one of them ever asks *who* he might ever have been cruel to, *who* he might have engaged in regrettable conduct towards.

'Because no cunt gives a shit, do they?' Lydia spits aloud.

She goes to YouTube and finds the video for 'Up For It', uploaded by an account called Stink Pop. Plays it on mute. There she is.

A version of Lydia anyway. Pandora too, but Lydia is so drawn to her own image she can barely perceive Pan over herself: emptily beautiful as a champagne coupe, with all the disposable utility of a wire coat hanger, wafting about the screen.

Her image lies back on a bed and pushes her skirt up. Her mouth is a wet red hole, singing silently in close-up.

She is not the person on the screen.

She is the answer to an obscure trivia question.

One of her busiest days on social media had been triggered two months ago when two accountants from Dundee won *Pointless* by naming 'Up For It' in answer to a question about one-hit wonders.

Lydia is not a pop star, not a musician and she is not even really a writer.

She is a loser.

She is nothing.

And she wishes Pan had never called that day that was meant to be her last.

A notification appears on her phone screen, popping up on top of the video, covering Lydia's nineteen-year-old eyes like a censorship bar, as her pink tongue licks an outsized heart-shaped lollipop.

Lydia? Please?

Henry.

She feels sick at the sight of the message and sick at the sight of herself at nineteen pretending to be both more innocent and more knowing than she was.

Snackable, fuckable, ephemeral, disposable. So full of love and rage at that girl who'd taught herself to play guitar and written the songs that snared the record deal then allowed herself to be milled into a puff of candyfloss.

The impossible, intolerable burn and yearn to reach back through all the years and say: *you don't have to let them do this.*

She catches on the word 'let'. That shock-stop of catching a cardigan on a door handle. Not *let* – 'let' burdens that incapable girl all the further. A spurious moral imperative that conflates unhappiness with weakness, pain with failing, implying that resilience is the ability to keep taking punches without extending any responsibility to the person throwing them.

Lydia thinks of that dusty old thought-terminating cliché: don't let the bastards get you down: What a scam – it's entirely reasonable to object to bastards, it's incumbent on *them* not to *let* themselves be bastards, especially the ones who are trying to grind you down on purpose. Walk away from the bastards, the formulation should be, popping the finger at them as you go.

And that's what Lydia longs to tell the video version of her still pouting in silver hotpants on her phone; she longs to give her permission to trust the disquiet she dismissed the day the footage was filmed, tell her it's not just unease, it's instinct, you're right to feel this is wrong for you and you don't have to do any of this. It's OK, *you don't have to.*

Unable to bear a second more, she banishes the video as another message from Henry arrives, longer this time.

> I know all this has been hard for you, but
> it's hard for me too and look, sorry, I know
> it probably seems a bit rich, I know it does,
> honestly, but I'm on a deadline and I'm so
> stressed out I can't write and it would just really
> help if we could have a chat and settle this,
> put it to bed you know? So we can both move
> on and . . .

Put it to bed?

The phrase conjures an optical illusion: a stubborn image that defies resolution.

Lydia is a sad old hag. She is a young girl.

Which?

Both refuse to go quietly.

Refuse to be *put to bed.*

Henry has stolen Lydia out from underneath herself: dismantled and handed back with the instructions missing.

And it is time to put herself back together.

Enough, she thinks, *enough.*

Lydia will not move.

She will not make an inch more space in the world for Henry than the vast acreage he has already grabbed for himself.

She will be the endless possibility of public revelation.

She will be the sudden shriek of fear that shakes him awake in the small hours.

The cold sweat on his nape.

The maggot in his apple.

The sand in his Vaseline and the thorn in his side.

And this time, she will not make it OK, she will not reassure him or bag herself up like a dog shit and climb into the nearest bin.

How conveniently she'd ingested Henry's implication that dirty laundry must be disposed of by tearing it in two. He can air it in public, he can live with the stain, but Lydia will have no part in decontaminating it.

Taking none of the time, care or craft she's squandered on composing every sext, text and passing communication for the last sixteen years, hastily she types:

> You are an abuser. I don't care if you know
> it or not. It is enough that I know. Don't
> contact me again.

She hits send, sees that Henry is online. Then Lydia opens her contacts and does the one thing she thought she never would and which, at that moment, feels like a statement of intent, that this time, enough really is *enough*.

She blocks and deletes Henry's number, the only way she has of contacting him since he isn't on social media. And the bridge between them is burned.

So, Lydia wonders, why does she feel nothing except loneliness?

Unless, of course, she thinks of Lol. And what Lydia would want for Lol, which is all the happiness and comfort Lydia has been deprived of herself. And she realises that that is something that is really starting to matter.

Chapter 11

Saturday comes round again and this week, as Betty and Joyce enter the club, Joyce's insides feel like she's on a rollercoaster, poised above a drop. Jangly waves shift back and forth.

'There's Shandy!' exclaims Angus, rousing Joyce from her introspection.

A big, blonde woman walks towards them, everything about her spangly and bouncy. Pink nails like candy daggers; constellations of diamante bedazzling every inch – earrings, shoes, dress. Dress so low cut that breasts the size of Joyce's head threaten to spill from the sweetheart neckline. Behind her follows a square-jawed man in a smart, tight-fitting shirt, hair gelled into crispy points.

'Hi!' Shandy waves and grins like a winner celebrating on a game show. 'Kiss, kiss, Uncle Angus,' she says, planting one on each of Angus' cheeks.

'Scott,' says Angus, pumping the younger man's hand ostentatiously. 'Pint?'

'G and T please,' Scott replies.

Angus wrinkles his nose. He introduces Betty and Joyce.

'What can I get you, sweetheart?' Angus asks Shandy.

'Fizz, please,' she winks at Joyce. 'I love my fizz.'

She squeezes onto the pleather banquette beside them, oblivious to Betty's look of fascinated horror. Joyce can see her mother stockpiling disapproval to feast on later.

Shandy radiates warmth and expensive scents. When she smiles, her teeth have the blue-white luminescence of cosmetic dentistry. 'I *love* your look, ladies!'

She fingers Joyce's hair the way children impulsively touch things that catch their attention, 'Super retro and cool, so vintage – it's just amazing.'

'Yeah, gorge, love the matching,' Scott chimes in. '*Love. It.* Such a ... strong look.'

Betty insisted that she and Joyce wear plummy-velvety tonight. Full-skirted with leg-of-mutton sleeves. A very special dress.

'Class never goes out of fashion,' Betty snaps, and makes a face like someone has let off.

Overthrowing the frail outrage she'd experienced when Shandy first sailed in – not behaving as she thought a 'bigger' lady ought to – and shamefaced by her knee-jerk distaste for Shandy's brazen comfort in her own skin, Joyce thinks: *I like you.*

'Thank you, Shandy,' she says. 'You look pretty, I love all your sparkles.'

'Got to have a bit of bling on Saturday night, Joyce.'

She smiles as Angus comes back with a bottle of budget bubbles and three glasses, exclaiming, 'Thought I'd treat you beautiful ladies to a little something special. There's your G and T, Scott.'

Angus rolls his eyes as he places Scott's drink in front of him.

'Oh, Angus,' swoons Betty, 'how *luxurious,* so *extravagant.*'

Suddenly it doesn't matter to Joyce that Martin still hasn't

113

arrived. She listens to Shandy and Scott talking about people they know while cheap bubbles tickle her tongue, the drink slipping down easily.

'You should let me do your hair sometime, Joyce. Ever thought of going shorter, maybe a few nice highlights?' Shandy says, catching a strand of Joyce's hair between her fingertips.

'Oh, I've just ... Mum and I do it, we've always ...'

'With your vintage style, you could totally carry off a bit of pink or purple. Just a few streaks, or a dip-dye. Couldn't she, Scott?'

Joyce bursts out laughing, 'Pink hair? Purple? Like a punk rocker?'

'Yeah, really in right now and you two have gothic vibes, you would totally suit it. Top up?'

Scott grabs Joyce's glass.

Joyce looks to Betty for a cue, but she's simpering at Angus who is showing her a photo of golf clubs on his flashy mobile phone.

'Yes, please,' she replies hesitantly.

'Didn't your lot used to own The Palace?' asks Shandy.

A column of froth overspills from Joyce's glass. 'Oops, clumsy me,' Scott laughs.

'Well, yes but, we ... anyway, how long have you two been married?' Joyce sloshes back the contents of the glass in one go. Scott fills it up again.

'Married?' They look confused.

Angus overhears. He roars with laughter, 'These two? Married?'

Scott and Shandy are giggling.

Betty looks snappish and discombobulated, 'What's this hilarity here? Has Joyce said something amusing? She can be a card, a real card, can't you, Joycey? Did you tell a joke, what did you say?'

Joyce's cheeks feel like a boiled kettle.

'Joyce just asked this pair,' chuckles Angus, wiping his eyes. 'She asked how long this pair have been married, but Scott here's, well he's ... what is it you call yourselves these days? I'm not up on the PC terms, you're not allowed to say anything these days, he's – ' Angus purses his lips, holds up his hand and flops it about at the wrist ' – aren't you, Scott?'

'Uncle Angus!' remonstrates Shandy, turning to Scott and Joyce, 'Sorry. He's such a fossil sometimes.'

'Gay is fine, Angus. I'm gay, Joyce,' Scott says, mouth smiling, eyes dead. The way, Joyce thinks, the way that eyes go dead when a person is so sick of something, so bored of something that used to make them angry, that all the anger is used up and burnt out. She can feel that flatness behind her own eyes, but she doesn't know why, can't think exactly when she might have felt that way herself.

Everyone is stiffly quiet. Betty looks as if she's just watched Scott pull his trousers down and wave his bits about, then Angus starts talking to Betty about a dead man they once knew, and the elderly DJ in his bow tie begins spinning records. A few couples take to the small dancefloor, performing ballroom moves to arcane pop.

'So, The Palace,' says Scott. 'I heard Shandy saying your family used to own it. Fancy! That must have been fun.'

Joyce picks up her glass, but it is empty.

'Oh, we used to, we, my dad ... did, once but ... well, he, there was—'

'Bit of bother was there?' Shandy refills Joyce's glass.

Joyce swings it back to the dregs.

'I think I heard. Oh!' Shandy claps her hands, 'I love this song, so cheesy, let's dance. Scotty? Joyce?'

Unsteadiness overtakes Joyce. She hopes it is just the unfamiliar drink, the unusually immoderate amount, but she knows it is the words going to work: *purple dip-dye, gothic vibes*.

Joyce feels as if she has inadvertently stepped out of her skin and is spectating herself from the other side of the club.

She feels exposed – what can Shandy possibly know about Joyce and Betty's private business? *A bit of bother; I heard about that.*

She was talking about Daddy.

Then thoughts are whipped from Joyce's head: Shandy and Scott are pulling her to her feet, onto the dancefloor where she shuffles woodenly to 'Build Me Up Buttercup', glancing at her mother who, to Joyce's surprise, gives her a little wave, smiles, and turns back to Angus, who never stops telling stories in which he wins.

Sadness swamps Joyce. She's sick of feeling like a great big baby who doesn't understand anything about the world or how to live in it. She doesn't even know how to dance, not really.

She observes Shandy and Scott – the song seems to issue them with friendly suggestions of when to spin and how to sway, so Joyce begins to copy them. Her movements loosen; the music feels like some dizzy fairground thing she is taking a ride on. And yet her mistake feeling keeps on blaring, insisting this will have to be paid for, costly installments which will far outlast her pleasure.

The song ends, Joyce is hot and queasy, her stomach is crampy.

As another song begins, Shandy and Scott continue dancing.

'Sorry, powder my nose,' Joyce says, mouth soupy as she lurches away.

The toilet is astringently bright, reeking of plastic pine. Simmering in her skin, Joyce hunches over in a cubicle; heart thudding, blood swooshing in her ears. She feels like a caged thing that doesn't know how to use freedom; she mistrusts the bigness of the world, which is only opening a little, such a tiny corner of life folding outwards, just maybe.

Mum's blasé wave: alien. It's as if there are no rules in the world.

Joyce wants to go home, where no one can see her but the dolls and the budgie and her route through the hours is as familiar and limited as the lines on her palm.

She takes some deep breaths and walks out, still flustered. The fire escape is open, a bartender puffing curls of pink-smelling vape outside.

Joyce steps into the car park, guzzling down cold air.

A perfectly round moon hangs in the sky. Pearly light makes the tarmac look like deep water. Headlamps turn it solid and grey as a wheezy banger pulls up.

Martin.

Joyce walks over to the car and he opens the passenger door, 'Joyce! Get in – you must be freezing.'

She hesitates.

She gets inside.

'I'm so sorry, Joyce,' says Martin. 'Gran's not well again, I had to get her settled in for the night before I could leave. I didn't want you to think I wasn't coming. Shall we head in?'

'Let's have a little minute right here. Just us, you know?'

Martin pats Joyce's hand. 'Whatever you like, Joyce.'

'You're very thoughtful.' Joyce smiles, she is trembling, her body thrums like a pylon. She's aware of her own absence indoors, minutes mounting.

'Talking about thoughtful, Joyce, *I've* been thinking . . . I just, I hope I don't sound like a weirdo but . . . '

Martin looks at his hands. Joyce notices a bald patch on the back of his head, his hair sits up around it, sticky looking, as if he's tried to cover it and failed.

'But?' she coaxes.

'I've been thinking about you. I can't stop thinking about you actually, does that make me sound like a creep? It does, doesn't it? Sorry – I don't know what's got into me.'

There are sweet wrappers crumpled in the cupholder next to the gearstick – Freddos and Curly Wurlys. Martin smells of cheap aftershave; the impersonal Christmas gift kind that comes boxed with an embroidered flannel.

Joyce feels as if she is seeing exactly how Martin must have looked as a boy; solemn, earnest and perhaps a little lonely.

His inability to look at her grazes her heart, but the gnaw of time passing, the wormy possibility of Betty marking the minutes, fills her with panic.

'We must both be weirdos, Martin. I keep thinking about you too, but I need to get back inside.'

'Well, I can come in . . . '

'Just Mum, Martin, she's . . . do you mind if we just sit here and then I'll go back?'

Martin looks confused, 'If that's what . . . whatever you like, Joyce. But when can I see you again? *Can* I see you again?'

'Here, next Saturday?'

'Can't you get away in the week? We could go for a meal. We can go anywhere you like. What do you like? Chinese? Indian? Fish and chips?'

The very impossibility of what Martin is asking collides with the heat of Joyce's skin and the fizz in her head, and before the idea has passed through any channel of conscious thought, she leans over and kisses Martin on the mouth.

He stiffens, turns into a plank in his seat with his mouth shut so Joyce has a horrible feeling of pushing her lips directly against his skull.

She pulls away and hangs her head, 'Oh God, I don't know what . . . '

Then Martin's mouth is on hers, licking her tongue. He is wrapping Joyce in his arms and gathering up handfuls of her hair, sliding his hands under her skirt. For the first time in years, Joyce has a body; a ravenous one, tingling, touched and wanting.

'I've got to go,' she breathes, palm cupping Martin's jaw. 'I've got to go.'

'I've never, nothing like this, Joyce. I can't believe . . . ' Martin sighs and rests his head against Joyce's.

'Me either, never.'

Liar. Fingers, an open mouth; another man in another car appears in Joyce's memory. Rain battering the windows, the luxurious, pheromone smell of the reclined leather seats and the bodies lying back on them, reaching out for each other.

'I haven't, I don't want you to think . . . '

Liar. Joyce wipes a hand through her hair, recalling one big suntanned hand catching up a fistful of it, pulling her head back, the other one pushing up her skirt.

'I don't,' Martin says. 'I don't think anything except that you're lovely. A lovely lady.'

Instinctively Joyce believes Martin isn't judging her, that he doesn't think anything unkind and that he never would, no matter what.

'I've got an office,' he says. 'Cupboard really, in the business centre in town. I'm there every day. Do you think you could ... pop in even?'

'I could try. I don't even know what you do.'

'Loss adjuster,' he says and fishes out a business card from the glovebox. 'Oh, Joyce.'

They kiss again, swapping smiles.

Then Joyce steps back into the cold and Martin drives away, leaving her to wonder for a moment what it could possibly be – this sudden, unevidenced certainty that she is known and understood without having to explain herself.

And as she walks back into the club, with her skin tingling and her heartbeat detonating in her ears, she knows exactly what it is: it is falling in love.

Chapter 12

Shandy lost her husband, Mick, twice. First to a hurricane in the Azores, then to angry men on the internet. Now their sixteen-year-old son Tyler is following his father into that spite-raddled darkness.

Shandy is fretting over this as she does during every quiet moment of every day. Fretting over Mick and Tyler, money and the future, as she lifts dead lilies from the vase on the reception desk of Beauty Box.

The lilies give off a rude, intimate smell. Shandy wrinkles her nose as she folds them into the bin. Ten pounds for a new bunch had seemed pricey with the appointment book empty for the second day running and the rest of the week looking sparse.

In the queue for the till, she'd dithered, snapping her purse open and shut. She'd almost put them back. But it's the little things, Shandy thinks; little luxuries blunt the pain of big disappointments. You have to hold these things in balance for life to feel worthwhile, for tomorrow to feel possible. She has learned she must count carefully, *choose* carefully what she holds on to and what she permits to fall away.

In the small hours, she'd heard Mick trip over the potted

bay tree on the doorstep, heard him carving at the front door with his key. Eventually, once it had begun to feel like he was scraping the inside of her skull, she'd stamped downstairs in her dressing gown and opened the door.

'Fuck you doin' up?' Mick had slurred, gaze skittering across her.

'Get inside. Don't you *dare* wake Tyler. Absolute state of you.'

A gust of booze and perfume had sniggered in with Mick as he'd lurched over the threshold.

Shandy had gone back to bed and watched the hours rack up on the radio alarm. Had listened, seething, to Mick pissing and farting, and later, throwing up in the downstairs loo.

'Shithead,' she'd hissed into her pillow. 'Wanker.' Refusing tears that needled her eyelids. 'Enough, enough, enough.'

Shandy had cried over Mick so many times since he'd quit the merchant navy that tears felt like a waste, like continuing to plough money into an investment that had long ago turned out to be a scam.

About two years ago, actually, bloody hell, nearly three, Mick had returned from four months at sea, thrown his hold-all on the floor, kissed Shandy on the cheek as if she was a distant relative and declared he was done, he was home and he wasn't going back.

That evening, after Mick and Shandy had sunk a couple of bottles of wine, Mick had sketched out a few details of the storm; skyscraper waves, the ship rearing and diving, crew-mates praying in languages Mick didn't understand to gods he didn't recognise the names of.

After that, Mick had steadfastly refused to discuss what happened. He'd flown into unspeakable tempers whenever Shandy had tried to coax more out of him. And after he'd found the leaflet for a counselling service she'd picked up from the GP's waiting room and left casually on the coffee table, the name-calling had started.

Gathering up mail from the salon floor, Shandy sighs at the stamped red threats and slips them unopened onto the pile under the reception desk.

In her nicest writing, she adds some special deals onto the A-frame blackboard with a pink chalk pen, in the hope of snaring walk-ins. She'll only make a tenner on each treatment even if people bite.

She unfolds the board, chains it to the lamp post outside, yawns and steps indoors to put the kettle on. She just needs a cuppa and then she'll be fine.

From his first day back, Mick had been quiet and remote. Then after a while, he'd grown more truculent; more resentful of Shandy's every word and action than their teenage son Tyler, who with each passing day looks more and more like the boy Shandy fell in love with decades ago, and who acts more and more like the man she is growing to despise as the weeks and months go by.

Somehow, for the first year after Mick stopped going to sea, it had been OK.

Not *OK* OK, but manageable.

Shandy had carried on, doing her best to keep things steady for Tyler. She and Mick established a way of staying on opposite sides of the barrier between them. Orbiting the elephant, was how she had come to think of their relationship.

Mick had found casual work at the Amazon warehouse inland. Zero hours, which was fine; Shandy's salon had been doing all right, tiding them over. But business has grown slower and leaner, and Mick phones for shifts less often.

Instead, he stays at home, baleful on the couch, watching

the news in a doggy-smelling dressing gown Shandy longs to burn; scrolling on his phone, uttering ugly words about people coming here and taking jobs and getting benefits. In the evenings, ostentatiously going 'out, just out all right' as soon as Shandy comes home.

Of course, it grew harder as Tyler got older: more independent, more observant, then eventually as contemptuous of Shandy as his father is.

Tyler and Mick had grown together in a way that forced her out. As if she was nothing but a splinter. They made her feel by turns superfluous and hated: no tender part of them she could soothe, nothing vulnerable; they were neither consolable nor inconsolable. It was just as if all the kind parts of Mick and Tyler had been bricked off from Shandy, dividing the household into *the lads* and *her*, one nasty shared joke at a time. One comment about benders and muzzies, one 'why don't you go and live with them if you love them so much?', one wet towel left on the bed, one skid-marked pair of pants left on the bathroom floor, one sulk, one storming out at a time.

The gulf between them broadened and rotted, became an infected wound, then a few weeks ago, during a stupid argument about doing homework versus meeting friends, Tyler had called Shandy a fat cunt and pushed her. Not hard, though. Hard enough that she'd stumbled before catching her balance but at least not hard enough to knock her over.

He hadn't wanted to knock her over.

He didn't know his own strength.

He was still only sixteen, still only a boy, even if he rarely seemed like one any more.

It's hard to find the child Tyler was in the man he is becoming. Shandy can't quite couple the sweet boy who used to cradle her cheeks between his palms when she was tucking him in at night, who'd gaze into her face and tell her she was the prettiest mummy in the world, to the teenager who laid his hands on her.

She doesn't even recognise Tyler's smell any more. The washing-powder home scent exchanged for a grubby fug that makes Shandy think not of motherhood, but nights long before it. The backseats of cars, hasty moments under the pier.

She finds herself wondering how her son behaves towards girls. She assumes the posters on his walls mean Tyler *does* like girls. Not that Shandy would care if he didn't.

Tyler being like his father would once have assured Shandy that her son would be considerate, kind, a caring boyfriend. Maybe he is, maybe he would be, maybe it's just that loving their mothers is a thing boys grow out of like dinosaurs and football stickers.

Or maybe it's her own fault.

Shandy often wonders if it *is all her own fault*.

The misbehaviour she let slide throughout the years because, well, it was never easy for Tyler; confusing the way it was just the two of them, him and Shandy, for months on end, then Mick would swagger back from sea, all costly toys and cheap promises. Promises to do things with Tyler that somehow, Mick never quite got round to before it was time for him to leave again.

Shandy was always the villain: taking Tyler home to eat his greens despite him screaming for a Happy Meal, Mick no help. 'It's just a couple of nuggets and some chips, Shand. You love Maccy Ds as much as he does, what's the problem?'

Making Tyler do his homework. When Mick was there he'd tell her, 'Relax, Shand, it's Sunday night, he's just a kid, let's all just chill and watch a movie.'

Maybe she should have fought harder to keep things stable, pushed back harder on the whole Magic Dad business so that there wouldn't have had to be that rancorous first week or two every time Mick left: re-establishing their routines, just Shandy and Tyler again.

Anyway, all that regret stacks up and doesn't make a hole in anything, Shandy thinks. She didn't even know that kind of contemplation was in her nature until she found herself with so much alone time.

After a bitter Christmas last year, Mick had begun to go out more often, to come home later, drunker, and more flagrant about the lipstick on his clothes, the animal scent of other women's bodies on his fingers until it became a boast, a goad, a dare. Come on, say something.

Shandy refused.

She refused and she hated it.

She hated it, she hated it, *she hates it*, but she was, she *is* also relieved, because whatever Mick does, whoever he does it with, means a reprieve for her.

Mick had always made Shandy feel so good about her body. From their very first night together he'd been so delighted that there was so much of her. And where she'd felt for so long before she met him that there was something rude and clumsy about her size, shameful about her appetite, he, from the first moment, had fed all her hungers, praised and encouraged them.

Out for lunch, out for dinner, filling Shandy's plate for her again and again at party buffets. 'Look babe, there's cheese-cake, you love cheesecake, go on, enjoy yourself, be a devil.'

Nowadays it's all, 'Are you really having seconds? Haven't you already had a bag of crisps? Have you finished all that ice cream by yourself? Fuck's sake.'

126

Back in the day, Mick had punched his own cousin in the face at their Grandad's wake for making a dig about Shandy's size.

Nowadays — if they ever went anywhere any more — Mick would probably laugh, maybe throw in a wisecrack of his own, stare Shandy down until she laughed to dispel the tension.

Mick used to want to show Shandy off. Unlike previous boyfriends, who were circumspect and sometimes wouldn't even hold her hand in public, Mick wanted everyone to see them kissing.

The first time Mick had kissed her, on the dancefloor in Jesters, Shandy had stopped feeling like the stereotypical fat girl of her most mortifying and multiple memories. Taking a joke, *making* a joke before anyone else could, grateful for scraps, telling herself to be bubbly, up for anything in bed even if she didn't really fancy it herself and all that shit, that dismaying *shit* that fat girls of a certain vintage learn by rote. The first time Mick had kissed her, Shandy had felt plain gorgeous, just mad about herself, like *she* was a great thing, so that naturally the more there was of her the better.

But, for the last two years Mick has moved in Shandy like a stranger; like he hates her, like he's trying to punish her and pull her apart, grabbing handfuls of her flesh like he wants to tear them off, jackhammering at her as if he is trying to smash right through her into the darkness behind, muttering that she's a dirty fat bitch, that she likes that doesn't she greedy bitch, fat bitch, fucking fat fucking slag.

For a time, Shandy had felt obligated to submit to and forgive the demands Mick started to make in bed in the hope that he would get it, whatever *it* was, out of his system.

She'd close her eyes and sort of curl up into a ball inside her own head to make room in her body for whatever Mick was trying to exorcise, roll to one side of whatever he was doing. But her submission only seemed to make him more brutal in the night and more callous during the day.

After a few months, Shandy had begun to complain of headaches and stomach aches, back pain and tiredness. She could feel him glaring at her in the darkness, the infectious seep of his disgust fouling her insides, then he'd pick his phone up off the bedside table and take it into the en suite, making sure she could hear tinny shrieks of performed pleasure coming from its speaker.

Often, Shandy wakes before Mick and watches him sleep; mussed hair exposing the balding he's so vain about, soft pink belly like a puppy's. So prone without his bitterness that love rushes in like grief, something akin to the panicky hope and fear she'd felt for Tyler when he was tiny. And in those moments it seems possible, *almost* possible, that when Mick opens his eyes, he'll look at her the way he used to.

But the last time, Sunday morning just gone, Shandy had been a bit hungover and she'd had that feeling, watching Mick, of possibility: reconciliation as abrupt as their estrangement. His eyelids had pulsed, fluttered, opened and she'd seen his consciousness latch slowly onto her face.

'Morning, babe,' she'd smiled.

'Breath stinks,' he'd spat and rolled over. 'The fuck were you last night?'

Shandy's heart had shattered quietly.

'Went to see Uncle Angus at the social club.'

'With bentshot Scott?'

'Don't you *dare*.'

'Well he is. Fat fag-hag, go and clean your teeth. Breath absolutely stinks.'

And Shandy had said, 'Please stop, *please*.'

She'd said please over and over and over, trying to call Mick back to her, as if the version of him that existed before the storm might hear her and come rushing home from the sea.

She'd said please and she'd cried please. Tears coursing down her face into her cleavage, onto the pillow under her head.

She said please until it was a burning, a drowning, a begging bowl, a prayer. Until it was just a feeling, until it was just a noise.

The whole time Mick had kept his back to Shandy with the covers pulled tight as a drumskin, pretending to be fast asleep.

But it isn't that which has destabilised her, not really.

Shandy doesn't know why, what it was about that poor strange Joyce on Saturday at the social club. All she knows is that it's not just the contempt in Mick's words or the pitiless wall of his back turned towards her that have been careening around her brain like a trapped bluebottle repetitiously bouncing off the double glazing.

Shandy remembered Joyce from school, even though Joyce didn't seem to remember her.

Joyce always seemed stuck up back then.

Always by herself.

Always watching everyone else without joining in. Thinking she really was a princess just because her dad owned The Palace and picked her up from school in a Bentley. Thinking she was too good for the rest of them.

So, naturally, it had always seemed fair enough that Joyce took a lot of shit.

Needed to be brought down a peg or two. Deserved to be.

Except she never seemed to be. Brought down, or even affected.

Shandy used to see Joyce leaving the loos with wet hair at lunchtime or knocking her school bag out of a tree with a stick after the playground emptied.

Hard-faced it seemed back then.

But on Saturday, something about the skinless, stupid rawness of Joyce – the kicked-dog vulnerability she'd radiated – had made Shandy first want to crush her and then want to care for her. Realising it had probably been there all along.

Poor Joyce. No husband, no children, no one to pal about with but her bitch of a mother. The pair of them bizarre; dressed like twins in clothes last fashionable in the nineties. Their black-dyed poodle perms and harsh make-up, flaky-powdery like dusty plaster masks.

They'd looked like a vaudeville act; twin clowns, refugees from the kind of cheesy old cabaret the father, the husband, persisted with for far too long in The Palace, before he lost his shirt and cleared out.

Or was made to.

No one really knows which.

Everyone just knows it was a bad business; that The Palace was going under, that Chick Wilson had taken a lot of loans then disappeared suddenly, and that it was something to do with the McMaster family.

Anything that ever involved or involves them is a *bad business*. Round here, the name McMaster is just a shorthand for violence, another word for fear – nobody with any common sense knows or wants to know what goes on under their shadow. Shandy's heard every version of the rumours about what went down, but all she knows for sure is that you never cross the McMasters.

They will disappear you or leave you with no choice but to disappear yourself.

Anyway, Shandy had only gone to the club to try to sweeten up her horrible old dickhead of an uncle, see if she couldn't tap him up for a loan, just a small one, just to see Beauty Box through these lean times, but she couldn't get near him for that ridiculous Betty.

Betty had sat there simpering at Angus, who'd lapped it up even though his wife, Shandy's Auntie Mo, was still alive. In a care home up the coast, dotty as you like, but alive.

Betty had glued herself to Angus all evening, radiating superiority, her judgemental gaze all over Shandy like tar and feathers, which was fine because *fuck her* and also what could you really expect a person to do when they'd been dragged as low as she had? You sort of had to have a grudging admiration for Betty Wilson's commitment to the pretence that she was still *someone* in this town.

But Joyce, Jesus. Her eyes darting under all the hair and make-up like a bird in a cage, or ... no, like a little child hiding behind their hands, thinking they couldn't be seen because they couldn't see you. Joyce was what Shandy would call 'a poor cow' and what her own mother, eight years dead, would have called 'a soul' – a catch-all description for those in need of sympathy which had never made much sense to Shandy, because didn't everyone have a soul?

And yet Joyce – her bungling attempts at conversation, not noticing that Shandy had been taking the piss out of her, her panic when Shandy had deliberately, meanly, asked Joyce about her father and The Palace.

Shandy had felt wretched; it was as though she'd pulled Joyce's knickers down in front of everyone. *Then* the idea had fallen into place that 'a soul' meant a person whose inside was on their outside. Joyce had seemed as if she was carrying her soul in her hands, as if she was one of those unfortunate babies born with some of their organs on the outside of their body.

Anyway, it had been apparent to Shandy that Joyce had no idea how naked she was, how humiliatingly visible, which had yanked some loose thread in Shandy and made her feel unravelled, or as if she had walked a few steps to the left of herself, of her life, and could view herself as though she were a dispassionate observer, seeing with scalpel-precision how miserable and lonely she was. Sealing the entrances to all her hiding places.

Shandy stands behind the reception desk, breathlessness overtaking her. She keeps thinking *ten pounds on those lilies was a stupid waste*, she feels like one of those escapology acts, a magician in chains inside a tank rapidly filling with water.

She thinks of Mick, a surge of rage, damn him to hell. A surge of pity, as if for a trapped animal which in its panic has gnawed a free leg off.

Maybe it's time, Shandy thinks.

Scott keeps offering to get Shandy work with him in a spa on one of the cruise liners which leave from a port a few miles down the coast. They'll be starting up again in March, Scott said on Saturday after she'd poured her heart out to him about Mick and Tyler.

There are plenty of jobs going, Shandy only has to say the word and Scott can get her in.

March is only a handful of months away. If she can only hold on until then.

If she can just get through Christmas with Mick and Tyler. If she can just hold her nerve, keep the salon open and her heart closed until then.

She almost believes that she can.

And that is fine Shandy thinks; almost is enough.

It *is* the little things, the little things and the big, held in balance that matter. It is knowing what to catch, what and *who* must be left to fall.

She stands behind the reception desk, smiling in the warm air of the bright salon, beside the lilies which are slowly beginning to open, like lips parting to speak, or the fingers of a hand letting go of something.

Chapter 13

'What have you got your coat on for?' Betty asks Joyce between wracking coughs.

Frail light trickles through the lace curtain.

It's Monday morning, Betty is wan and sweating, propped up in bed, hands clawing the eiderdown. To Joyce, she looks impossibly small and bird-boned. Without her make-up, Betty's face has an ablated quality; grey and blank like the flat stones that pock the shoreline at low tide.

Joyce fingers the business card in her pocket and digs her court shoes into the pile of the bedroom rug.

'Listen, Mum, you're so poorly and, well . . . ' She stares at the fluff banking up round her toes, pushing the corner of the card against her thumb until she feels it bend. 'I just thought I'd pop to the shops and fetch you some soup and some painkillers. Maybe get us a little treat for when we're watching our programmes – a fancy cake, or a packet of Viscounts.'

'Viscounts? Joyce! We're not made of money. Take your coat off, I'm too sick to be left alone.'

'Oh, Mum, you'll hardly notice I'm gone, and I'll bring you back some nice soothing soup, some painkillers and a fancy cake, then we can get you all propped up on the sofa in time for our programmes.'

'I said *no*, Joyce.' Betty folds her arms and pushes her lips into a pout. 'I don't *want* cake, I couldn't eat a bite. I need you *here*.'

When Joyce had walked back into the club on Saturday night, Betty had questioned her prolonged absence. Joyce had told her mother she had a dicky tummy and Betty snapped, 'For goodness' sake, Joyce, don't be coarse. No one needs to hear about your lavatory habits.' Then she turned on a Broadway grin for Angus, who had barely paused for breath.

Joyce had sauntered round the dancefloor with Shandy and Scott for a few more songs, so full of secret happiness, so lifted by it, she'd felt like a helium balloon, spinning and shining and catching the light.

It had carried Joyce along, she'd floated through Sunday. But with each hour of distance from the kiss, the idea she might sneak away to see Martin became more preposterous, imbued with the wistful humiliation of remembered teenage dreams. Unlikely heights that once seemed scalable.

Then in the evening, Betty had begun to cough and splutter and had woken this morning so obviously sick that Joyce felt like a witch; as though the dark magic of her desire for freedom had cursed her mother.

'Poor Mumma, you need stuff to make you better, paracetamol and hot soup.'

Joyce patted Betty's leg through the covers.

Betty whisked them away, turned onto her side, turned back, 'There are sardines in the cupboard, Joyce, and some Rich Tea biscuits.'

'The Rich Tea are finished and we ate those sardines on Friday and besides you—'

'Those were pilchards. We had pilchards on toast, double fish this Friday we said, I distinctly remember because we had a lovely little laugh about that, and we shared a can of Fanta Orange so there's no need for you to go out.'

'But . . . '

'Anyway, how would you pay, Joyce? You haven't a penny, not a penny if I don't give you—'

Joyce fumbles with the belt of her trench coat, 'I've enough in my purse to—'

'Where did *you* get money?'

Earlier, Joyce had sneaked to the kitchen and withdrawn a note and some coins from the tartan biscuit barrel where her mother hid their savings. The Scottie dogs in Toorie hats on the side of it looked as if they were laughing at her, glancing over her shoulder as if she was committing the crime of the century.

'Oh, just from the tin, I—'

'Unauthorised!' Betty shrieks, 'I did not give you permission!'

'It's *our* money,' mumbles Joyce, 'yours *and mine* – Daddy gave it to both of—'

'Gave?' Betty slaps her palms against the covers. 'He didn't *give*, Joyce! He's not . . . he wasn't a benefactor, it's what I'm owed, not a brass farthing more than what I'm owed for the trouble you . . . he . . . the burdens I've had to . . . ' She begins to cough as if she is drowning, until spittle flows down her chin.

Joyce takes her hankie from her coat pocket and mops at her mother's mouth. 'See, Mum? You're really not well, not well *at all*. That's why I need to pop out, and you always say no good ever comes of talking about—'

'Your father?' Betty snatches the hankie from Joyce and

tosses it away. 'No, no good ever comes. No good ever did. A handful of hush money! A pittance! Barely enough to survive since he abandoned me ... us ... you! Abandoned *you*.'

Joyce puts her hands over her ears like headphones. 'Don't, Mum, please. Let's not talk about horrible things.'

'Now you're upset,' Betty gives a satisfied smile. 'So pop your coat off and park yourself. There is absolutely no need for either of us to leave this house today.'

Joyce sits up very straight, tries to imagine the burning inside her is molten metal pouring into her spine, forging it into an unbending rod.

She imagines Martin, his delighted face. Happy kisses in a neat cosy office.

'Don't be silly. I will be gone for an hour, *less than an hour*, and when I come back everything will be much nicer.'

'Silly? The language!' Betty swoons back onto her pillow. 'I can't believe it, calling your sick mother names, swearing at your bedridden mother, casting up the past, making me think about your father. *Yours*. I feel even worse now.'

'I am only going to the shops.' Joyce clenches her fists and clamps them to her legs.

'You're not. You are *not* going to the shops.'

Sweat has matted Betty's hair. Her pink scalp shows.

'I *am* going to the shops. I didn't swear. I'm sorry I called you silly. I'm worried about you, about your illness. It's not nice.'

'Not nice for who, Joyce? You, of course, self, self, self. Wanting to treat yourself to a shopping trip when I'm flat on my back.'

'I'm going to the shops to get things to make *you* feel better.'

'I'd feel better if you stayed,' Betty contrives a baby voice, putting a hand to her head. 'I feel ghastly, Joycey.'

Joyce touches Betty's cheek, 'Oh my goodness!'

'What?'

'Oh, Mum, you're burning up. You're so hot you could faint or have a fit if I don't get something to take your temperature down. Then we'd have to call an ambulance and they'd take you out past the neighbours in your nightie with your face not on and your hair a mess.'

'Oh, don't Joyce, don't.' Betty fidgets with her hair, plucks at the top button of her nightdress.

'I don't mean to scare you, Mum, but if you go downhill there could be a palaver. A *scene*.'

Betty bites her lip, 'You'd be gone for less than an hour?'

'Less than an hour.'

'Perhaps we could stretch to some Viscounts after all,' Betty says ruminatively, tucking the covers around herself, plumping her pillows. 'Some Viscounts and a fancy cake, cream maybe, nothing with nuts in and make sure you get it from Gregg's or the bakery section in the Co-op, not The Copper Kettle. Angus said the new owners are Polish.'

Joyce smiles, 'Yes, Mum, of course.' She kisses her mother's cheek and her light feeling returns in such a rush, such an overwhelming surge, that as she stands, Joyce feels like she's rising into the air, a helium balloon again, slipping off its string this time, floating suddenly upwards; free, fast, impossible to catch.

Chapter 14

Lydia goes upstairs to the apartment, exchanging the mildew fug of the Flamingo Suite for expensive aromas of Penhaligon's and Diptyque.

Pan wanly raises a hand and returns to talking to a man whose glasses make Lydia assume he is an interior designer. She sees fabric and wallpaper rolled out on the sarcophagus-like kitchen island, luxe patterned swatches that probably cost more per metre than most people's wedding dresses do in total.

She heads back towards the door but hears a quiet strumming from Lol's room and is compelled to knock.

She pops her head in – the room has a grubbily evocative miasma of sweat and sugary perfume; the candy kind which appeals when you're young and want to feel like an edible little confection.

Lol puts the acoustic guitar on the floor as if it's contraband.

'That sounded nice.'

'No, it didn't. I'm not good.'

'Yet, maybe, it's just practice.'

Lydia suddenly realises she hasn't owned a guitar or even touched one in, well, she doesn't know.

'Can I come in?'

Nodding, Lol picks up the instrument and holds it out to Lydia.

'Oh, Lol, I can hardly . . . I probably don't even know . . . '

But she takes it, curves her fingers round the neck and lets the other set fall across the strings.

The embodied haunt of all those diligent, frustrating, thrilling hours in her teenage bedroom feels like the specific rush that comes from touching the skin of old love who'd hurt you after many years have elapsed; conjuring the pain they caused and the pleasure preceding it.

The stiffness in Lydia's fingers softens, the chord shapes flow, finding their way out through her hands like water assenting to the shape of a glass, as though there's only ever been one direction of travel: the way back.

Moved by the inexorable physics of muscle memory, Lydia starts to play 'Who Knows Where the Time Goes?'

The lyrics leap to her lips, almost embarrassed at first, then the sentiment swells in her; astonished to find she still has a voice, huskier, lower, than before, something weary but maybe a little wise in the cadence.

Lol clears her throat, an awkward little squeak like someone tuning an instrument, and begins to harmonise.

Lydia hears her own smile inflect her voice, like the sunniness of yearning finding its object and turning to joy. The two of them, Lydia and Lol, filling the room with music, as uncomplicatedly, unabashedly as speech.

Lydia looks at Lol, eyes closed, plump, moist lips moving on the words and it makes her heart feel as if it is straining against her ribs, like something winged aching to fly.

Then the door opens and Pan comes in and says, 'All right, *X Factor*, any chance you could knock off the caterwauling? Jonathan and I are trying to get the room schemes nailed for a pre-Christmas start to the work. So, don't take it the wrong way but could you ... stop? For now, totally nice thing to do later, super cute, and joking apart, you sounded quite nice, but it's just far too difficult to concentrate, thanks.'

And then she's gone, like a neighbour putting a knife through a mis-aimed football and kicking it back over the wall. Leaving Lydia and Lol suspended around the silence where the music was moments ago, as if they are looking at dissipating ripples where water has healed seamlessly over a skimmed stone.

'Lol, love, she—'

'Can you go now, please, Auntie Lydia?'

Lol is holding her stomach rolls through the shapeless black and red striped jumper she's wearing, kneading at them catlike with her knees drawn up to her chest and her head canted down, staring into her lap, the bulge and glint of tears massing in her green eyes – so like Pan's, regardless of how differently they see the world.

'Lol, I think—'

'Can you *go* now, *please*, Auntie Lydia.'

Lydia feels that despicable desire to say something wise, apposite, aphoristic. A selfish adult desire to insist that she, rather than Lol, knows what's best, when the moments that matter most when you are sixteen and feeling hurt or humiliated are the all too rare ones when an adult respects your boundaries.

Reaching down to squeeze Lol's shoulder, Lydia says, 'OK. That was so nice you know? Singing with you,'

Lol shrugs her off and Lydia, fingers still feeling the press of the strings, the vibrations of the last note in them, with unsung verses curdled in her throat, has no choice but to do as she is told.

Craving air and light, she grabs her coat and goes out.

Lydia pinballs along the street between the sea and the stained Babygro pastels of the empty seafront hotels and everything appears abrasive with pathos.

Every view confronts Lydia with sadness too absurd to be heartbreaking and absurdity too sad not to break your heart.

Outside the snack bar stands a grinning fibreglass hotdog the size of an eight-year-old. The hotdog has arms and legs and is lubing its sausage body with ketchup. Someone has kicked a hole into the corner of its demented grin.

Letters have fallen off the sign above a shuttered arcade so that it reads USEMENTS.

Gobstoppers fester inside a gumball machine with *Britain First* and *Free Tommy Robinson* scrawled across the Perspex.

This decrepit town, thinks Lydia. *What am I doing here?*

Pan alleges it's poised to become the next fashionable place to move away to from London. But Lydia's seen scant evidence to support this assertion other than an office block with some canvases by the windows, suggesting they're artists' studios, and a poky, metro-tiled coffee shop with hoyas hanging from the ceiling, owned by a girl with green hair and a huffy demeanor who serves oat-milk lattes in pottery vessels.

But Pandora's a hip-seeking missile, powered by FOMO and fashion. More than that, she's incredibly financially shrewd. And she's here, so Lydia supposes it must be true that this place is about to 'happen'.

As Lydia's thinking this, she passes the same pair of big pink knickers she sees every time she walks over this spot, noticing that they've moved a little each time. Now they are thick with dirt and balled up small in the gutter, migrated there from the middle of the pavement, where they were when Lydia first saw them.

Maybe it was as long as three weeks ago – a Sunday morning when she and Pan were heading out for breakfast, walking with their arms linked. They'd just snapped a selfie because the light was good when they noticed the knickers at the same time. But where Pan burst out laughing – a smutty Sid James cackle, wisecracking, 'Someone had a great Saturday night!' – Lydia felt troubled, consumed by ugly imaginings, replying, 'Or a completely terrible one.'

'Don't be such a downer, Lyd,' Pan withdrew her arm from Lydia's. 'You used to be such a good laugh, wicked sense of humour, and now it's like, everything's so po-faced with you these days and I know you're depressed, but honestly, you're never going to cheer up if you keep seeing the worst-case scenario everywhere. It's a fucking dreary way to live.'

Lydia wanted to tell Pan she didn't know the half of it, wanted to clap back that she no longer enjoyed the luxury of laughing at the things she would once have found funny, and that without deliberately keeping a running tally of them, she notices every one, aware of her altered emotions each time she perceives the mechanism of a joke, its power dynamics instead of the punchline.

Lydia's sense of humour: another theft of Henry's. Taking her trauma seriously has made Lydia earnest in a way she would once have found excruciatingly embarrassing.

She is retreading this resentment, as well as remembering the conversation with Pan about the discarded underwear, and she is back on the creaky hamster-wheel of self-examination again. *Oh, stop. Just try to have a day,* Lydia tells herself, make something of being here instead of London, and so she veers into the stairwell which leads up to the small local museum.

A much older woman stands behind the till. She has one of those faces that appears to have settled into a permanent look of reproof, presumably from a lifetime of disapproving of people. Certainly, the flinty, head-to-heel look of appraisal she metes out to Lydia makes it seem that way.

Lydia feels sixteen, on a school trip.

Arranged around the cash register, fading postcards sit in a cracked Perspex holder next to decorative spoons and thimbles entombed in individual plastic vitrines; badges, bookmarks and novelty erasers emblazoned with the town's coat of arms. All of them gather dust under a grinning cardboard sun sporting shades and a fedora – a leery prick if ever she'd seen one – blurting a speech-bubble claiming that this bric-a-brac is a gift shop.

What an arsehole, thinks Lydia angrily, then: *This is how low Henry has brought me – I am genuinely railing against the imagined misogyny of a cartoon sun.*

She picks up a giant souvenir pencil and imagines plunging it into her jugular.

'Are you going to buy that?' the woman asks.

Lydia wordlessly places it back into the jar and starts to tour the fusty, irrelevant museum: three rooms filled with an incongruous mix of pottery shards and circus memorabilia, vintage souvenirs and arcane fishing equipment.

There is a large original travel poster on the wall: the Come On In Girl in full colour, bright beachball and scarlet bathing suit, more pneumatic and cheerful than her bronze golem on the prom. But she still appears so trapped to Lydia, jammed on top of her beachball, arm raised like she's trying to hail a taxi to take her the fuck away, smiling and smiling like face-ache.

On a small, wall-mounted monitor, a clip plays: a plummy

144

older man, captioned with the name Stanley Lisle, being interviewed for a BBC documentary about iconic designs.

'Oh, I'd been having a blighter of a time trying to come up with the design for this poster and I'd gone out for a stroll, a stomp, actually, might be more accurate. And, all of a sudden, I saw this girl.' Girl pronounced to rhyme with 'belle'.

'She was pretty: the very soul of good cheer and health. And, at once, it was quite as if the poster designed itself. It materialised: complete, exactly as you see it today.'

Offscreen the interviewer asks, 'And did you ever find out who she was?'

Long-dead Stanley Lisle laughs, 'No, no, not the faintest idea. Just some rather attractive girl I saw on the beach. Nothing particularly *special* about her, I don't think. She only caught my eye because I was in a jolly foul mood that day and she struck me as absolutely carefree.'

Rage surges through Lydia, thinking of that old man, young then, seeing some girl on the beach unselfconsciously enjoying herself, unaware that a stranger was at that moment consuming her, helping himself to her body like a buffet laid on for him, uncoupling her breasts and buttocks, her smile and her beachball from her name and taking them away without her consent.

Callous, purloining cunt.

And bloody hell, it is so boring, Lydia thinks, to be unable at any moment to divest herself of this tormenting awareness of herself as a person to whom things have been done.

Done and now *written about*.

A *comedy*.

Jesus fucking Christ, it hits her anew like an arrow finding its bullseye: in a few months' time, for the whole of April, *every fucking night* from 7.30 onwards, Lydia will know that there is a London theatre full of strangers laughing at her and applauding Henry, and she will have to try to make that OK.

She cannot imagine how she will possibly make that even slightly OK.

Now, it is as if the massed junk of the museum is creeping closer to her. Second by second, the scrimshaw and clown shoes, the eel spear and the disembodied torso dressed in Home Guard's uniform, the Roman coins, ammonites and gas masks seem to encroach on her. The bunting festooned around the display of vintage bathing suits feels as if it is wrapped tightly round Lydia's neck, and above it all that bastard of a sun, smarming away inanely above cheap trash no one wants.

Lydia scuttles out into a day so uniformly grey that the sea, sky, sand and streets are indistinguishable from one another. It is unseasonably muggy; moist and tainted, like halitosis.

Right now, Lydia is unsure if she hates Henry for what he did to her, and what he is intending to do, or herself for letting him do it, and the spores are multiplying so rapidly and poisonously that Lydia wants to march across the promenade, wade into the sea and let the waves wash her clean, freeze her numb, or just shut over her head.

Chapter 15

Joyce scurries along the prom with every nerve alive, worrying her armpits might be dampening inside the pink mohair sweater she'd chosen to make her bosoms look alluring. In a demure way.

Fine rain drifts from grubby clouds that squat over the waves, obscuring the boundary between sea and sky.

Pride comes before a fall, cautions a voice inside her head.

She withdraws the creased card from her pocket and checks Martin's address.

The business centre is far down the dock end of town, where Joyce and Betty never venture.

With such distance left to walk, the minutes move faster than Joyce's feet.

Hustling along, she grows hotter and hotter. Lately, she always seems to be roasting.

She is preoccupied by the possibility that she might be beginning to smell.

How romantic, the voice pipes up inside Joyce's head again, as if it comes from somewhere else. *What a stinker*, it sniggers. *How unladylike.*

Shut up, Joyce commands. *Leave me alone.*

The gloom makes Joyce feel as if something is wrong with her eyes. Incipient headache pincers her temples, induced by the effort of trying to work out whether she should run her errands before she surprises Martin or on her way back home.

If she shops first, her mother's cake might get crushed, or telltale sweatiness could seep into the paper bag. But if she shops afterwards there might be a poor selection of cakes to choose from. Mid-morning is a bad time for buying dainties, as her mother always says. Too close to elevenses, and what then?

Joyce can't work it out, freedom has imported so many variables into her day – trip hazards in every permutation. Just like always, she can't keep things right in her head.

Outside the shops, a small dog is doing its remarkably huge business while the elderly owner pretends not to see it. Joyce's nostrils fill with stink.

Private and intrusive, reminiscent of Betty's new fug, the way it burrows into Joyce's nostrils.

Images pounce: Betty's black hair plastered in strands across her head, the way the exposed parts of her scalp had looked vulgar.

A pillow: soft and white in Joyce's hand.

Joey in his cage, always scrabbling and gnawing, flitting at the bars. The little door open, the window wide.

And the dolls: all those inscrutable faces, all those brittle fingers reaching into the stale air of the living room. She imagines them toppling: cleaved faces, sockets emptied of glass eyes, the astonished look of headless bodies.

Not nice, Joyce, not nice at all. What is wrong with you?

You?

Me.

What is wrong with *me*?

She picks up her pace and speeds past the shops.

Approaching the pier, Joyce's body becomes so humid inside her coat that claustrophobia overwhelms her. *Oh, not now*, she thinks, *not here*, but her heartbeat feels so erratic, the sweatiness of her skin so intolerable that she has to stop and undo her buttons.

She faces the sea, leans over the handrail and lets the puny wind cool her. Her coat fills with soothing air.

Listening to the waves shush and boom round the barnacle-crusted pier legs, watching them gather in lacy swirls, Joyce experiences the freezing peace of sea swimming. The moment holds her, secure in the stillness, time irrelevant; Joyce has no thoughts to speak of as she savours the cool bliss of solitude.

'Don't jump!' A voice cries out to her, she turns.

In the doorway of The Palace, a drunk man with a black eye puckers his lips round the browned stub of a roll-up and laughs.

The scintillation of contact; the shock of this man, cloaked in smoke and with his loud laugh, stampeding at her.

'Only joking, sexy, only joking,' he stares at Joyce with his one good eye, waiting for her to do – what?

She has a part to play in this but has not been issued with lines. Joyce doesn't know what to do except ignore him and turn away.

She hears him call her a stuck-up cow.

When she looks back, he has gone and left his cigarette end coughing its last in the gutter.

From The Palace, brash sounds and urgent bass lunge out. An electronic voice keeps exclaiming 'Winner! Win, win, winner!' It is inconceivable to Joyce that this place was ever familiar to her.

Bright flashes of memory sizzle and zap: the thick carpet, silver forks clinking against china plates and a long-lost version of her mother – the blowsy, astute chatelaine, syrup and flint in her sequins, welcoming but formidable.

Long boring evenings just 'being around' so that Betty would know she wasn't anywhere else, getting *up* to anything. Drifting into her father's office to find her parents poring over documents, how they'd shut up and shoved the papers out of sight when they saw her.

Anger that her parents considered her so simple that she couldn't see something was wrong, some kind of tightening noose around their necks, clearly connected to the men who had always loomed on the margin of their lives, but who had by then become omnipresent. Men who hung around The Palace in smart coats and shiny shoes, with low voices and smiles like knives. Daddy, such a big man once, seeming dwarfed by them.

He was there, he was one of them – that man who'd surged so potently through Joyce's head when she'd been kissing Martin in his car outside the club.

In that other car, with that other man, with his expensive suit and sharp haircut, Joyce's body had understood what she desired, long before her head did.

Don't, Joyce pleads with her brain. *Please don't think about old things.*

Got some bats loose in the belfry there, Joycey? her brain rejoinders. *Getting tired?*

She tries to imagine Martin but can only picture his shoes, clumsy looking, scuffed not polished, his rusty jalopy, not like, so unlike, don't think, *please*.

Too late: already Joyce remembers pricey hand-stitched brogues, rain on car windows, leather seats reclined, squeaking and whispering as she lay back, stubble under her fingers, the greedy want in her body, hunger for: *don't* she begs herself, *don't say his name, not even in your head.*

Martin's kiss had awoken that appetite.

Joyce had taken for granted that she was no more likely to experience it again than to return to living in a nice big house with a garden, a fridge that was always full and new clothes in the wardrobe.

Until Saturday, it had appeared as impossible to Joyce that her body's aches and demands would rekindle as going back to school. It was a phase she'd been through, got past, finished with.

Ended well, did it, Joycey, before? smirks the voice in her head. *How did that turn out, all that business with—*

Don't! she begs herself or the voice or her brain but it's too late.

All that business with Paul.

Gulls leap from the pier rail. A huge quantity of them cackle and scatter, slicing around the sky like a sheaf of paper cast against the wind. Alarmed, Joyce's heart batters and bucks, heat even more insistent in her body than before.

The wind is stronger now, Joyce's coat streams out behind her like wings. She stretches out her arms and steps up onto the railing.

She cannot stop imagining what a relief it would be to peel off her mohair jumper, strip down to her unmentionables and let the wind blow all over her skin.

At this moment, it feels horribly possible that she might.

At this moment, Joyce feels like she might be capable of anything at all.

Not good not to know, is it, Joycey? Remarks the voice. *Bit of a fix, isn't it, not being certain that you're not going to take your clothes off on the prom?*

A pressure in Joyce's head makes her fingers tingle; her legs feel like noodles and she can't catch her breath.

Joyce can't seem to fill her lungs.

Above her gulls guffaw, below her the pavement is so watery and unsound that Joyce can't tell if the ground is dissolving or if she is falling.

Her mother looked so little in the bed, body barely tenting the covers.

Her poor, sick mother, who put her back together, who took control when everything was falling apart and who hauled them out of the mess Paul and Daddy left them in.

Her poor, sick, strong, brave mother who keeps things right in Joyce's head when she can't do it herself.

Joyce stares down into the water, thinking of those raw gaps of scalp where her mother's hair had gone askew.

Joyce will comb it for her.

She will make it nice.

Like a bird done with flying, folding its wings away, Joyce tugs on her coat, does up the buttons and belt.

She turns on her heel and scurries back towards the centre of town.

Joyce will go to the chemist.

She will go to the Co-op.

And then she will go back home.

Chapter 16

Lydia takes off down the prom. Catching her reflection in the window of a charity shop, she sees herself tripled, bleached and blurred, interpolated with a mannequin dressed in the frumpy finery of a bride's mother. Wan and threadbare, body adrift in loose garments like a victim straight from central casting, Lydia is a stranger to herself. Faceless and flying apart. Even obliterating the means of communication hasn't severed the tie between her and Henry; the strangling vine, the tumorous tendril, still lashes him to Lydia.

She watches a skein of geese stitch a dark line across pale clouds; the ease of their leaving feels as though it unravels a thread, one which spools out from Lydia's navel and tugs at her gut like a thirst, like a hunger.

The day's slender grey light takes on a wistful quality, the non-specific nostalgic cadence of a thousand days long past; the numberless, nothing, drift-through kind which leave no specific impression.

She can't imagine being fully free of Henry any more than she can imagine flying.

But it's the first aesthetic thought Lydia's had in days, summoning her favourite poem to mind, and as the geese become

153

a single V-shaped brushstroke on the overcast sky, she thinks: actually, the soft animal of my body would love everything and everyone to fuck right off now.

In the shop window, the dummy's feet are speared by metal rods and surrounded by curios and tchotchkes, like offerings to a blank-faced god: a frog on a log, a cottage-shaped teapot, a knitted scarecrow – all the loving hours of its becoming not enough to save it from The British Heart Foundation, woolly legs straddling an elderly set of compact binoculars, upon which Lydia zeros in.

Her parents are twitchers, or more accurately, her father is. His hobby, really, everyone else's by extension. Until Lydia was old enough to be left behind, they'd spend most weekends and holidays as a family, hunched in hides, haring from one chilly mildewed hut to another as Dad added ticks to his list.

And it wasn't that Lydia hated it wholesale. What made her miserable was the restive, relentless marking off, the 'right, bagged a Willow Tit, pack up, on we go to the next stop', just when she'd been revelling in the stillness of the scene.

Whenever she complained, asked 'Can't we just stay here a minute?', her parents would call her lazy, a daydreamer. 'On your feet. Goodness' sake, Karen, you'd always lollygag if we let you.'

She and Pan had always found that word so hilarious – *lollygag* – and it had become their band's name – The Lollygaggers – because it summed up the woozy, mystical *Picnic at Hanging Rock* languor that was their aesthetic obsession back then. When they'd first performed, they'd dressed in drifty Victoriana dresses, long hair loose, but the record company persuaded them to shorten their name to *The Lollies* and convinced them to present as candy-pop sapphic snacks in minidresses and space buns. Lydia was no more allowed to linger where she loved to be than when her parents snapped binoculars into their cases and moved the family on after half an hour, because Dad had clocked another wader.

As an adult, Lydia thinks that the moments of presence on those trips – the ones in which she was not worrying about homework, or who'd next chase her through the suburb's desire lines and culs-de-sac trying to pull her ponytail or steal her dinner money; too present in nature to be anxious, enjoying finding words to describe what she was seeing to herself, were the ones that taught her the consoling power of looking to the beauty.

Acute and poignant noticing has always helped her out of herself, escorted her away from pain and the past and coupled her to small, instrumental wonders outside herself.

Look to the beauty.

She darts into the shop and buys the binoculars for ten pounds from a slow-moving woman dressed in more shades of beige than Lydia ever realised could exist. She peers over her gold-rimmed glasses, breathing audibly through her wet, puckered lips as she taps on the till at a glacial pace, fingers knotted and striated like bark.

I will never get like that, Lydia thinks, and is sharply ashamed by her revulsion and impatience, remembering the distance of distaste doesn't keep anyone safe from ageing.

It's happening to everyone all the time, she thinks, accelerating in middle age with every conversation about interest rates or spatulas conducted without stopping to note what a fucking boring topic it is or to ask, 'When did we become the sort of dullards who have this kind of chat?'

Increasingly, Lydia's become convinced those unresisted, unremarked upon instants are the ones that change people:

stepping-stones from one iteration of self to the next, moving in such small increments that they cross boundaries of becoming without perceiving the distance covered, until they stop to look back and are astounded by how far behind they've left themselves.

And she believes that her years-long relationship with Henry also resulted from travelling such a spectrum of unnoticed alterations: feeling stuck, directionless, trapped in repeating their destructive dynamic was easy to mistake for going nowhere. But now Lydia can see that life was carrying her along like a travelator nonetheless and she's determined to regain her capacity for noticing and the sense of presence and purpose it lends her.

Transaction finally complete, Lydia hangs the brown leather case round her neck and starts to walk, the swing of the binoculars against her chest creating a pleasant sense of hobbyist purpose.

Discreetly, holding her hand at thigh level, she flicks the vickies at the Come On In Girl as she passes. A sadder sight than ever: hair even more thickly ombréd with bird crap than before, a pair of blood-red bullseye nipples spraypainted over her swimsuit.

Poor pathetic thing.

Salt wind paper-cutting her face, crunching over shingle and sand, Lydia walks, stooping to pick up litter. Every day on the beach she sees traces of selfishness, waste, lack of regard for the natural world. Furrows of rubbish the sea washes up then drags back into itself – cans, condoms, sanitary towels, friable icebergs of polystyrene shedding white hailstones as innumerable as shells and as durable as stones, pop bottles and plastic bags whose lifespans will exceed the humans who discard them by decades.

Callous.

Careless.

Selfish.

Litter is just an object lesson in the fact that all human beings believe they are the centre of the universe and the exception to the rule.

All human beings think just this once won't matter, they rely on everyone else to conduct themselves more decently, they promise not to do whatever unthinking, inconsiderate thing again, furtively or flagrantly, and then they do it anyway.

Because all human beings lie to themselves.

All human beings instinctively create extenuating circumstances to validate their venal choices.

And all human beings permit themselves not to inventory all the one-offs, in order to avoid confronting the fact that if they did, they would inevitably see the number of occasions on which they had taken the lazy, egocentric option mount up to the sum of absolute dickhead.

Just like Henry, granting himself exception after exception over the years. The version of him who forced himself on Lydia not an abuser, but a nice guy who misinterpreted her saying no as flirtation; one move in the inevitable dance towards sex, just a powerplay in a game of withholding and folding.

Which was how the equally selfish, older version of Henry had tried to frame it in the coffee shop: we were young, we were unhappy, we were so fucked up, we'd had some pretty heatedly messy sex on previous occasions, all the things he said before *sorry*. Letting another error in his perception violate Lydia's consent.

He'd even used the actual words 'I know I'm a nice guy' on either side of *sorry*.

He'd been so open about the fact that it was the MeToo movement that had motivated his self-scrutiny, leading him to conclude his behaviour did indeed merit an apology, however fudging, half-hearted and egoistic. And yet at no point had he truly seemed to include himself in the sum of abusers and Lydia in the number of the abused.

Protected from having to do so by his privilege, because men like Henry who are white, who are straight and cis, middle-class and degree-educated, articulate and artsy, men who read books and go to galleries rather than lifting weights and going to pubs, don't abuse people. They make stupid mistakes in the heat of the moment, which are unreflective of the truth of their characters.

And it feels to Lydia like she walked out of the coffee shop seeing all life's pipework and sewerage exposed, understanding how one group of people's effluence is allowed to poison another group's drinking water; finally, meaningfully, aware of all the world's inequalities for the first time in her life,

And it is all that fucker Henry's fault, this hateful growing decency: a burgeoning need to really be good inflicted by his badness; the need to be thoughtful exacted by his thoughtlessness.

Nothing has been the same since Lydia's cosy complacency was rent away from her like blankets off a sleeping body, shaking her awake to race and class, sex and gender, abled and disabled. All the *o-phobias* and *isms* present, pressing, egregious and exposed.

Lydia's own complicity in almost all of them a source of guilt.

She steams along, all this burning and churning through her head as she tramps the estuary's flatlands and sandbars, where ebbing waters have left old boats leaning tipsily in the silt.

Slowly, steadily, thoughts begin to evaporate as Lydia observes topographies of time layered on time; places where the past speaks through pocked concrete pillboxes, decomposing factories, the fire-gutted chalets of an old holiday camp where the only residents are birds overwintering in the charred rafters.

Turning the coast's corner, Lydia follows a chalky incline which starts to pull the breath from her lungs as the terrain rises from kneel to stand, eventually becoming cliffs.

She pauses, stands at the very edge, looking out, looking down; exhilarated and unsteady, she feels the woozy, seductive pull of gravity and starts retracing her steps.

Back on the flat, out on a shingly, scrub-topped finger of land where wind streams across the rough mane of grasses, she notices a squat hut: a bird hide.

The door admits her with a squeak, releasing a friendly creosote and damp smell that reminds Lydia of her father's shed.

She opens and clips the stiff shutter and clambers inelegantly onto the rough wooden bench, walking-boot treads imprinted on it in crumbly dried mud.

Taking the binoculars from their case, raising them to her eyes and adjusting the dial, she finds the focus and it pulls the world towards her, bright despite the grey, the stones turning to little brown birds.

All sense of time evanesces as Lydia watches flurries of sanderlings and plovers, glittering down to feed at low tide, light gilding their wings as they bank against the air currents.

Buoyed by the way birds travel in instinctive patterns, by how fathomable they are, lacking the elliptical complexities of people which are so easy to mistake and misinterpret. There is no subterfuge, no game or argument, no question of possession or abandonment; this is the beauty. To cease dwelling on human things and be present in the centre of the moment.

Lydia notices an Arctic tern, the red dart of its beak, black prayer cap, the funereal edging of its elegant, geometric wings.

It should not be here at this time of year, should be thousands of miles away.

At the sight of this bird blown off course, a species out of season, Lydia experiences an almost insufferable tenderness for another lonesome, buffeted being.

The door of the hide opens and there is a blip, a beat and leap in Lydia's chest, similar to the one she experienced walking alone into that spit-and-sawdust pub the other night, an instant in which she can all too easily imagine her coat and shoes, binoculars and underpants in evidence bags.

An older white man, carrying the ostentatious apparatus of expertise, walks in. He appears surprised and displeased to see her, but mechanically mutters, 'Morning', all the same.

He sets up a big scope, places the caricature accoutrements of the kind of man he is on the bench beside him: flask and foil-wrapped sandwiches, a Moleskine notebook and Parker pen.

Lydia intuits that the writing inside will be small and fussy, ant-sized and neat as newsprint.

When she looks back out, the Arctic tern has gone and in its place, three male mallards huckle and flap round a female, trying to mount her.

Shoulders crunched up in discomfort, Lydia feels her mouth downturn into a rictus of distaste.

The female duck tries to outpace the jostling males, waddling out from under them as each tries to press her to the sand.

'Fucking hell,' she exclaims. 'Fucking leave her alone.'

From the opposite side of the hide, the man tuts and shushes.

A scalding build of steam bulges inside Lydia's skull and she shocks herself by saying, 'Don't you fucking *shush* me.'

'I beg your pardon?'

The man turns from his scope and Lydia lowers the binoculars from her eyes and turns to look at him.

'I *said* don't you fucking *shush* me.'

'How dare you! I've never seen you here before. I come here every day.'

'So what? So what if you do?' Lydia rails. 'That doesn't make this place any more yours than mine.'

There she was in her moment, held gentle in a peace she's scarcely experienced in months, almost a year, and now some entitled arsehole has ripped it away.

'Whatever is the matter with you?'

The man looks at Lydia as if she has escaped from a locked ward, or maybe a zoo.

She rises from the bench and steps towards him, 'No. What's the matter with *you*? Actually, don't answer, I know what's wrong with you: nothing more and nothing less than that you're a prick, you're a fucking prick and—'

She stops mid-stream because although the man's cheeks are jam-splashed with anger, he also looks intimidated, maybe even afraid.

It strikes Lydia that he was once conventionally handsome. Unexpectedly, it's apparent that before time dragged his cheeks down and mulched them into his wattle, before his mouth settled into a gape, before hair started sprouting from his nostrils and stopped growing on his head, the man might have been desirable to her.

Some younger version of him drifts in front of the suddenly vulnerable, grandfatherly figure cringing in the corner of the hide, looking at Lydia as if she's contaminated or criminal.

Like a television with a bad signal interposing pictures from two channels, Lydia receives an unwelcome vision of him kissing her on the mouth and is beset by an intrusive curiosity about whether this man still fucks, still wants to, if he can get it up and if he's ever forced himself on anyone.

'Sorry,' she says. 'Sorry, sorry.' And she blunders out, dashed by wind and light.

She powerwalks back towards the town, the distant diorama of it recalling Minitania, buildings growing as Lydia draws nearer, half horrified by how quickly she'd made the shift from aggrieved to aggressor, half-thinking *fuck him*, he'll dine out on the incident of the psycho-bitch in the bird hide for months.

He struck her as the kind of man not to mull her motivations, whose default setting is probably to divide the world neatly into people like himself – solid, sensible, reasonable – and people like Lydia – rude, oversensitive, hysterical. He struck her as a man who'd be comfortable with the words 'people like them, people like that', using them to hierarchise humanity into the deserving and the dismissible.

But then, Lydia thinks bitterly, that's just what she's done to him by thinking it in the first place and he's a cunt and she's a cow and she'd never have got into a thought-spiral like this before Henry said what he said in the coffee shop and she is so sick of hating herself and Henry and the world and everyone in it.

As Lydia draws level with the half-derelict pier, from the building called The Palace – which she and Pandora jokingly call The Pathos – she hears an electronic voice yelling,

'Winner! Win, win, winner!' over and over. It feels so delib-erately contrived to mock her, so spiteful. She thinks she is about to cry. But just as she's sure she will, she sees the most heart-stoppingly beautiful and optimistic sight.

A sharp wind has started up, teasing the clouds apart. Crepuscular rays sing through the gaps; slender, vivid chan-nels of light, and where they brush the surface of the sea like God's own loving fingers, the waves glow gold and white.

Directly beneath the parted clouds, a woman stands facing the sea with her back to Lydia.

This woman is so still, surrendered to her moment, so emphatically contented that it appears as if even the weather has made room for her to step into the centre of the universe.

The woman's jet-black ringlets draw themselves sinuously on the air and the fabric of her long black coat ripples and bil-lows, streaming out behind her as if she has wings of her own.

Above her, gulls hang as if time has stopped, as if the woman is holding the birds in the sky by some invisible magic emanating from her outstretched arms.

It is impossibly romantic: she is a real-life, real-time *Wanderer Above the Sea of Fog*.

She is the freest person Lydia has ever seen.

Lydia takes out her phone and snaps a photograph so that later she will be able to reassure herself that she didn't imagine her.

Then as a statement of intent to herself, and to all 35,000 of her followers, she posts the photograph of Joyce on both Twitter and Instagram and captions it #goddess #lifegoals.

And somewhere in the South of France, an extremely famous actress, whom Lydia once did a few lines with at an album launch in the aughts, sees it and retweets it to all 98,000 of hers.

Chapter 17

'Sweet suffering Jesus, Joyce, I feel sick, I could faint. I thought you were dead! I was about to call the police! Where have you been, what have you been doing? You look like the wreck of the *Hesperus*!' Betty croaks, wringing the eiderdown between white-knuckled hands.

Joyce, returned from an absence that lasted fifty-six minutes, leans against the doorjamb, heartbeat flailing. She feels life boxing her up; the constricting safety of home enclosing her.

'It's very windy out there, very windy, and … And there was a huge queue in the chemist. Just enormous. You wouldn't believe how long I had to wait.'

Joyce rakes uselessly at her hair with her fingers. There had been only one other customer in the chemist – an elderly man with a Zimmer buying sticking plasters.

Betty looks disgruntled but her grip on the bedclothes loosens. 'Prescriptions for happy pills, I expect. Everything's a mental illness these days.'

Joyce bandages up her hand in the belt of her coat, 'Probably, yes – they didn't look like our sort of people.'

'Fatties were they, Joyce? Foreigners?'

'Every last one,' Joyce lies, guiltily, even as diverting fibs continue to materialise. 'And some of them had pyjamas on under their jackets.'

'Oh *no*, Joyce. Imagine! *Pyjamas*. How simply *dreadful*.' Betty relaxes into the pillows with a look on her face like she's sampling dessert.

Joyce slips her coat off and folds it over her arm. 'It was, Mum, it was awful. And I knew you'd be worried, so I was too, worried sick. I could have killed them, the people in the queue, I practically ran all the way home.'

'Poor Joycey. My pillows could do with a plump. Look at the state of you. I'm parched, Joyce, I'm starving, I'm completely past myself. Go and put the kettle on. What kind of cake did you get?'

'Belgian bun.' Joyce smiles uncertainly.

Betty wrinkles her nose as if Joyce had bought her dog's muck.

'Rather an unusual choice. Not a favourite, I'd have expected you to know. But any port in a storm, I suppose. Pillows, Joyce.' Betty gestures imperiously.

Joyce walks over to the bed and, seeing the patchy thatch of her mother's hair, begins to comb it tenderly with her fingers.

Betty recoils, crunches up her shoulder, 'Stop pawing me. Joyce. What are you trying to achieve?'

'I wanted to make your hair nice.' Joyce looks down; black strands of Betty's hair graffiti her palm. 'Sorry, I, I just wanted to make your hair nice, let me just ... '

Joyce reaches out once more.

'Hell's teeth, Joyce,' Betty taps Joyce on the hand, bats it away. 'Am I about to take part in a fashion parade? Leave me alone. Honestly, lady, I don't know what goes through your head sometimes *and* your own hair is a rat's nest, you should see yourself, Joyce, people in glass houses.' Betty is beset by a coughing fit, 'See? I feel perfectly wretched already without you manhandling me. Now, pillows.'

Joyce throttles and punches the pillows until her mother snaps, '*Enough*, Joyce, goodness' sakes, it's not a boxing match.'

Joyce goes to the kitchen to make tea and put the wrong cake on the right plate, still feeling as if lava is coursing around her veins.

In the narrow little kitchen, the lino is clean and scuffed.

A pall of bleach and stale meals hangs in the air.

Two plates, two cups, marooned in the draining rack.

A pair of aprons hang by their necks from a hook.

The tap drips.

It has been dripping that way for months.

Maybe for as long as a year.

The Formica counter has chips and cracks in it that Joyce could accurately point to wearing a blindfold. The brown open bracket of a burn where she once placed a pan of potatoes.

Careless.

Stupid.

The kettle whimpers as it begins to boil.

Defeat and relief vie for position as Joyce thinks of Martin. Martin and—

Him. That man. But she will not think of him, or her father or The Palace or the past. The things she used to have. She cannot understand the unsanctioned part of her that insists on it.

It's like her brain is a badly tuned radio allowing bursts of static and garbled transmissions to break into the neutral music of her thoughts. And she couldn't help but note the alarming ease with which her mother's prejudices appeared in her own mouth. Convenient untruths that don't represent Joyce's beliefs and yet, when she sweeps Betty's doctrines aside, nothing of her own steps forward into the room she's cleared, other than a general sense of being more open-minded than her mother, too confused about her own life to judge other people's.

Instead, complex equations flock into Joyce's head.

If her mother is still bedridden tomorrow, should she try to go to Martin again, could she, does she even want to? If she does not want to, what does that mean?

I want to, she affirms to herself, *I do*.

As Joyce absentmindedly lifts the kettle and begins filling the teapot, their kiss grips her; a hot, honest rush dives through her body.

She thinks that blazing belongs to Martin, is sure it does, but for a moment she doubts it — just because of this lady's stuff, the time of life business. All these strange feelings, sometimes akin to a sensation of worry, fizzing and foaming in her tummy, untethered to any emotion, heart tripping syncopated beats and at other times, well, she gets a hungry heat in her bits and pieces that makes her squeeze her thighs together.

But the sudden reaction she experienced a moment ago, when she thought of Martin kissing her, was more intense than all of those occurring together, so she thinks it must be love.

Why, then, less than an hour ago, had something cemented Joyce to the spot, then carried her home? Why can't she summon Martin's face but can visualise every one of the chocolate wrappers littering his car? Pocket money sweets. Something about it hurts her heart. That too Joyce names love; love flexing its muscles.

Then the kettle burps boiling water over her hand; shock, pain, humiliating somehow. She yelps, begins to sob and rushes to the sink, cold water pummels sore skin. Her mother limps in, 'What's the commotion, Joyce?'

'My hand, I burnt my hand,' tears run down Joyce's cheeks. 'It hurts, it really hurts,' she cries.

'Oh, calm your passions, Joyce, anyone would think you were being disembowelled. Take some deep breaths.'

Betty stands in her nightdress, arms folded, mouth chewing over nothing, slowly shaking her head.

Joyce clenches her unharmed fist, tries to gulp in oxygen, but she's howling too hard to force a breath down.

'What has got into you, Joyce?' demands Betty. 'Drama,' she sighs. 'Dramatic.'

Joyce crushes her lips between her teeth, screws her eyes shut but tears keep thundering out of her.

Opening her eyes, Joyce turns to her mother.

Betty looks so little: wizened and pale, eyes and nostrils ringed with wet redness. In her nightdress, without her face made up, Betty appears as insubstantial as a cobweb, throwaway as a paper hankie.

Old.

A poor thing.

She looks like a poor old thing.

'Mum,' exclaims Joyce, rashly reaching out for a hug. Water flies from her fingers, spatters and pools on the linoleum between them.

'Joyce, you're wet,' Betty says. 'Look at the mess you're making. Look at the floor.' But at the same time, as if brushing crumbs from a table, she strokes Joyce's arm, 'There, there, Joycey, come on, there's no need for all this. We've both been in the wars, not a nice day today, is it?'

Like a disconsolate child, Joyce shakes her head.

'No,' says Betty, patting Joyce's back. 'Not a very nice day. That's what happens, isn't it, when you don't have me to keep you right? Our routine's all out of kilter and now you seem just a tiny touch *tired*. Let's get this water mopped up and then we'll have ourselves a tea party in front of our programmes, shall we?'

Joyce nods, wipes her palms across her wet cheeks, sucking in sips of air. Then she picks up a cloth, kneels and begins sopping up the puddle at her mother's feet.

It will be OK, Joyce assures herself between sniffs, it will all be OK. Today will be a day like any other and that is fine.

That is good.

That is perfectly nice; a nice cup of tea in a nice china cup, a nice cake on a nice plate on a nice doily in front of our programmes. And that will be enough.

Tonight, I will go to bed and sleep soundly in the knowledge that nothing has happened to me but today. Today contained in itself; finished and neat as a bead.

'For crying out loud, Joyce,' gripes Betty, 'not *that* cloth. What are you doing? That is a J-cloth, for surface use only, stop grovelling about on the linoleum and get the mop.'

But Joyce doesn't move. She remains on the floor. On her knees.

Chapter 18

In the apartment on top of The Hotel Duchesse Royale, Lydia, Lol and Pan are sitting at the boardroom-style dining table, each holding a phone and a fork, picking over an insipid risotto with one hand and grazing all the horrors and attractions of the world with the other. Each of their faces blue-lit like something from a watercolour painting of cholera victims.

'Bloody hell,' says Lydia, 'this tweet is popping like a right mad bastard.'

The little digits beneath the photo of the woman keep rising in real time, likes and retweets and quote tweets growing in number, reaching figures Lydia has never achieved before.

'That lady?' Lol asks without looking up. 'The no fucks thing?'

'Have you seen it? What no fucks thing?' Lydia puts her phone down on the table next to her bowl.

Lol turns her own phone and holds it out to Lydia like a warrant card, 'It's everywhere, Auntie Lyd. My friend sent it to me.'

On Lol's phone is Lydia's photograph superimposed with block capitals that read ZERO F G.

'Right,' says Lydia. Her voice sounds rubbly and rough as if it is emitting from a blown speaker. She struggles to keep it even, 'And this is a ... thing?'

Lol gives Lydia a *fuck's sake, grandma* look. Completely despairing, but not entirely unkind.

'Well,' she nods, 'can't you see it doing numbers?'

'Yeah, I just ... '

Then Lol's expression hardens and her brows knit, 'It's kind of gross, Auntie Lydie. Sorry but, does the woman in the picture even know she's gone viral? I guess at least her face isn't visible but, like, still. Or,' Lol smiles uncertainly, 'did you maybe ask her? Before you took it. Did you ask?'

'No,' says Lydia staring dumbfounded at the photograph of the self-possessed woman as if she is standing outside her own house while it's being burgled, important things being nicked, or ... no. *No.* She's the thief. Lol's right.

Lydia *took* the photograph.

And seeing the theft in it, refracted through the terrible, clarifying prism of Lol's disapproval, makes Lydia feel like she's eaten a bad oyster.

Lydia stares at her own photograph on Lol's phone, as the digits below her original post spin relentlessly upwards, making it real to her that every one of those numbers represents not just validation and approval for Lydia, but someone else, somewhere else, actual people holding their phones in their hands, looking at a photograph.

A photograph of a woman that, in the last few hours, has been unglued from Lydia's original tweet, that has sped around the world, multiplying, mutating like a virus, getting stickier and stickier, picking up meanings, gaining mass and momentum like a rolling snowball, having text added and subtracted, making strangers in distant continents and near ones feel better and worse about their lives, being subsumed into private jokes and public ones, being shared and shared again on Facebook and Twitter and Instagram, being liked and laughed at and admired and criticised and mocked, and of all the words these people have attached to the photograph, the one nobody has uttered in connection to it is *Joyce*. Joyce, who is staring out of her living-room window with a mouthful of chocolate biscuit, stoppering a scream.

'Pushy madam.' Wielding her finger like a shiv, Betty slashes at the Duchess of Sussex's smiling face in the *Daily Mail*. 'She's trouble, Joyce. She'll come between those brothers, you mark my words. I'll wager their mother wouldn't have liked her one bit. In fact, I expect she's spinning in her grave as we speak, God rest her. A tragedy that we lost Diana and now we're stuck with madam here, Joyce. Pushy, grabby, just dreadful, isn't she dreadful? Joyce? *Joyce*. I said isn't she dreadful?'

Joyce's scalded hand screeches under a bandage applied by her mother the previous evening.

'I like her hat.'

'You like her hat? Which hat are you looking at, Joyce Wilson? Because that hat there is an abomination, honestly, heaven only knows what kind of a dog's breakfast you'd make of yourself if you didn't have me to keep you right. Saints preserve us, would you really wear a hat like that?'

Pain in Joyce's palm surges and recedes, blinking like a Belisha beacon.

'I suppose it's a bit of a funny shape.'

'It looks like it's been trampled by horses, Joyce, is what it looks like. So, do you really like her hat?'

'No, actually, it's not very nice.'

'Not very nice at all, just like the wearer.'

172

Joyce drifts backwards through the hours, this second day of her mother's illness. Replaying the shock of waking to discover Mum still feverish and spluttering, suggesting herself this time that Joyce pop out for more tinned soup, another nice cake. *See if you can't improve on yesterday's debacle, you could hardly make a worse choice, Belgian bun, for goodness' sake, and a newspaper thank you very much, even though it will probably make me feel even more dreadful than I already do, but one has a duty to remain informed I suppose, and Joey needs some Trill but don't be long or we'll miss the start of our programmes.*

Joyce had found herself skittish and reluctant.

In her head the route along the prom stretched and warped, far and open; so much street and sky, so many strangers. And halfway between home and Martin's office, The Palace and all the memories that spilled out of its doors, ones it did her no good to confront, especially the ones involving Paul.

Paul. Joyce has begun to find his name forcing itself into her consciousness. Every time she thinks of Martin, Paul steps in front of him, the weight and musk of him, the savage hunger tumbling inside her body when he climbed on top of her in his car, reminding Joyce that the reawakened parts of her once belonged to him. Even though, once Daddy was out of the picture, Paul hadn't wanted them or the future he'd started to strongly imply they'd share.

Vivid as videotape, Joyce sees herself in the jeweller's window: a spectral reflection of her smiling face, Paul's handsome head resting on top of hers, his big strong arms inside his impeccably tailored coat wrapped round her body, pulling her into his as she admires both how attractive a couple they make and the rings glinting on cushioned on black velvet squares. 'Just say, Joycey, just for fun, if someone was going to buy you one of these sparklers, which one would you choose?'

And the pellucid spring day Paul picked Joyce up from the villa in his gleaming black car and pointed to a house up the road with a garden carpeted in cadmium daffodils. 'Smashing house that. Nice and close to mum and dad, could do it up really pretty, just like you.'

Joyce had rubbed her hands all over her face as if washing it, until the image was scrubbed away. She'd pointed out to Betty that there were bits and bobs actually, plenty of bits and bobs, so they could manage another day's meals. But her mother replied, 'Well you couldn't get out of here fast enough yesterday when I asked you not to go, breaking your neck you were, and now I'm asking, Joyce – and you *know* I *never* ask you for *anything* – I am just asking you to pop out to get your sick mother a few little things to brighten her day, Joyce. You always were a contrary Mary and I expressly said Joey needs some Trill, not that you seem to care since you don't like anything that takes my attention, he's down to the last scratchings, poor thing, and—'

'*All right!* Mum, all right, I'll go.' Joyce had conceded and without time to collect herself properly, was back on the prom.

Joyce's make-up felt like an oily mask and the dress her mother had bid her wear – navy-sailory – she thought made her look rather matronly. Gave her a bust rather than bosoms.

She'd marched past The Palace with her face turned away as if from a nasty accident and before she knew it was outside the business centre. It had felt very important that she manage it this time.

When Joyce entered the foyer, a bored-looking receptionist had been pecking at her phone behind a perfunctory plastic flower arrangement.

'Hello, good morning, I'm . . . I have an appointment . . . a meeting with Martin.' The girl had glared as Joyce fumbled the business card out of her pocket. 'Mr Ballantyne, Martin Ballantyne.'

The receptionist flourished a nail file like a magic wand, 'Through the double doors, second office on the left.'

Down the corridor, behind a small window sliced up by a dusty Venetian blind, Joyce saw Martin at his computer, one hand fumbling in a bag of Monster Munch as he tapped numbers into a spreadsheet.

Joyce's only sensation had been the burn gnawing under the bandage.

He looked like any middle-aged man; a bit bald, slightly chunky, nothing particularly smart, nothing particularly slovenly about his clothes. The kind of person, Joyce thought, you could sit beside on a bus without being curious about where they might be going or wondering about them after they got off.

A sudden pluck at her heartstrings: poor pet, she'd thought. Outraged, almost, that good, kind, quiet people could be so easily overlooked and underappreciated. Determined to show Martin she understood what was special in him, gently, she tapped the glass.

When Martin turned and saw Joyce, his face was like the first night the fair opened back up in spring; a sudden switching on.

'Joyce!' Martin opened the door, 'Come in.'

'I can't stay, Mum's poorly, I said I wouldn't be gone long, I just, I don't know really.'

'What matters is that you're here, and I'm so glad you are.'

Martin had pulled the cord on the blinds.

His wet kiss tasted of pickled-onion crisps, which struck her as schoolboyish.

Paul always smelled of expensive aftershave, the chic scent of a bottle bought in London and under that something feral, lushly animal, clawing at Joyce's controls, ripping up the rules her mother wrote.

But the rules had been suspended then. Paul had been her mother's suggestion, she'd insisted actually. 'A nice business-man,' she'd said. 'He's been asking your father about you. It would be helpful to the ... *situation* if you could just be ... *nice* to him.'

Joyce had lost her balance and she and Martin stumbled together. She bumped her bad hand on the desk and cried out.

Martin mistook the mewl for desire, spiked Joyce in the hip with the bulge in his trousers and sighed into her neck, 'I want to make love to you, Joyce. I've been thinking about you. And now you're here, you've got me hot, Joyce, worked up.'

Joyce looked at Martin and pulled away.

'Oh, oh, Martin, I'd love to ... well, what you said, but there isn't time. Not here. How are you? How's your gran?'

Martin leaned back against his desk, upsetting a pot of pens which rolled onto the floor, 'Yeah, better, thanks, a bit. I'm going to kiss you again, Joyce. Is that OK?'

Joyce clutched her injured hand, 'Well yes ... but, careful. I hurt my hand, Martin.'

'Poor Joyce.'

'Don't,' she said sharply as Martin's mouth brushed the shiny pink skin peeping from the bandage's cuff.

'You should never have to hurt, Joyce.'

The way Martin had looked at Joyce, with the preposterous gravity of a nobody copying a leading man's line from a film, struck her as inauthentic.

Joyce glimpsed some darkness in herself, something

snide; akin to standing over an ant, the urge to push down with her shoe.

Then Martin had sighed heavily and pushed his face against Joyce's, held her a while, and irritation was subsumed into the pleasure of being held. It was so nice to be held, to be wanted. It was all just a bit quick; just the time, Mum waiting, the distraction of her achy hand causing the confusing feelings.

Martin's breath was humid against Joyce's neck, 'I think about you all the time.'

'I do think about you too, Martin, I do, I just ... '

'What, Joyce?'

'Mum, I've got to get back, I've errands to run. I was only popping, a quick, you know, hello?'

'I could drive you.'

'Really?'

He kissed her again and she tried harder to surrender.

'Joyce, you're a beautiful woman, you know.'

Martin looked at Joyce like he was waiting for her to say something, but she'd only smiled, mouth taut and distant.

As he drove they'd talked about nothing much. It was like being with a kind friend, someone nice you could tell about trivial things: household chores, what you might eat later. A clean warmth had settled into Joyce, like dozing in a bath.

When Martin had dropped Joyce at the shops, she'd kissed him gently on the cheek, 'You're such a lovely, sweet man.' They'd arranged to be in the club on Saturday.

A pleased little pull carried Joyce round the shops, the promise in her like a future holiday. And yet none of that feeling had followed her home.

Instead, what had remained loyal was the thought she'd had about Paul, about how she had ended up with him in the first place. Among the smoggy memories one fact shone out clear and true: her mother's insistence. *A nice business-man, Daddy's dealing with him, he likes you, it would be good for everyone.*

Everything present dissolves, leaving Paul's fingers and lips all over Joyce inside the car, always the car, making her shudder and moan, holding her in his arms outside the jewellers, dangling diamonds over her as if it was only a matter of time until he slipped one over her finger. And then after: Daddy gone, suddenly gone, the hard, secretive hurry in her mother, the abrupt move from villa to flat, Paul no longer calling – she never had his number.

'No point, Joycey sweetheart,' he'd explained, 'I'm hardly home and I always give my girl a bell as soon as I am.'

After a couple of weeks, in the grip of a desperation so bodily it felt like flu, Joyce had gone down to The Palace. Billy, the doorman, whom Joyce had known since she was a little girl, couldn't meet her eye. His gentleness when he insisted that he was unable to let Joyce in was mortifying.

Joyce had felt like she was being gutted – her belly physically sliced, pried open, innards dragged out – when she saw that Billy's hand was ready by her elbow to escort her away, as he told her there was really nothing to be gained by causing a scene. 'Go home, Joyce, walk away. Joyce, you must understand, don't you understand, Joyce?'

Billy's face. Bafflement and pity as it dawned on him how little Joyce did understand. And at that moment Paul had arrived, giving Billy a look like he was pressing a blade against his jugular. The doorman didn't blanch, but his eyes flicked back to Joyce, soft and sorry. 'Leave it, Joyce sweetheart. You don't mess with that lot. Try and think of it as a lucky escape, eh?' Joyce had called Paul's name as he walked away from her into The Palace without a backward glance;

only a flinching tilt of his head, like he was ridding himself of a neck crick, to denote he'd heard her.

'Sorry, love,' Billy had patted Joyce's arm paternally. 'Head home now, Joyce, there's a good girl.'

'But we're meant to be getting married,' Joyce wailed. 'We were looking at rings.'

Billy's face set itself into that tolerant, pitying 'bless you' expression people make in the presence of the extremely ill, the completely mad and the totally stupid. 'Joyce, love,' he'd said, 'Paul's already married. He's got two kids.'

And Joyce remembers how she'd stood there, feeling that if she just stayed still enough, for long enough, something, someone, would come and press rewind and all of this would turn out to be a nasty prank or a misconceived joke. Even after the rain came on, even after it began to get dark, even after her clothes were soaked. Until, eventually, her mother came and manoeuvred Joyce into a taxi, which carried her off in a fugue tide that washed the weeks away, the months and years, and fetched her into life the way it is now.

Now. Joyce sits with her mother who is still flipping the pages of the newspaper.

'I don't know how these hippy-types can believe all that twaddle about global warming when it says right here it's going to be the coldest winter on record, Joyce. Do you see what's globally warm about the coldest winter on record, because I don't.'

Joyce thinks of Martin, not a bad bone in his body, no darkness or deceit lurking under the surface, nothing but the milk of human kindness running through him, and reassures herself that in the car with him it had been nice: the low-watt flattering glow had been happiness. It *is happiness*, just talking to someone who wants her, who, of course, *she also wants*.

Betty is onto the next page of the paper. 'I don't know why these people didn't say anything at the time if what happened to them was so awful, attention-seeking, that's what it is, attention-seeking.'

A punctured feeling sighs through Joyce; a tired, airless sensation.

She drifts over to the window and looks out at the rain pummelling down on the bin sheds and terraces, slickening the patchwork of gardens, paving stitched with dandelions and trimmed in litter, upturned patio furniture, potted palms with their dukes up, convulsing in the wind, sheds, a massive garden gnome leaning drunkenly on a barbecue, and in a gap between the rooftops, if she twists and squints, the sea.

The gas fire whinnies.

Joey rakes the sandpaper floor of his cage.

From every corner of the living room, dolls stare blindly, haughty madam looks on their dumb faces, flounced and frilled to their frozen china throats and wrists.

'Stop pacing, Joyce. What are you pacing for? You're getting on my last nerve, lady, I'll tell you that for free,' croaks Betty, babied up under a crochet blanket. 'Just park your backside, have a biscuit and content yourself, Joyce Wilson.'

On and on and on Betty rattles. Joyce craves silence; just a second to parse all these thoughts she is having. The need for peace an itch, a crimson, vermiculating itch, scorching in a place so deep inside that it feels as if her soul has hives.

She is allergic to her life and the words 'shut up' are a spasm in her diaphragm, but she sits. Joyce sits down in her chair, next to her mother, and chomps a Viscount so that the 'shut up' stays there.

Chapter 19

The weather is violent. Battering and squalling against the window.

Gulls huddle on the balcony and Pan is grousing on again about bird spikes. Chuntering about whether she could install them herself or if she'd have to get someone else to do it.

Lydia paces round the living room, putting her phone down and picking it up, watching the counters on the picture of the woman ticking up; fervently wishing they would stop so that her anxiety levels and the picture itself would subside instead of spiking.

The sound of Lol's strumming bleeds from her bedroom and Pan tuts, 'I don't mean to be a bitch, Lyd, but I can't wait until she quits the guitar like she's quit every other hobby. Can you sit, please, you're doing my absolute nut in padding about like a caged tiger. Are you all right?'

'She could be good, you know?' Lydia perches on the edge of the cream leather couch. 'I think she just needs a bit of encouragement.'

'God, that girl gets nothing *but* encouragement, Lyd. Who do you think bought her the guitar? And it's a good one.'

Lydia thinks twice about it – remembering how

excruciatingly awkward she felt when her parents told her to 'give us a tune then', shifting awkwardly in their armchairs when she did – but then she calls through to Lol regardless. 'Come through,' Lydia shouts. 'Why don't you play us a song?' The strumming stops

Pan harrumphs, a hollow sarcastic snort.

Lol appears with the guitar. She smiles shyly. 'I've learned something actually,' she tells the toes of her Converse. 'Like, I'm not super good or anything . . .'

'Doesn't matter,' Lydia looks encouragingly at Lol. 'Your mum and me weren't very good and it didn't stop us getting a record deal.'

Pan laughs. She sits up and actually gives an honest raucous hoot.

'She's got a point there. Why don't you play us a song?'

'Can you not look, please?' Lol asks, almost in a whisper. 'Can you please just listen but not look.'

And Pan's face is love, the bruised and buttery glow of absolute adoration, a cherishing that is almost painful.

She and Lydia utter 'of course' in unison and swivel their bodies away.

Lol clears her throat, her fingers strike the strings and the chord hits Lydia in the tenderest meat of herself. The girl begins to sing in a slender voice, lucid and flowing as water, gaining power as she goes, until the music is a cresting wave.

> *I'm a missile, I am magic, I'm a movie*
> *I'm a star, I am ready, feeling groovy*
> *Watch your heart, gird your loins, lock up your daughter*
> *You're in flames, you're in love, with me,*
> *just like you oughta*
> *Be, so just stand back and see*

Pan and Lydia look at each other, astonished and delighted, they grin and shake their heads at the joyful, confusing beauty of Pan's daughter singing their song. All the shock and beauty of a firework out of season.

And the chorus comes and all three of them sing in unison, the old disused song burning to life.

I'm up for it, up for it, going out and up for it.

The cheesy lyrics and empty sentiment – stale and brittle as the sun-bleached plastic of an abandoned beach toy – somehow ardent and alive now they're singing it together.

Pam and Lydia do the chorus's double handclaps seamlessly on beat, in perfect time with the ones their teenage hands had first laid down on a decrepit four-track in Pan's parents' garage.

When the song ends, they all whoop and cheer and stomp.

'That was amazing, Lol,' Lydia stands and puts her arm over Lol's shoulder as she lays her guitar on the couch.

'Brilliant, darling,' Pan stands too and puts her arm around Lol from the other side. 'Proud of you . . . Lol, really proud.'

Pan and Lydia put their arms around each other, closing the circle.

They linger that way, enmeshed in each other like *The Three Graces*.

'What was it like?' Lol asks, voice muffled by her face against Lydia's arm. 'When you were in the band?'

Lydia says, 'Shit.'

And Pan says, 'Fun.'

They let go of one another.

'It was complicated,' Lydia says eventually.

'It wasn't really,' counters Pan. 'It was fun and it was exciting, then it was . . . not fun and, I guess, maybe a little bit . . . shit. But it was a long time ago and the PRS money buys you some nice stuff. Even pays your school fees sometimes. Which we need to talk about, because after Christmas, you'll have to—'

'They treated us like dirt,' Lydia can't stop herself from saying, 'even before it all kicked off, all the tabloid stuff ... the furore, like I don't even mean that. Right from the start we were surrounded by pricks and pervs who treated us like ... I dunno, a product, a commodity and—'

'We were though, Lydia, be real,' Pan sits down on the couch and pours another rosé into a glass like a goldfish bowl on a stick. 'We weren't exactly artists. I mean, come on.'

Lol balls her babylike hands and retracts them into the sleeves of her hoodie, black with a little Progress Pride emblem over the left breast.

'No, Pan. We were practically children and they dressed us up in next-to-nothing and all those men in their fucking suits seduced us and cajoled us into acting like ... looking like ... they took our music and they turned us into puppets and a peep show, and they made us pretend, or, if not pretend, at least imply we were lesbians. We weren't even bi and—'

'What about Harriet, Auntie Lydia?' Lol asks, sounding shocked.

'Oh,' Lydia sits down and helps herself to the glass of wine she'd sworn she wasn't going to have. 'I forgot you met Harriet.'

'I liked Harriet,' Lol's mouth-corners flick up.

'I'm surprised you remember Harriet,' Pan says, 'you were only little.'

'I don't think ... ' Lydia starts with caution. 'I just really liked ... *loved*, Harriet.'

'Well,' says Lol, 'that's not being straight then, is it?'

And it lands in Lydia that Lol might have a point. After all, she still fancies some women, still wanks over lesbian porn. Maybe Harriet, a 'proper' lesbian, calling her straight when they broke up had made Lydia feel invalidated, exiled from a community that perhaps she belongs to after all. And maybe that, in killer combination with how often Henry – the straightest of cis men – had pulled Lydia's focus from everyone else to the detriment of other possibilities, had caused her to forget that being bi or pan, or in some way queer, was, is, *could be* at least, part of her identity.

But mentioning Henry to herself returns Lydia to the subject she was talking about before, and she gulps half a glass of wine so hard her throat hurts. 'Anyway, me and Harriet, that was years after those sleazes made me and your mum—'

'For heaven's sake, Lydia. They didn't coerce us. We would have done anything, don't you remember? We would have done anything to get that record deal, get out of that town, away from our parents. You can't, you *cannot* rewrite *our* history just because *you* don't like your life now.'

'Or maybe you can't force me to pretend it was all fine any more, Pan. You were always the one who said *Fuck it, let's just get on with it, let's go out there.* You always—'

'Because every time I tried to ask a question or push back or sound even the slightest note of caution around all that stuff you're moaning about now, *you* said, *It's fine, Pan, leave it. Stop, Pan, they're getting annoyed.* It was always *you* saying *Don't make a fuss, don't piss anyone off, let's just do what they want, take our bras off for the record cover, pretend to get off with each other in the video.* Every single time. *It. Was. You.* And I went along with it then but I'm not going along with this now. You *do not* get to decide *my* past was all misery and abuse just because you've chosen to view *yours* that way.'

Anger roars inside Lydia's skull, so fiercely it feels like it might blow the top of her head off. 'Fuck you, Pan.'

'Please don't, Auntie Lydie. Mum, come on, please don't.'

Lol's voice is a frightened child's.

'Don't what?' Pan snaps at her.

'This is horrible,' Lol says tearfully.

'Then go to your room,' Pan replies, slugging the last of her wine and refilling her glass. 'Stay out of it.'

'Don't speak to her like that,' Lydia hisses.

'She's *my* daughter and this is *my* house. I'll say whatever I want to either of you,'

Pan looks blotchy with drink, a sotted, marshy raggedness round her words, and she grins, manically and raises her wineglass as if she's chinking cheers against the air.

'Come on, Lydia, lighten up and stop acting like a crazy bitch. It's really not cute. We were having fun. Give us another song, Laurence.'

'Mum, why can't you just respect that my name is Lol now?'

Lydia barely notices Lol's plaintive plea. Surging up in her, hurt and rage like a molten bubble, an aneurysm mushrooming inside her skull, a sensation of swelling so bodily that she imagines trepanning herself with the nearest sharp object just to release the scalding steam of it.

'I don't want to be *cute,* Pandora,' Lydia stabs her index finger at Pan. 'I don't *need to be cute.* Look where *being cute* got us in the past and anyway, I'm ... I'm ... hurting and I'm a mess and ... I'm a hurting mess of a person, Pandora, not fucking Hello Kitty, so there is absolutely no need *at all* for me to be *cute* now. Or. *Ever.* And you're a bad friend for saying that, Pandora,' she spits. 'And in general. You are a really lazy, shitty friend.'

Pandora performs an arrogated gesture of feistiness: she lunges her face forward and snakes her neck back, snaps her fingers and jabs her index finger at Lydia. 'Hell no!' she fumes. 'I mean, what the hell, Lydia? How dare you? No. I can't,

I can't even, you are being ... seriously ... I can't even. I cannot even, do you hear me? You are staying in my hotel, house, making me feel attacked in my own house. You are *being* very attacking right now after everything I've done for you, OK? Not cool, Lydia.'

'Stop it!' Lol puts her hands over her ears and bursts into tears.

Lydia goes to comfort her but Lol tenses and shrugs away.

Pan laughs and drains her glass again, 'Guess you're not flavour of the month any more *Auntie* Lydia.'

'Fuck,' Lydia gets up, walks over to Pan and squats down on her haunches. 'I'd forgotten just how nasty you can be when you've got a drink in you.'

Lol is wailing like an ambulance, still begging them to stop.

'Get out,' Pan leans forward and spits the words at Lydia. 'First thing tomorrow, you can piss off out of here. Lol, stop that silly bloody noise, would you?'

Lol keeps on and on.

'It was such a mistake to get back in touch with you,' Pan slurs. 'I wish I hadn't phoned you that day.'

'Well, the feeling's mutual. I wish I hadn't answered,' Lydia says, not in anger but with a sadness so heavy her skeleton might snap like a match.

She tries to go to Lol, but Lol makes a barrier of her arms, a gesture like some kind of cinematic CGI superhero sending an enemy flying through the air.

So that's fucked too.

Lydia takes out her phone to use as a torch as she descends the dim stairs to the Flamingo Suite and sees the screen is cluttered up with missed calls, WhatsApps, Twitter and Facebook DMs, text messages too.

She feels bombarded.

For the last decade, Lydia's phone has been glued to her hand – she's always relished the sense of connection, of never being alone, *not really*. Drawing pride from popularity. Feeling *wanted* and *real* when communications flurry in; comments, likes, replies, invitations and gossip.

So often, the world inside Lydia's phone has felt more vivid and desirable than the reality in front of her, not least because her phone was where Henry lived.

Now Lydia is afraid to be in the moment and afraid to see what the onslaught of emails and voicemails and texts are about, who they are from.

Entering the room, she begins to read:

Photo!!! Who is she??? OFG Style Feature?

> New HERO! *Love heart emoji* *crown emoji* *painting nails emoji*

Most of them are about the photograph – which has become a meme – and offer Lydia work. Opportunities to track the woman down, write an article on how to recreate her look, do a piece about 'everyday style stars'.

She tots it up. There are several hundred pounds' worth of jobs being offered. And although the time it will take to get paid as a freelancer will be geological, at least Lydia would know the cash was on its way, could start to plan accordingly.

Plan *what?* Lydia's shoulders sink. With profits from an image of a woman who never asked for any of this?

Fuck.

Fuck.

She never meant this to happen. Knowing that it is already

underway and unstoppable is akin to the nightmares Lydia has where she realises she's committed murder but finds she is unable to explain that she was outside herself during the commission of an unintended act of violence, that she's a nice person who didn't mean to hurt anyone.

And Lydia knows she's not an abuser, nor a predator or aggressor, but the way she feels right now about the harms she may have inflicted on the woman in the photograph, and her urgent instinct to wheedle in her own defence, to separate what she's done from who she is, points towards a painful parity with the record execs whose conduct she was just lamenting. And Henry's. Or at least there is insufficient unlikeness to feel chastening.

And somehow it calls to mind being on the train leaving London, the one that brought Lydia here.

How, as it departed, and Lydia embraced being alive to experience autumn, she'd pictured herself returning to London after a handful of days, rested and refreshed; walking through the city on some frosty morning, brave, cute and scarf-wrapped. Swamped by a school-hearted Sunday-night sensation, which felt like all the inarticulable sadness and beauty of the world ballooning under her sternum, climbing her throat so she could hardly swallow.

She'd been filled with a tenderness towards herself so vast that she'd popped her headphones in and cued up 'Never Enough' from *The Greatest Showman* to enhance the image of all those who hadn't noticed Lydia's suffering realising how tragically they'd failed her; their self-rebuking at Lydia's funeral, which she'd come so close to bringing into being.

Dissenters cleared their throats just outside the frame: inventories of cares and kindnesses committed by the very individuals Lydia was damning as all take and indifferent.

Thoughtful acts and intended efforts Lydia had been so sated by savouring that she'd never quite got round to doing those things, sending those messages or replying to all the loving ones from friends saying they hadn't heard from Lydia in a while. *Are you OK? I'm here for you if you need anything.*

She'd pushed the nuances back into comic-book outlines, redivided the world into heroes and villains, then cried silently and steadily all the way to the end of the line, where an ombré of candy colours had been striping the sky above the sea.

During the eleven months after meeting Henry in the coffee shop, Lydia's loneliness, the interior kind not proportionate to company, had blinded her to the fact that she wasn't really alone. She recognises that now and damns the clarity of sight which shows it to her and exposes exactly who she is in the world: her pliable lack of selfhood, her utter selfishness, her inability to receive kindness. So aware of her own wounds she failed to account for her capacity to damage others, identifying too strongly with her own victimhood to imagine such an eventuality, too obsessed over inequalities and power imbalances in the wider world to focus on the ones right in front of her.

That's the thing about MeToo, she realises. You're never not included. No matter how tired she is, no matter how heartsore, overburdened, burnt out or incapable, every essay, article, tweet and headline insists on a conversation with her own pain and that of others, demanding she triangulates her own damages against those inflicted upon friends and strangers alike. And in the case of the photograph, Lydia completely, catastrophically, miscalculated her position.

And it is *too much.*

It is all too much.

It is all too much.

It is all too much.

And Lydia feels like she will die of this.

Lydia really feels like she will die of this.

She can't even cry. She's as dry and lost as someone caught in a sandstorm.

Pan hates her and Lol hates her.

It probably is time to leave. To get away from Pan and the past and from Henry, who haunts The Hotel Duchess Royale.

She still doesn't know what to call his actions.

Coercions?

Invasions?

Assaults?

The other word? The most serious one.

Whatever.

Those events somehow seem to belong more now to the hotel than the places where they happened, and she needs to leave it all behind, even though she wishes she wasn't leaving like this.

Going back to being alone with everything that has been done to her.

And everything that Lydia is beginning to realise she has done to someone else.

Chapter 20

'A second Viscount, Joyce, really?' Betty shakes her head. '*Really?* A second? I mean, you know me, Joyce, I'm not one to make remarks. But if I was, well, I'd say those biscuits are disappearing down your gullet at quite a rate of knots and you are hardly fading away to nothing as it is.'

Betty makes the gesture of a bragging fisherwoman exaggerating the size of a catch.

All afternoon, Joyce's brain has been steaming inside her skull. Torment rising towards a scream with the television yammering and Joey's beak snip-snipping at the bars of his cage.

It's Paul and Daddy and all the things she can remember scrabbling among all the things she can't. How it unfolded, how it felt and how it fell: the twin abandonments of both these men and the subsequent move to this flat, this flavourless life. And now Martin, harmlessly suggesting there *is* another potential life. And yet it is distant and impossible as a far-off planet, because of Betty.

Betty who goes on and on, abrading Joyce, until Joyce says, 'Well, Mum, it's just as well you aren't the sort of person who would make remarks, isn't it? Because that would be mean.'

'I beg your pardon, Joyce? What did you say?'

Betty's eyes flash a warning but if Joyce recognises the mistake, she fails to heed it and follow the rules accordingly.

Joyce abruptly rises from her chair.

A strange, strident giggle geysers out of her: 'I *said*, *Mother*, although I'm fairly sure you heard me, *actually*, I said it's just as well you'd *never* make a remark about me having a second Viscount because that would be awfully mean, wouldn't it? It wouldn't be very *nice*. And I know you wouldn't want to be *not nice*.'

Betty draws her body up in her chair, 'I don't think I like your tone, Joyce Wilson. I don't think I like it one bit actually, *madam*.'

The atmosphere becomes taut.

Joey appears to still, beak closed around the bars, even the dolls seem rapt. Joyce's heart is cantering. 'I think I'll go out,' she blurts truculently. 'Yes, I think I am going to go out.'

'Out?' Betty snorts derisively. '*Out?* And where in the name of all that is good and holy do you think you're going to go? I never heard such nonsense, whatever is the matter with you, Joyce? Sit down. There's nowhere you've any need to be going. You already had yourself a little jolly when you left me *alone,* remember, and me feeling simply awful. Selfish, *un-be-lievable*. There's not a reason I can think of for you to go *out*. There's nothing we need. Not one single thing.'

Joyce walks over to the window, which is dressed in a prim little blouse of Roman blind; pink, cut from a much larger one that framed the sea view from the picture window in the living room of their old house.

The rain has stopped. Under a stark, low sun, long shadows bend across the yards as if tidying the day away; evening folding over the light hours, packing them up.

In other houses, lamps are blinking on, tables are being set for evening meals. Three places, four places at the table, maybe even more. Dishes are being laid down to be casually scooped at, conversed across, tales to be told of days spent in separate places, anecdotes to be listened to, laughed at, picked over and commiserated with.

In other houses, there are cots and playpens, jotters and homework. There are dolls to be played with instead of looked at and not touched, toy cars abandoned mid-crash on the rug, school uniforms being laundered, pyjamas being readied for warm, sleepy bodies, baths being run, bedtime books being chosen or the same ones read again, pictures pointed at by two sets of hands, a small one following a large, new words sounded out hesitantly.

In other houses, competent people are arriving home, tired from having done their jobs, satisfied or stressed after days spent in hospitals and hairdressers, docks, warehouses, shops and schools, gladdened by the sight of their spouses and belongings, of pets that rush happily to greet them instead of attempting to escape.

In other houses, the occupants look forward to evening hours which pass too fast instead of too slowly; a glass of wine, and then perhaps another, might as well finish the bottle now; ice cream mined casually from the tub, running jokes called back and embellished, a new episode of an old show on in the background and spoken over.

In other houses, welcome-home kisses gain heat and turn into something so urgent that meals dry up in the oven, pots boil over.

'Do you ever look out the window, Mum,' Joyce asks Betty, 'and think that the world doesn't really look so much like the world but more like a poem about the world instead?'

Betty sits up straight in her chair, clears her throat, sniffs. 'Joyce,' she says very cautiously, 'I don't quite get your meaning. I don't think, Joyce, this is ... what's this funny talk, Joycey? *Out* and *this*, this *funny talk*, are you feeling tired ... dear?'

'I'm feeling, I'm thinking, just ... Mum?'

'Joycey?' Betty's voice is strained, she works the crochet blanket through her fingers.

Words swarm up from every place inside Joyce, stinging until her throat feels packed, bruised.

'Joycey?'

Now.

Now, like ripping off a plaster or nothing will ever change.

Now, or I will never let the dinner burn while I tumble into bed with my clothes half off or speak with my mouth full or drink a glass of wine in front of a soap opera or eat ice cream straight out of the tub.

'I think ... I think, maybe, I think maybe I might have met someone. I *have* met someone.'

Betty's face freezes like a clock stopped mid-chime and for a moment, only for as long as it takes for her heart to beat, Joyce thinks that Betty's features will soften into her smiling Miss Halcyon face – shock becoming delight as the revelation of success takes hold. Then she will say, *How wonderful, how clever, tell me everything you sly little minx*, the way she did when Joyce told her she'd agreed to have dinner with Paul all those years ago, after Betty had manoeuvred her to do so.

But no.

No.

Of course not.

'Who someone? Where someone, *how*?' Betty demands.

Her expression is hard and sharp; catastrophic as shards of an heirloom smashed by a curious child.

'When have you had . . . at the shops, Joyce? What kind of, Joyce, what's this talk?' Betty throws the blanket off, fruity blotches of anger redden her neck and cheeks.

The blanket hunches on the floor like a sleeping baby.

Joyce picks it up and folds it neatly over the arm of her mother's chair without speaking, without looking at Betty.

'Joyce? *Joyce*. What is the meaning . . . you have got yourself in a muddle here, lady. I think you'll find there isn't anyone, Joyce, what is the meaning? I ask you. What kind of, Joyce? No. Joyce. Joyce?'

'Stop saying my bloody name.'

Joyce's name doesn't feel like it means anything any more, her head does not feel as if it is attached to her body. She feels like a person on one of their programmes: a stranger doing things she never will, a stranger living a life unlike hers.

'His name is Martin and I met him at the club, and he is a wonderful man. A kind and wonderful man.'

'Martin? Joyce! At the club, Joyce? Is this a prank, Joycey? Is this meant to be some kind of joke, Joyce? Because it's not very funny. How could you possibly have met? When? You couldn't. I'd have noticed. I feel sick, I could faint. However could you have? You were never out of my sight. I'd have noticed. Oh, my heart, Joyce, my head hurts. I don't feel well at all.'

'I *was* out of your sight. You were intent on Angus Stirrup and I went to the bar and I met Martin. I don't want to sneak about and I don't want to lie. I am forty-six years old and I have met a man and I want to invite him round for tea.'

Betty's voice is a gull's raw yawp abrading the air.

'*Deceit!* The absolute barefaced deceit, Joyce! After everything I've done, everything I've sacrificed. Sneaking around. How long has this been going on? What is wrong with this man that he ... what is wrong with you? I can't believe, I simply *cannot* believe, there has been a mistake, hasn't there? Joyce, hasn't there? *Joyce.*'

Joyce pats the blanket, smooths it out.

'No mistake,' she says breezily.

'How could you? We go over everything, on club nights, when we get home we go back over *everything*. Together. Everything together.'

Betty clutches her chest like a rotten actress overplaying a minor part. 'Joyce? I feel sick, I could faint, Joyce.'

She wobbles about, one hand grasping a handful of her nightdress, the other against her brow.

'I've got a pain in my head, Joyce, an unbearable pain.'

Betty swoons melodramatically into her chair.

Joyce snorts.

'I'm going to go and put the kettle on and switch the television off and then we can have a talk about this, OK, a sensible talk about it all. I know it's a lot but please, Mum, take some deep breaths while I make us a cup of tea. You are *OK*.'

Betty slips down in her chair. 'My mouth feels all funny, Joyce, and my eyes and—'

Without pause, Joyce walks out of the living room, feeling as if she is rolling between rooms on castors, as if she is not inside her body, as if she has been pumped full of rather marvellous drugs. Thrill and terror sparkle in her heart and gut, her hands shake – the bandaged one and the good – as she drops a teabag into the pot, is careful with the kettle.

It *was* time.

Time for a change.

Everything must change eventually.

Martin *is* wonderful.

And in time her mother will see.

Joyce envisages them all going out together, her and Martin and Betty, maybe to a beauty spot up on the cliffs, picnic in the boot of the car, or perhaps one of the hotels further along the coast, the ones that have *grounds* and *spas* where the three of them will have afternoon tea and glasses of champagne will arrive with the stand of sandwiches and cakes. Perhaps Betty will say to Joyce, as Martin goes to hang up their coats, 'Champagne, Joyce, imagine! How sweet of Martin to arrange for us to have champagne!'

Stifling a smile, Joyce carries the teapot into the living room where Joey drills frantically at the bars of his cage, where the dolls look down disapprovingly and everything is as neat and pink and flouncy as it normally is, except for a patch of carpet at the centre of the room where Betty lies spatchcocked on her back with her nightdress flipped up to her underclothes.

Chapter 21

Just to breathe fresh air, just to leave this frowsty, chaotic room which appears to Lydia as a diagram of how stymied she is, she walks out of the hotel.

A wall of wind comes slapping in off the sea.

I could run. I could wade right into the water and all of this would be over.

She finds herself recalling the recording of *The Lollies Are Legal*, the way it had felt as if they were making something groundbreaking.

How easily the record execs had convinced them that the lesbian Lolita image they were suggesting was edgy and important.

The thought of shocking the world had been thrilling and the snug, smug, valedictory feeling of everything coming into bloom had thrived inside Lydia while the record was being mixed.

On the night of the listening party and launch, Lydia had been dressed in designer clothes: a psychedelic mini-skirt cut about a millimetre below her labia which made her look like a slutty Barbie. Hair in a big beehive with bow-embellished pigtails. Sixties-style make-up, borrowed diamond chandeliers swinging from her earlobes – feeling valuable and precious. Pan beside her dressed the same, both of them ready to take over the world.

Fuelled with champagne and anticipation, everyone sat down to listen to the album. 'Up For It' was already a hit, number two in the charts – only for a couple of weeks, but still – and the room went wild when it came on. A couple of songs later, though, something had begun to feel indefinably wrong. The atmosphere had turned brittle, a bit too hushed, as if people were witnessing something shameful. The jewels in Lydia's ears weighed on her like a lie about to be exposed.

People began to talk over the songs and when the music stopped, most barely noticed, some even failed to conceal their relief. As a smattering of applause sounded through the private members' club like spits of rain, Lydia's humiliation had been complete.

The album was a jalopy. A death trap.

Now, Lydia feels this moment is imbued with the same pitiless, elemental clarity. But the disaster in question is not forty-five minutes of disappointing punk pop – it is Lydia's whole life.

After the billboards went up and the outcry about The Lollies' image began to grip the tabloids, the record company stopped saying *all publicity was good publicity* and started distancing themselves. Their second album was shelved. And Lydia had, in some way, to confront that she had been part of something despicable.

Headlines which read things like LESBIAN LOLITA POP DUO IN BARELY LEGAL BOOBS OUT BILLBOARD SHOCK weren't just harmful to Lydia and Pan, they were extensively, egregiously harmful to lesbians, about whom nobody in the whole wretched process, least of all them, had thought. The whole thing had been a sort of catch-all, tantalising titillation. And it could never be undone.

Sometimes, Lydia googles The Lollies, searches Twitter for mentions of them, finding solace in occasional complimentary tweets.

> Give The Lollies their flowers! Up for It still absolutely slaps and there's actually a couple of bangers on The Lollies Are Legal and at least they wrote their own songs

> Controversial opinion but tbh, The Lollies should have totally been bigger than Spice Girls

But equally, Lydia is mortified by the far greater number which use The Lollies as an example of what a harmful time the late nineties and early aughts were for teenage girls and the queer community.

> Was thinking how my mum brought up that fake lesbian shit about The Lollies back in the day when I tried to come out to her and used it as an example of how I probably just hadn't met the right dude SMH

> Remembering being sixteen and thinking I had to starve myself and dress like a total slut and kiss other girls at parties bcuz all the boys at school fancied those fake gay twats The Lollies.

> Remember the 90s when that shit was "feminism?" LOL

And on those occasions, there's nothing Lydia can do but sit in the discomfort of knowing it's true that Lydia and Pan wrote their own songs and equally true that the image they acquiesced to was part of the callous culture of a damaging time that the majority of people, herself included, had accepted as the status quo for women and queers.

Lydia is slowly coming round to believing she does belong to both groups: women *and* queers. She feels contrite that The Lollies' faux-sapphic marketing hurt strangers in demonstrable, material ways and sad for herself that it left her feeling as if loving other women was only ever a thing she'd performed as a straight woman for the male gaze. That accusation was, after all, absolutely true: Lydia never felt even the slightest stirring attraction towards Pandora, despite the dry snogs they'd performed on camera.

It feels ridiculous to have dismissed the two years she went out with Harriet and the sexual explorations she'd enjoyed with other girls when she was an adolescent.

Two years. Jesus Christ, Lydia went out with Harriet for two years.

And it feels like maybe there is some beautiful, optimistic possibility in this realisation, but it is too sedimented under other sadnesses right now to mean much.

Lydia walks up the street past an empty Chinese takeaway where a young woman leans on the counter beside an algae-furred tank full of tropical fish, one finger skating across her phone screen; past a drunk in dirty joggers with the waistband pulled down and his junk flopped out, pissing in the doorway of the Cash Converters with racist graffiti daubed on the shutter; past two seagulls fighting over regurgitated rice.

Then, there is a sudden deafening bang.

Lydia jumps, a clinch of fear takes her body.

The pissing man looks round, eyes wide.

The woman in the takeaway rushes to the door.

Then there is another bang, followed by a blitzkrieg of fizzles and pops.

The pissing man continues pissing, unruffled.

The woman in the takeaway recedes behind the counter.

Normality resumes in an instant and Lydia realises the sound is only fireworks, although she thinks, perhaps if they were not, if it were instead the sound of violence happening just outside people's purview, even then they'd cling to normality.

That's what people do – hold fast to the little things for dear life, especially when disaster is near. *We'd all still be shopping and ordering pizza if the apocalypse found us here,* Lydia thinks.

When her mind releases the thought, she remembers seeing a poster for the grand opening of some Winter Wonderland affair in the park, including a firework display.

Oh, bloody hell. Christmas. I don't want to be anywhere this Christmas. Everything is just waiting for April when Henry's play opens now. Waiting to have to cash the humiliation cheque Henry is writing her as he drafts his *comedy.* Fuck.

The thought sends Lydia into the supermarket, where she buys a pack of cigarettes.

Starting to smoke again feels like permission to relinquish all sorts of onerous intentions: eat more fruit, read more, drink less, practise yoga, be better at staying in touch with friends.

Lydia goes back to the hotel, puffing all the way, taking perverse delight in how perfectly disgusting each drag feels.

She grinds the cigarette out under her heel and lets herself into the foyer, which smells of new paint and old mould.

A dark shape is shifting behind the dustsheets and for a

second, Lydia – who isn't even superstitious – entertains the notion that she is seeing a ghost.

Then a sight far more haunting and horrific materialises from behind the plastic.

Lol, with her hoodie pulled up over one shoulder, rivulets of bright blood coursing down her arm from a series of livid slashes.

'I hurt myself, Auntie Lydie,' she sobs.

'I'll get your mum,' Lydia makes for the stairs.

'Please don't, *please*. She's so wrecked, Auntie Lyd, and she said ... and she said ... ' Lol's broad back hitches and kicks with wracking sobs.

'OK, OK,' suddenly Lydia is capable: practical and present.

As she bashes open the swing doors to the big, empty industrial kitchen, Lydia calls a minicab and tries not to make it sound too much like summoning an ambulance in case they won't accept the booking, snatching up clean tea towels as she goes.

She wraps the cloth around the bleeding gashes and grips Lol's arm, vice-like, as she walks her out, steering her like a pram onto the prom where the recently strung Christmas lights swing like boats in a storm.

The taxi pulls up and the middle-aged man at the wheel raises his eyebrows when he sees them and hears Lydia say, 'Hospital, please.'

As Lydia and Lol are driven away from the hotel, Joyce sits in the relatives' room in the accident and emergency department, sobbing into her cupped hands.

Joyce did not believe her mother's collapse was real. Not at first.

So many times, Betty has claimed sickness and faintness,

headaches and chest pains, to terminate conversations not to her liking.

And given that Joyce has never challenged or shocked her mother so extremely or penetratingly before, when she walked in and saw Betty on the floor, she initially assumed it was an escalation of existing behaviour.

But then worry had wormed through Joyce, then panic.

'Mum?' Joyce got down onto the floor next to Betty and patted her shoulder.

'Mumma, come on, stop this,' she shook her mother.

'Please Mumma, please, I'm sorry, just talk to me, please?'

By then, Joyce's heart was beating hard and she noticed her mother had had an accident; wetness darkening the gusset of her underpants.

'No, no, no,' Joyce had thrown her body on top of her mother's inert form. 'No, no, no, I'm sorry, I'm so sorry, stupid, stupid, stupid.' And she'd hit herself as hard as she could in the head with a closed fist, then sat there for a while clutching her mother's body and sobbing before realising that any normal person would have called an ambulance by now.

With trembling hands she'd grabbed the telephone, screaming at the operator who kept telling Joyce she needed to calm down, just calm down and tell her what had happened, to whom and where, and was her mother still breathing, did her mother have a pulse and the ambulance was on its way.

And when the paramedics rushed in with their trolley and apparatus and began to work on Betty, Joyce had stood there, hyperventilating, but disgracefully unsure whether she was willing the two women bending over her mother to say that it would all be OK or to say *Sorry, it's too late, she's gone, there is nothing we can do.*

Chapter 22

The harsh fluorescence of the hospital has leached all meaning out of time.

Lol is off being treated. Lydia sits in the waiting area watching the automatic doors parting with slow deference, almost ceremoniously, as people come and go.

Each time they do, Lydia catches a glimpse of a nurse smoking in front of a large photographic window decal of a model dressed as a nurse, declaring the hospital grounds a no-smoking zone. It's a perfect metaphor for something, but she doesn't quite know what.

She keeps taking out her phone to call Pan, then putting it away because Lol was so upset and emphatic about not wanting her to know, not yet anyway.

Lydia still doesn't know what Pan said that triggered Lol to self-harm.

Instinctively, she touches her own thigh through her jeans, right where she knows the row of white tally marks are.

A low moment, a sharp razor after The Lollies imploded.

Assuming she and Pan would pull each other out of the wreckage, Lydia had been devastated when, about a month after Pan had broken up the band, she'd had come home to the flat they shared with her hair dyed chestnut brown and bobbed, no more silver ring in her nose, and announced she was going travelling, delivering the news as a fait accompli.

A nurse with a contemptuous expression calls Lydia through. Lol is lying on a trolley looking doughy and pale. The wound on her arm stitched and dressed.

'Doctor needs to write a discharge note and then you can go home.'

'Will there be . . . is there going to be another appointment?'

Repercussions, Lydia means, or maybe help. She imagines social services coming to the hotel, or mental-health appointments.

'There's no on-call psychiatrist and this young lady seems very sorry. You know it was silly, don't you?'

Lol nods but Lydia says, 'She was distressed. That is not silliness, it is serious.'

The nurse looks at Lydia over the rim of her frameless glasses. They make her eyes appear like little silver fish in a tank. She barely tries to conceal her derision.

'I'd say you need to keep a better eye on her,' she says, waspishly. 'Kids these days with phones – I'd ban them – the internet, very contagious ideas. Teenagers need boundaries.'

Badly boundaried, Lydia's therapist said, back when she could afford one, and it always felt horribly correct. Automatically Lydia would imagine herself as flat, featureless countryside – beige and soggy and low-lying. Marshland or a fen. A place without fences or landmarks.

But no one chooses to be powerless, Lydia always wanted to say.

No one chooses to be hobbled by excess politeness.

No one chooses to let a misplaced sense of responsibility rob them of the ability to say no and ask for what they need.

Being a feebleton chooses you. It's a vocation. Like the priesthood. But Lydia never said that, in case she appeared touchy and resistant; unwilling to accept her faults.

Then she feels disgusted at the alacrity with which she milled the nurse's warning about Lol into navel-gazing about herself. Still, as the nurse walks out, Lydia scowls at her back and gives her the finger. Lol laughs.

On the other side of the wall, Joyce weeps in the waiting area of the MRI department while Martin cuddles her close, rubbing her back in circles like someone drying up a plate with a tea towel. *It will be OK,* he tells her, *whatever happens he will look after her, whatever happens, he's got her now.*

And he's not going anywhere.

A stroke plus a chest infection is what the doctors told Joyce: neither catastrophic with the right care, both treatable, but Joyce couldn't really take it in.

Joyce couldn't hook the words onto any meaning and instead kept obsessing over details. Her mother not having clean underwear, not having her face on or her hair done. Hoping against hope Betty wouldn't make a scene when she woke up and saw Doctor Ekdawi or heard sister Agnieszka's accent.

Everyone kept asking Joyce questions. First paramedics, then doctors and nurses. Treating her like she was a proper person, a capable adult, but Joyce did not know anything. Not even Betty's date of birth.

Joyce had tried to explain that Betty had been Miss Halcyon Holidays in the summer of 1959 or maybe '60, '61 even, when she was probably, oh, about seventeen or eighteen.

The medical staff had tried to conceal their frustration, but Joyce knew it was apparent to everyone: she is someone who cannot keep things right in her head.

Back in the waiting area, spiralling into a panic so intense she was afraid where it would end, she had found Martin's business card in her pocket and knew she had to call him.

Martin had been discombobulated when he answered, but he'd soon understood his role and as he'd spoken soothing words softly, Joyce could hear the jangle of his trouser belt and then his car keys as he readied himself to come and find her.

Why, then, had she thought of Paul, unbuckling, scintillating wants, her ache to be touched?

Vile, inappropriate . . . just . . . what is wrong with you? With me. Stop it.

Joyce's thoughts had carried on careening until Martin arrived and folded her into his arms. He had held her against his anorak, which exhaled the smell of an unfamiliar house: mothballs, fried food and fabric softener.

After that, adequate would have been an overstatement, but at least Joyce had felt more solid. Almost like a person. She'd liked the way the nurses and doctors spoke to Martin and the way he spoke to them. Calm and serious and pleasant.

'I know the drill, don't I?' he'd said when Joyce complimented him. 'Been in and out of this place with Gran. We'll get it sorted Joyce. *We* will get it sorted.'

And even though it had felt, well, a bit illicit, Joyce had kissed Martin on the mouth, standing right outside the room where her mother was being examined. She kissed him with her mother just behind the door and felt a snaking, liquid sensation in her down below which made her grab Martin's jaw.

In the cubicle, now the nurse has left, Lydia probes Lol gently. 'Can I ask . . . you said . . . Pan, your mum said something, and it seemed like, well, that's what, maybe it's why—'

'Not one particular thing, just tonight, she made a comment. A crack.'

Lydia nods in disconsolate recognition.

She takes Lol's hand in both of her own, shuts it like a pearl in a shell and says, 'Not the worst thing, just the latest thing, the one thing too many, is that what you mean?'

'See,' Lol looks at her with an admiration which is almost like wonder, 'you always understand, Auntie Lydie. You're a good queer elder.'

Despite what she'd been thinking earlier, reflexively Lydia disowns the idea. 'I just loved Harriet, Lol. She's the only other woman I've ever really, you know, done anything with.'

'But would you go out with another girl or like a non-binary person or a trans person or . . .'

Yes.

Lydia realises the answer *is* yes and an emphatic one, so says it.

'Yes.'

Which, at that moment, feels a bit like unsealing a room in her house whose door she bricked up years ago, or like a more profound, pronounced version of what she'd felt when she'd played 'Who Knows Where the Time Goes?' on Lol's guitar. Returning something to herself that she'd made disappear, like palming a coin and forgetting where she'd put it.

She cannot quite take in the sleight of hand she has pulled on herself.

Magic is only magic if you choose to let the deception escape your attention. You must disconnect the moment from its context. That is what brings the trick into being.

The thought sharply vomits up the incident with the magician, behind the scenes at the TV taping, but in this recollection, the details are different: closer to the actuality of what occurred.

After he had squeezed her breasts, *she* had been the one who said, 'Just a bit of fun.'

Not him.

Then Pan had come back into the room and he had pulled up his sleeves and said, 'Show you a little trick, love?' Winking over at Lydia.

Maybe she even winked back as he asked Pan, 'There's nothing in my hands, is there, darling?'

And a moment later there had been something in his hands. The alarm on Pan's face.

Fuck.

She and Pan need to talk.

'Auntie Lydie? You believe I'm pan, don't you, that that's a *thing* and . . . that I am who I say I am?'

It takes Lydia a second to catch on that Lol is using pan to mean pansexual, not her mother.

'Look, I don't often feel like I know *anything* but, lately, I think I've learned that one of the most important things in life is knowing the difference between the feelings you have to claim for yourself and the feelings you must refuse to let other people force you to claim. Like, think of it as if you were at the baggage carousel in an airport and your own suitcase comes out, but at the same time, so does another identical one.

'And imagine someone else tries to give you the identical one and you know it's not yours. You pick it up and it's far too heavy, too heavy to hold, and you even tell them *This isn't mine*, but they insist it is.'

Lol nods, serious and pleased; Lydia can see the words working on her and is encouraged.

211

'Maybe they're really mean, or older and in authority, so you are scared and intimidated. Or maybe they're really nice but they make you feel like you would upset them if you contradicted them, so you heave it out of the airport, this suitcase that weighs more than you can easily lift, and which is packed with things that are no use to you, leaving the other one behind. The one you knew was yours, full of your own comfortable stuff, clothes that fit you, wishing you had just said *no*, wishing you'd spoken up for what you knew all along, grabbed your own suitcase and taken it home instead of being persuaded to take the one that didn't belong to you.'

It strikes Lydia that this analogy is as true and useful and new to her as it is to Lol, born of unabashed earnestness where archness used to reside. That in the past she would have cracked a joke at Pan's expense or proffered some forgettable platitude.

'Always trust that you know your own suitcase when you see it, Lol, and always pick it up and walk away with it no matter who tries to tell you you're wrong.

'You can trust yourself, Lol. You can believe yourself, you can claim yourself as you know yourself to be. Actually, I'm pretty sure you have already and I will always love and support you, whoever that turns out to be. Do you know what I mean? Does that make sense?'

Lol beams, 'It really does, thank you, and Auntie Lydie?'

Lydia's eyes are brimming with tears at having said the words to Lol she has needed so badly to hear herself, and she thinks that whatever Lol says now will set her sobbing uncontrollably.

She leans forward on the creaky plastic chair, 'Yes, sweetheart?'

'I'm hungry, is there anywhere to get a snack?'

Lydia laughs, 'Of course.'

She walks out into the corridor to find a vending machine and heads back towards the waiting area, following a middle-aged couple, holding hands, not talking. The woman's dark curly hair and long black trench coat an uneasy reminder of Lydia's photograph.

Her husband in his grey anorak and slacks strikes Lydia as one of those men who washes his car weekly even if it isn't dirty, who constantly tiddly-pom-poms tunelessly under his breath and has a transport-based hobby: train spotting, plane spotting, a model railway layout. He is one of those men who appear always to have been middle-aged.

Lydia's imagining that he has a shed like her father's – tools neatly pegged up on a board inside their own outlines – and thinking it's high time she gave her parents a call when the woman stops and wobbles on her heels like a toy.

The man looks stricken by her discomfort. He fusses and clucks and points to a row of chairs bolted into the wall.

Lydia overtakes them, catches the woman's eye as she walks past, and smiles at her.

The woman looks startled. She shrinks in behind her husband like a nervous child who does not know how to behave in front of adults. The kind of child Lydia had been. It makes her feel tender towards the stranger.

She sees the vending machine and takes out her purse. Annoyingly, she only has a fiver, which the machine doesn't take.

Thinking the anorak man looks like just the sort of grown-up Boy Scout to carry a little coin purse specifically for such situations – again much like her dad, who does exactly that – Lydia turns round to head back and ask. As she does, she sees the woman spreading her arms to remove her coat, making her long black curls sway.

It hits Lydia like an uppercut and sends her reeling: it's her. *It is her.*

That fiercely fucks-free moment Lydia captured and released into the ether to breed a few days ago was only that: a moment.

An anomalous one.

Or perhaps, in Lydia's desperate need to believe that there was a way of living that was an afterwards rather than an after*math,* some grace and glory in the mere act of survival, she had misunderstood it completely.

As Lydia watches Joyce crumple into the chair, observing her servile conduct as she listens to Martin telling her to take some deep breaths, put her head between her knees if she feels faint, Lydia understands that she has stolen something from this woman, or foisted something upon her for which she bears no responsibility, and at a terrible time in her life.

Lydia's legs feel like they can't hold her weight; she has to pause.

Joyce looks down the corridor and sees Lydia staring.

They lock eyes momentarily, gazes catch, spark and unhook and Lydia feels as if she has been force-fed something essential about Joyce, about her life. A sort of stripped wretchedness – a profound floundering Joyce emits like a pheromone. One which transmits that in the mere act of looking at Joyce, Lydia has embarrassed her.

In her pocket, Lydia's phone takes on a hefty tonnage and seems to burn, as if sending out an SOS or maybe just like it will burst into flames. The phone with which Lydia glibly snapped the woman's image transformed into an instrument of abuse.

Lydia wants to say something. Sorry?

Yes, Lydia wants to say sorry.

How would she even explain what she has done, how would she start a conversation with a stranger that is essentially reducible to, 'Sorry I took a photo of you without really considering that you're a person and now I know you are, and, funny thing actually, hundreds of thousands of strangers are sending your picture to each other.

'Hundreds of thousands of strangers call you the Zero F G woman, but I can see you have plenty of fucks to give about whatever terrible thing is happening in your life tonight and it's all my fault. Please, forgive me,'

And Christ, Jesus suffering fuck, shitting hell, Lydia really is the Henry here, to even consider it.

Unsought apology, she understands, is for the person doing the apologising, not the person being apologised to. It is handwashing, conscience laundering, an imposition.

Just *Bam!* Cramming dirty sheets into another person so they will hand them back clean and sweet smelling, so you can sleep better in them at night.

Horror restores power to Lydia's legs and she speeds back to the cubicle shaking, to tell Lol that unfortunately the vending machine was out of order.

Chapter 23

Joyce sits on the living room floor, stripped to her undergarments, staring at a slim black address book in her lap, open at the page headed 'C', which contains only one number: a long string of digits, a foreign country code.

Joyce has been sitting this way for some time, knowing she must dial the number, unable to do it, feeling the lack of stable foundations.

In the hospital, Joyce had sat by Betty's bed, having shooed Martin away to wait in the canteen, worried her mother would wake up and see him.

Joyce had noticed Martin had an irritating way of singing tunelessly under his breath, the same handful of dissonant notes going nowhere. She had also noticed that in repose, his mouth hung open, making him look, well, if Joyce was being entirely candid, a bit gormless.

Further down the ward, a woman with an immobilised arm and leg, clearly in the later stages of dementia, kept making a great fuss about leaving, though she was clearly incapable of going anywhere.

'Show of herself,' Betty had said when she'd briefly been awake. 'Ridiculous,' slurred out of one side of her mouth, an oxygen tube under her nose. 'Making an absolute show of herself. She ought to be in the batty-boo hatch, that one. She's obviously wrong in the head.'

'I don't think she feels very well,' Joyce had replied.

Half of Betty's face had a slack, melted appearance, but she'd still managed to look reproving.

'I don't feel very well listening to her fucking racket,' she snapped.

The F-word hit Joyce like a backhand across the cheek.

Her mother never swore.

Betty seemed to Joyce to be blurred at her edges, like a pencil sketch that someone had started erasing. Jabs of familiar complaint and rebuke kept petering off into silences, during which Betty's – Joyce didn't quite know the word, *essence* maybe – seemed to shrink back from her eyes, replaced by a fog like the dense felty wad that often hangs above the sea first thing in the morning.

Betty's simultaneous sameness and difference so uncanny that Joyce feels like she's meeting her mother in nightmare.

When Betty had fallen asleep again, the nurses told Joyce to go home for a while, get some rest, come back later.

Outside the hospital, Martin and Joyce had sat in his parked car, kissing.

'Oh. Joyce. You've got my blood up.' Martin writhed in the driving seat, humping the air next to Joyce with tented trousers and Joyce kept slipping in and out of her body, the car, the kiss, the moment.

Desire clunking on and off like a hazard warning light.

'Can we go back to your place, Joyce?' Martin had panted.

'Oh,' Joyce said, 'I'm ... I'm tired, Martin. I'm just really, completely exhausted. And we'll have lots of chances ... together.'

'Sorry, Joyce.' Martin had rubbed his hand across his head so the sparse hairs around his bald patch stood up like ducky fuzz. 'You must think I'm an animal, poor you, your poor mum.'

'No, of course not,' Joyce had sighed. 'Just it's been a bit of a saga, hasn't it?'

'Poor, Joyce,' Martin had taken Joyce's hand, squeezed it, gazed at her earnestly. 'But Martin's here now.'

Squeamishness had cantered up Joyce's spine and down into the place below her waistband.

'You're lovely, Martin,' she'd said. 'You are such a nice, *nice* man. Can we go now, please? Would you mind awfully taking me home?'

'I'll take you anywhere you want to go, Joyce.'

Romantic, romantic, he is so, this is so, *romantic*, Joyce had insisted to her scrambled emotions as Martin had started the car.

'Shall I pick you up later? We can go back and see Mum. And then maybe . . .'

'Maybe?'

'Dinner. Spot of dinner then . . .'

Joyce had patted Martin's leg.

'Let's see what happens, shall we?'

'Of course, Joyce.'

Joyce had watched the coast road stream by outside. The day had been so clear that the sea looked like a sheet of glass, a huge cruise liner on the horizon had appeared like a paper cut-out in a puppet theatre.

Joyce's head felt very far away. She'd been unable to believe that the boat was full of people going to other places or coming back from them. She felt as though the world ended at the edge of town, as if she and Martin inside the car were a diorama contained in a snow-globe.

'Have you ever been on a cruise?' she'd asked Martin when he stopped the car outside the flat.

'Oh, no. Love to though. Imagine! One day, you know, we could, if you wanted, Joyce. I've got a nice little nest egg saved up and I haven't really had anyone to do nice things with. Work, work, work, save, save, save. So now I've got you, now we've got each other, we could spend a bit, you know, on . . . I don't know – whatever made you happy, really. You deserve nice things, Joycey.'

Joycey. Just like her mother says.

'You're so kind, Martin.'

They'd kissed chastely and after Joyce got out of the car, while she'd been climbing the stairs to the flat, she'd tried to imagine telling someone, Shandy at the club maybe, 'Oh yes, Martin and I are heading off on a cruise.' But the idea had remained flat, emptily unreal, sailing away without her like the distant ship she'd seen.

When Joyce unlocked the door, a sad smell rushed to greet her – old food and airlessness.

She had peered into the living room and seen it as if she'd only been a visitor. Jaded furniture, doilies and gonks and dolls crowding every surface.

A load of old rubbish.

'Hey, girls,' Joyce had called out the dolls, feeling unaccountably whimsical. 'Busy day?'

She'd high kicked her court shoe into the air, then shucked off the other and left them both where they'd landed: one on the telephone table, one halfway through the door into the living room.

All right there, Joycey? Having fun? the voice in her head had piped up. *Where's your mum?*

Shut up.

219

Have a nice time with sexy Martin, did you?

Shut up.

You've got my blood up, Joyce. The voice had done a spiteful impression of Martin's slightly nasal speech.

Shut up.

And Joyce didn't know why, other than that she'd been gripped by a sort of childish, transgressive urge, but she'd gone to sit in her mother's chair and started to stroke herself. First through her underwear, then she'd pushed up her skirt and slid a hand inside them.

Once in a while, she has, she does. Sometimes, in the bath, Joyce will get all hazy in the head and have the feeling for it, the instinct. She hadn't known how, before Paul. He had shown her the way with his own hands.

Joyce's fingers had gained speed. She'd let herself remember Paul as she'd lain in his car, her body screaming for him to do things she'd had no idea were possible. The first time it happened she thought she might die.

Then the reality of her situation had thudded into her head. Pulling her wet fingers away, she'd been overcome by self-disgust.

Dirty, she'd told herself, *you're dirty and you're wrong in the head.*

Get it together, Joyce, she'd commanded, *you're going to have to take charge.*

She'd flinched from the thought but had nonetheless gone to the bedroom and opened her mother's bedside drawer, where she'd withdrawn papers she'd seen Betty stash there. The mail that arrived addressed to Betty and which Joyce was forbidden from opening.

Joyce had scanned them, needles of cold becoming prickles of heat. She'd thought she understood their *circumstances* but the numbers read only in a handful of thousands.

Joyce had been incapable of stacking it up in needs and goods – foodstuffs and cleaning products, electricity bills, face cream and hair dye – but she understood it was not an amount of money equal to the years she and her mother have left to live, no matter how frugally.

Don't worry, Joycey – a sneer – *hunky Martin is going to look after you now.*

Smeared in sticky humidity, breathing rapidly, she'd told herself there were benefits – the ones written about daily in her mother's newspaper, ones people seemed to live on quite handsomely. Big tellies, fancy mobile phones. Oh, her mother would never countenance the shame, but Joyce realised that there was no point trying to predict what her mother might think or say any more.

Bit of a predicament, eh, Joycey?

'Shut up,' she'd replied aloud to the voice.

There must be help, she'd thought.

She could go to the job centre, the benefits office. They're there to help, she'd tried to reassure herself, and she'd been momentarily sure they would be glad to deal with a nice respectable lady like Joyce, matching shoes and bag, well-spoken and polite. It is their job, after all, to help, to explain what to do to people who are having trouble with their *circumstances*. Or she could get a job, Joyce had tried to tell herself.

Better start working on your CV then, Joyce, got a postage stamp handy? the head voice had sniggered.

Perhaps there was another account, another bank book. Joyce had taken down her mother's red vinyl suitcase from the top of the wardrobe.

It had fallen on Joyce's head and showered her with dust. The thump had felt humiliating and her temperature kept rising until she'd become so hot, just intolerably boiling. She'd grabbed her dress by the scruff and swiped it over her head, then thrown it on the ground and kicked it.

Then she caught sight of herself in the vanity mirror. Her stupid old body and her horrible, raddled, red-cheeked face; tan tights like a pensioner, foundation garments designed to hold everything in place and nip desire in the bud and her hair dyed far too black. Self-loathing had ballooned inside Joyce. Poisonous fumes that built and burned, and Joyce had opened her mouth and spewed out guttural raging noise until the people downstairs banged the ceiling with a broom handle.

Then, panting, staring at the carpet, Joyce noticed that among the things which had flown out of the burst-open suitcase – knitted booties, family photographs from The Palace days – was a small black book.

A very poised, methodical state had come upon Joyce, who picked it up on autopilot and flicked through to the section marked 'C', certainty congealing in the pit of her stomach. There wasn't a name, just a number.

Just the number Joyce has been staring at for heaven knows how long.

She hoists herself onto all fours and picks up the telephone.

She keys in the digits.

It begins to ring, the long bleats of elsewhere.

A female voice answers chirpily, 'Las Palmas Scottish Beach Bar, can I help you?'

Joyce's voice is stuck inside her throat as she listens to the background hubbub of music and laughter, clinking glasses.

'Hello?'

'Is ... can I speak ... is ... Chick there, can I speak to Chick, please?'

'Sure, one minute.' Joyce hears the muffled voice brightly call out, 'Chickie, love, it's someone for you.'

Shuffling as the receiver is handed over, Joyce is eerily devoid of feeling.

'Hiya.'

The greeting gusts out on a long-term smoker's wheeze.

'Daddy?'

Feathery breath marks out long seconds on either end of the line and it feels like Joyce hangs suspended over the moment, all the time in the world to observe the happy holiday noise the telephone imports into the shabby little living room.

'Daddy, it's me, it's Joyce.'

The wet pop of a mouth opening, a pause, 'Oh no, sorry pal. Wrong number. You've the wrong number there, sorry.'

And the line goes dead.

Joyce thinks she will remember on her death bed the amiable calm with which her father delivered the lie – the unruffled, companionable way he cut her off.

Joyce dials the number again.

She knows what will happen.

Joyce remembers the plaintive peals of the telephone questing through the rooms of the villa up on the cliffs in the months before her father disappeared, the bristle in the atmosphere, the stiffening in her parents' relationship, the silent electric consensus they'd arrived at without speaking, as they'd allowed the telephone to go on ringing. The palpable relief when, eventually, it stopped.

The telephone rings and rings and then someone picks up, says nothing and hangs up.

Joyce dials the number again and this time the phone rings and rings and no one answers until finally, Joyce understands that no one is going to and drops the handset back onto the cradle.

223

She keeps waiting to start being recognisably *Joyce* about this; for her mystifying dispassion to give way to agitation.

Joyce's wooden fortitude reminds her of Betty's, the day they'd first come to the flat and stepped into the dingy shoebox hall, doors open, displaying four equally dispiriting rooms.

Joyce had been unable to stop herself exclaiming, 'Oh, but we can't live here, Mum – look at it. It's so poky. It's just *awful.*'

With brittle grace, Betty had taken Joyce firmly by the arm. 'Now you look here, lady,' she'd said. 'When you're up against it, you just have to get on. You do what you need to do. You don't spoil yourself crying, you don't waste time on tears, there aren't going to be any scenes.'

Then Betty had reached into the shopping bag under her arm and pulled out two aprons, 'Get yourself into this pinny, madam, and get cleaning. We do what need to do, Joyce. *We do what we need to do.*'

Her mother's bloodless pragmatism directs Joyce to her feet, to the hall where she picks up her coat and feels for the business card in the pocket. She takes it out and goes back to the living room, where she rolls her shoulders, takes a deep breath and dials Martin's number. And as another phone begins to ring, Joyce casts an eye over the dolls, their pursed lips lending them an air of judgement.

'Don't you look at me like that,' she says to them. 'We do what we need to do.'

Chapter 24

Chickie came.

Chickie came back. Her darling Chickie, dear Chickie-doty who saved her. But now he's gone again.

Maybe it was not him, but someone who reminded her instead, after all. It's all gone strange.

Confusing.

She's having a hard time thinking. Saints preserve us, she's being more like Joycey than herself today.

Poor clueless Joyce, without a scrap of the sense you'd expect a person to be born with. She's been a life's work all right, a labour of love has Joyce.

Where is she?

Who?

Joyce.

Just like Joyce, Betty is having a hard time keeping things right in her head, sore head; blinding boom disjointing her thoughts, which are alternately jerky and slothful. It's not very nice, not nice at all – very complicated, very tiring.

Betty is so tired, she'd like a little nap, thank you, but that mad, daft cow in the bed a few along keeps making a racket, making a show of herself, a real show, but Betty is tired. Too tired to have a word.

You'd think someone would put a stop to her nonsense, one of the nurses or a doctor.

Normally she'd take the matter in hand herself, she's very diplomatic, but Betty is indisposed today, feeling peaky, exhausted actually, and she follows the feeling off into a drowse, or a memory, something confusing and comforting: Chickie-doty, her Chickie-doty.

In her bed in the hospital, Betty slides backwards through the years or maybe the memory steps forward to fold her up in it; unwomaned, girled again, seventeen.

Seventeen and snivelling in nothing but her pretty gingham swimsuit.

Someone is approaching.

'You all right there?'

She is not.

Betty is not all right.

She cowers in shadows cast by the thick bushes that screen the swimming pool of the Halcyon Holiday Camp from the rows of chalets behind. Musky night air is thick and warm as an eiderdown, but Betty cannot stop shivering.

Gentle music floats out of the Hawaiian ballroom.

The swimming pool filter purrs. Gold and silver threads cast by streetlamps weave a lamé of light on top of the turquoise water, where a discarded rubber ring glides silently in circles.

In a nearby chalet, a baby is wailing.

'What's the matter there, doll?'

She recognises the voice as he stashes himself next to Betty; the Scottish accent, the jokey intonation. Chick, the comedian, with a suitcase in his hand.

Betty can feel his body next to her own, humidity escaping his cheap suit.

'Something happen?' he asks.

'Everything,' says Betty. 'Just, *everything*.'

'Know exactly how you feel,' he says. 'Were you there this afternoon?' he asks. 'Did you see?'

She saw. Betty saw *everything* happen to him this afternoon: sweat beading on his upper lip, his reddening cheeks, trembling fingers plucking at his tartan bow tie.

Heard it too: the jeering silence, his hectic, amplified breath, spit clotting loudly in his mouth before the heckling started.

Betty reaches into the darkness for his hand, catches it along with an awkward fistful of leaves. Squeezes: 'No.'

The squeeze returned: 'Aye, ye did.'

Rapturous applause bursts from the Hawaiian ballroom, a flock of gulls pouncing into the sky, torrential rain battering down.

'I was meant to be in ... there,' Betty sobs. 'I was going to be in the ... I was invited to ...'

'You would've won as well. You're prettier than all of them. Much.'

Sweaty hand lets go of her own, travels down, glues itself to the small of Betty's back. Momentary recoil, then, a fizzy frisson of something intimate and illicit that drives Betty's bruised skin into Chick's hand.

She hears his breath catch.

'You're gorgeous, you know? I'm no' just saying it. You'd have won hands down.'

The Miss Halcyon Holidays pageant. The camp host had invited Betty to take part.

'Not a hope,' her father said. 'No daughter of mine is going to be parading herself like a streetwalker.'

'Just a bit of fun, mister. Bit of fun but done tastefully. She's a beauty, this one, a real bobby-dazzler.' The camp host in his checked sports coat winked at Betty, keeping his eyes on her. She felt delicious and devoured when he said, 'There'll be a place for you in the pageant if you change your mind.'

As soon as the host walked away, Betty's father grabbed her arm, hard enough to leave a mark, and pulled her into the King's Head pub, where she and her parents nursed lemonades under the mock olde-worlde beams and brasses, trading flurries of damnation about their fellow holidaymakers.

'The absolute size of that woman, like the Graf Zeppelin, what does she think she looks like in that dress?'

And, 'State of that family. Common, absolutely common as muck and proud of it.'

And, 'Whorish, brazen, not five minutes older than you, Elizabeth, acting like a prostitute and in front of her father too, not that he seems to mind, plastered, and in broad daylight too.'

When they'd arrived at the holiday camp almost a week before, its cheerful mood had made their home, a couple of hours away in the flat fens, seem horribly drab to Betty, who had seldom been elsewhere. She experienced a septic jag of dread at the thought of returning to begin her first job as an office junior in the tractor parts factory where her father was foreman.

But her gloom had ebbed as her father loosened his tie and started whistling while her mother rhapsodised about the nicely appointed chalet, clean paths and charming places to eat and it felt like they were all taking on the bright colours and gaiety of the camp, becoming nicer and cheerier than their home selves.

As the week went on though, it became clear Betty's

parents had brought their home selves along, folded in among the mothball-smelling swimming trunks and evening wear.

The chalet was poky, dim actually.

The meals too heavy, grotesque, far too much.

The music in the ballroom was too strident, their camp-mates raucous and common.

It was also true that there were moments during the early days of the holiday when Betty's parents had been unbuttoned and relaxed, allowing her freedom to roam the camp alone. Holiday spends burning a hole in the pocket of the sundress her mother had spent evenings sewing for her. White cotton patterned with yellow roses, a circle skirt floating on a paper lace petticoat.

Betty had bought potato crisps with a little twist of salt, peppermint rock and ice cream, ate them sitting on a bench, feeling furtive at her mother's imagined voice: 'You've a tendency to get thick-waisted you know, you'll have to watch that, Betty. All the women in our family are cursed with the tendency to get thick-waisted at the slightest crumb. Not attractive being a porky pig.'

Once she silenced the jibes, Betty luxuriated in her rebellion, senses feeling rich and acute; aware of every inch of exposed skin, she hiked her hem, letting sun stroke its way up her legs, cold ice cream beading sweet on her tongue, trickling from the cone down her arm.

Licking her wrist, she felt the sweep of eyes following the sunshine brazenly up from her ankles to the lace of her petticoat.

Cheeky Chick Chuckles. She'd seen his face on a poster on the noticeboard that announced the camp events.

He was big, imposingly so, but wasn't exactly handsome, with carroty hair and pop eyes. And yet, there was something about him, a sort of *edge,* a mischief he radiated which made him seem quite dishy.

Watching Chick watch her, a certainty woke inside Betty.

His Adam's apple bobbed in time with Betty's tongue moving on her own wrist and Betty realised she could play him like a note and then another, that all her mother's dim, elliptical mutterings about boys just wanting to mount Betty like a cow – farmyard rhetoric close at hand since they lived in the countryside – were untrue, or only part of the truth.

The truth recounted with its dangerous magic missing.

And just like that, the gap closed between the rutting Betty had observed in the fields back home and the screen romance she'd seen a handful of times at the picture house in town, and it was as if something had flown into her or been released.

Chick had run a hand over his pomaded hair and strutted over. 'Having a good time?' he asked.

'Very,' Betty pushed the last of her ice cream between her lips.

Chick ran another appraising look up Betty's legs and she felt it travel along her skin like fingers.

'Like your dress, suits you,' his cheeks flushed, 'You . . . uh . . . going to be, I mean, what are you up to later? Because, just,' he'd swallowed hard and run his hand over his orangeade hair again, 'there's dancing later, in the Hawaiian ballroom and, well, I'll probably go, I'm going to . . . go, like if, I dunno, will you be there? Do you think? Later? Will you be there?'

Betty let her fingers tinker with the hem of her dress – feinting to smooth it but lifting it a fraction instead – and watched fascinated as Chick's Adam's apple lifted and sank.

'Oh,' she smiled, 'I suppose. I suppose I *might* be.'

Later, weeks, months, years and even decades later, it

230

would appear to Betty that that moment with Chick, her tongue cold, fingers ice-cream sticky, skin sun-caressed, body alive with newly fluent language which every part of her knew how to speak, was the last completely simple one.

Because in that moment, as if it was its own animal, Betty's hand knew to wander up to the strap of her sundress with the yellow roses, her eyes knew to drop her gaze into her lap then to fly up into Chick's and rest there candidly for a second before her father appeared behind him.

It would always seem to Betty that had she been less languid when her father arrived – or if she had at least possessed the good sense to sit up at once, stand, assume a chaste demeanour, rather than giving her father the frilly little finger wave that she did, while exchanging a 'here comes trouble' glance with Chick – the moment might have passed more lightly and then she would have lived a different life.

After that incident, Betty wasn't allowed out of her parents' sight, not to the dance in the Hawaiian ballroom that evening, or to enjoy the camp alone during the day. The holiday became just as drab as life at home. Worse even, with the camp's pleasures near at hand but off limits, like the tantalus of full decanters her parents kept in the front room.

Somehow it made Betty more determined than ever that she just *had* to compete in the Miss Halcyon competition. Want hardened into need; just one special thing before home and the factory job, where each day would match the one before. Meat-and-two-veg days, crossing the fields to work with her father every morning and evening, church on Sundays.

Next morning she begged.

'Not a hope,' her father repeated, as Betty had tried out different cases and pleas until he put a hand to his belt buckle and her mother said in a breezy voice with only the slightest quavering in it, 'Enough, Elizabeth. Daddy said no, that's *enough* now.'

Betty hadn't mentioned it again, but carefully, over the course of the following days, she pounced on their every criticism of the evening meals and entertainments, seeding the idea that spending their last evening in town would be preferable to the camp.

When the evening came, Betty complained of tummy cramps, invoking the unspeakable spectre of woman's trouble so that her father was very keen for him and Betty's mother to leave her in bed while they went into town.

As soon as they left, Betty had flipped back the covers, applied her mother's make-up to her face, pulled on her red gingham bathing costume and stepped into her cork-heeled sandals. She'd just finished pinning her hair and was turning herself this way and that in front of the mirror, making a film star face and admiring how beautiful and grown-up she looked, when her father had walked in.

'I forgot my wallet, I— Elizabeth, what the bloody hell . . . what in the blue blazes do you think you're—'

Betty had seen the realisation of exactly what she was planning materialise in her father's eyes, yet his expression remained inscrutable, perfectly reposed as he walked towards Betty and thumped her. Once, twice, three times, calmly and brutally about the head as if he was hammering a fence post into the ground.

Betty fell to the floor with her ears ringing and fairy lights jigging across her vision. 'Slut, cheap slut, disgusting,' her father leaned down over her like an ambulance man. For a moment, Betty had thought he was going to help her up, but then he delivered another merciless blow to her face.

'Little liar, disgusting, cheap, bloody slut,' he spat, 'get to bed.' He stormed out and as his footsteps receded down the path, Betty got woozily to her feet and ran out into the night, not knowing where to go or what to do, which was when she'd heard footsteps and plunged her body into the bushes where Chick discovered her.

'That's me,' says Chick.

'That's you, what?' Betty asks.

'Scunnered. I was just on a try-out, an audition week, like. And you seen, I know you said you never but, I know you seen how it went, so that's me, eh?'

'I'm scunnered too.' Betty appropriates Chick's unfamiliar word.

'What happened?'

'My dad. He caught me trying to sneak out to ... and he ... '

A sob rips out of Betty and Chick takes her in his arms.

'Fuckin' arsehole,' Chick says, his breath a warm tickle on Betty's bare skin. 'Das are fuckin' arseholes, darlin', pardon my French. My da's one and all. Speaks with his fists is it, aye?'

Betty nods against Chick's cheap suit.

Chick kisses Betty's shoulder. She pushes her sore skin against the sweet, wet burn of his lips and he pushes his leg between Betty's, puts his hand to her cheek and lifts her chin.

Trembling, Betty presses her lips to Chick's, he kisses her deeply. A kiss of the kind Betty has only seen on the cinema screen – her head fills with music, orchestral strings, and she presses her whole body against Chick, who crushes himself against her before pulling away.

'No like this, darlin'. It's no' right.'

Betty wants clothes, she is ashamed and makes to step out of the bushes, away from Chick.

Gently, he grabs her wrist, 'Hey, no, it's no' that I don't want you, oh I *want you*. When I seen you the other day, I wanted you then. *That's some girl* I thought, but it wouldny be right just now. You're all upset, and I'd be taking advantage and I'm no' that kind of guy.'

He kisses Betty on the top of her head and pulls her in tight to him. Betty feels dizzy with desire and the thrashing her father delivered. But she also feels a vast trust in this stranger, whose honourable conduct is steadying her.

'What will you do?' Betty asks Chick, cheek against his chest.

'I know some boys down the coast. Brothers named McMaster from back home. They're making good, down there, they'll sort us out with something.'

'Us? Do you mean I can come with you?'

Chick laughs, 'I meant me. When I says us, it's just a way of speaking.'

'Oh.' Betty pulls away from him.

'But you could, you know,' he folds her back into his arms, 'if you wanted. If you didn't want to stay with that arsehole da of yours. If you wanted to come with me, then maybes I could mean *us* after all. As in both of us.'

'Not just a way of speaking?'

'Not just a way of speaking.'

'Are you serious?'

'Aye, you seen how I got on trying to be a comedian, so aye, I'm giving it up, I'm a serious man now. Can I tell you a wee secret?'

'Yes please.'

Chick kisses Betty on the top of her head again. He is so much taller than her, he makes her feel dainty and slight in the most thrilling way.

'I think maybe this is fate, like meant to be, you know? Mad, eh? But, see, when I seen you the other day, I thought – sounds nuts now I'm saying it – but I honestly just had this thought and it felt right: I thought, *that's the girl I'm going to marry.*'

It's like a film, Betty thinks, a beautiful romantic film.

'When would we go?'

'What's to hang about for? Me having to get in a square go with your da when he comes back?'

From the Hawaiian ballroom, the strains of Connie Francis pulse through the night air.

The music fills Betty with a shimmering sensation, a reeling, sparkling expansiveness, as if she had inhaled the whole night sky.

This man must be mad, she thinks, or even dangerous. What sort of man just invites you to walk out of your life into the night with him, into the unknown?

People don't just walk out of their lives into another one on a whim. And yet, Betty thinks, she has not chosen the life which waits for her: continuing to live with her parents, listening to the tap drip and the cows low, going to bed in the boxroom off the kitchen at 9 p.m., she and her mother keeping quiet enough, meek enough to stop father's hand from approaching his belt, working in the office at the tractor parts factory until one of the apprentices asks her out, until Betty has gone on enough outings with him for marriage and children and a poky house in the same charmless village to become a foregone conclusion. A colourless, compacted life that now seems intolerable. Impossible.

The song changes key, ascending and making Betty's heart feel too big to fit inside her body, affirming that her life is too small to contain someone capable of such titanic sensations.

'Then let's go,' she says to Chick.

'Serious?'

'Serious.'

Chick and Betty kiss.

The kiss feels to Betty as if it is lifting her off her feet, merging her with the swell of the song's crescendo, with Connie Francis' voice.

'This is mad, doll. I don't even know your name.' Chick breathes heavily against Betty's cheek as they pull apart, as the song ends.

'Eli ... Betty,' she tells him, she always wanted to be Betty instead of Elizabeth, but her parents refused to let her call herself that. Common they said. A slut's name.

Well, who cares what they think now, Betty abandons the extra syllables and smudges her throbbing face into the cheap fabric of Chick's suit.

And in the hospital, Betty wraps her arms round her pillow.

With one side of her mouth, she smiles in her sleep, as inside her brain, blood bubbles and races, breaching its vessel.

A cluster of Betty's synapses shrink and part company, which if visible to the naked eye would look like a small posy withering in timelapse. Or a constellation going dark.

Chapter 25

'Go to bed, love, I'll talk to your mum.'

Lydia kisses Lol's fading blue hair.

Padding into Pan's bedroom, Lydia sees an empty bottle beside the bed.

'Pan,' she says, sitting, gently shaking her shoulder.

Pan sits up blinking, with the knackered look of someone at the end of a bender. Sketchy lines on her face seem more deeply inscribed than usual — inked rather than pencilled. The skin around her eyes looks sore.

Pandora spreads her arms and beckons to Lydia with the tips of her fingers, 'Bring it in, baba, come on.'

Lydia is shocked that Pan doesn't seem angry. Although, she observes through a veil of fatigue, there is never really anything shocking about the conduct of a person as ruled by whims as Pandora.

Lydia submits to Pandora's embrace. A surge of relief as Pandora's smell fills her nostrils: Tom Ford, ethanol.

Pandora kisses the top of Lydia's head. 'Let me see you,' she holds Lydia out to arm's length.

'Jesus,' she says, 'you look like a dead dog's dick.'

'I was at the hospital,' Lydia says gently. 'Lol self-harmed,'

As if electrocuted or scalded, Pan starts to kick the covers off.

'Wait, Pan, please. Just a second. She's OK, she's safe.'

'Why didn't she ... why didn't you ... I'm her *mother*.'

Uncharacteristic tears gleam in Pan's eyes.

'Oh, Pan,' Lydia puts an arm round Pan and Pan allows it. Taking a moment to frame her next words, Lydia feels the muscular but bony solidity of Pan's back under her hand, her scapulars angular as wings.

It feels like no time at all since the teenage sleepovers where they lay on each other's beds designing band logos, writing lyrics, humming tunes; all the times the record company was too stingy to pay for separate rooms or even beds on tour.

'What if,' Lydia inches out cautiously, as if embarking on a tightrope walk, 'what if Lol just is who she says she is?'

'In what way?'

'Any, all. The stuff you're so resistant to – her sexuality, her name, her weight, all the other concerns she has about her identity. I know I'm not her parent or anyone's and I know I haven't been around.'

'You've been a total piece of shit.' Red splotches appear on Pan's cheeks.

'I have. I agree.'

Pan looks wrongfooted and suspicious, but she leaves a silence for Lydia to speak into.

'You're hurting her, Pan. I know you don't mean to and you're worried about her but she's already so full of her own worry, her own pain, that if you pack in more, well, I think she'll find any desperate way to get it out. She'll carry on self-harming.'

'I won't be held hostage, I won't be manipulated, her father's like that.' Typical of Pan that even in the deep seriousness of a

238

conversation like this one, she puts on a pretty offensive French accent, worthy of *'Allo 'Allo!*, to say, *'I can't live without you, Pandora my darling, I'll jump in the Seine if you don't come home.'*

'That's not the same.'

Pan's mouth moves like she's chewing the thought, 'No. Probably not, but honestly, all this pansexual palaver when I'm pretty sure Laurence hasn't even had her first kiss and this "Lol" thing – she's full-on rejecting the name I chose for her, well Alain as well, the fucking arsehole but—'

'Yeah, well, my birth certificate says Karen Cockley, not Lydia Lincoln, and I still love my mum.'

'You're not close to her, just the other day you called her a cunt.'

'Yeah, and that's exactly my point. It's her attitude to my name change and everything she can't easily grasp – so busy telling me who she wishes I was that she's never got to know me. Even so, we might not be close but she's still my mum.'

Lydia thinks sadly of an experiment she once read about, where a scientist gave baby monkeys a cold metal effigy of a mother and they clung to it for comfort regardless.

Then Pan's shoulders start shaking under Lydia's hand, 'Oh, Pan, don't cry.'

Pan hoots, 'I'm not, just – fuck, Lyd, I totally forget your surname was Cockley. It absolutely cracks me up every time I remember.'

'Piss off, you cow,' Lydia laughs too and for a second, everything else falls back and the two of them are teenage best friends, laughing together in one of their bedrooms. But Pan's always used humour to keep dreary things like emotion at a distance. So, capitalising on the warmth of the moment, Lydia pushes on, 'Look, I think what I'm trying to say about Lol is that recently, I've been thinking that life is one of those shape-sorting toys for babies and it feels like all of mine, I've been clashing my shape against an aperture it won't go through. Just in a panic, smashing myself and smashing myself.

'And I think it's time to stop and work out if I need to sculpt the shape of myself so that I fit comfortably or carve out a new gap ... and yes, it's pretty gap year of me and colour me mortified, but maybe that's why I understand what Lol's going through. And it's fucking nightmarish trying to work out who the hell you are at forty-eight, but Lol's sixteen so what if you let her work that stuff out now? What if you don't make her smash herself against the wrong hole?'

Pan gives a dirty laugh and makes an *ooh matron* face.

'You always loved mangling a metaphor, Lyd.'

Grudgingly, Lydia laughs too, but gravity returns immediately, 'I'm serious, Pan. Lol knows who she is. You can't let her or not let her become that person, because she just already is, whether you make it harder for her or easier. I honestly think whichever you choose, you won't change Lol, you'll only change how she feels about you. '

'Oh, Lyd,' Pan shakes her head, 'it's gorgeous, genuinely, how you and Lol have connected this last short while. It's sort of what I hoped for when I made you ... asked you to be her godmother. But it's like, all this stuff – like this *they* stuff Lol brings up every so often. You can't just check out of being a girl because it's hard, because you bleed, because you hurt, because—'

'Oh, fuck that shit, Pan. Let's not reduce being a woman to being a wound. You're the one who always says *Let's not be dreary*. What could be drearier than thinking of our own identity as a collection of sex tripe and gynae problems? What if Lol just isn't going to be a woman?'

'Then what the fuck exactly would she be then, Lydia?'

'Lol. She'd be Lol. Like I said – she already is.'

Lydia waits for the eruption. But it doesn't come.

'I want to see her,' Pan says and gets out of bed.

When she gets to the door she turns and says, 'Come on then, Karen Cockley.'

'Fuck off, Panzer division.'

Lydia follows Pan into Lol's bedroom, where they sit on either side of her.

Lydia will call Lol 'her' until such a time as Lol confirms she needs to be called 'them', if and when the moment comes.

Pan fingers the cuff of Lol's bandage, 'Darling.'

Then she doesn't say anything else. She and Lol put their arms round one another and Lydia says, 'I'll leave you to it. You two need to talk and I need to pack.'

'Where are you going?' asks Pan.

'You said it was time I left.'

'Yeah, well, you were being a cast brass bastard,' Pan says.

'So were you, Mum,' says Lol.

A stinky, meaningful quiet permeates the atmosphere.

That Lydia and Pan each believe the other should apologise, that neither plans to, dawns like a dreadful fart that each intends to blame the other for.

It is Lydia's job, she knows, to make this OK.

Her work is to be a good sport, do the mental gymnastics that will make last night's fight not worth minding about, not worth causing a scene over.

She can feel the teeth of it catching inside her, like a music box starting to play a tinny tune because someone else has wound it, someone else has opened the lid, and Lydia, as usual, is the tatty little ballerina performing plastic pirouettes on command.

'I can't,' Lydia says, sadly, 'I can't.'

'Can't what?' Pandora asks.

'Make everything OK.'

'Everything is fine, Lydie,' Pandora gives an anaemic smile. 'We *are* OK, aren't we, Lydie?'

It's not the things people need you to say that break you, Lydia thinks, it's the things they oblige you not to say that do most damage.

'I don't know.'

'Well, what if you stay and we ... I don't know, make everything OK? Hang out, spend time? I bet Lol would like you to.'

Lol smiles, 'I really would, Auntie Lydie.'

'And you?'

'Oh, of course, you silly bitch. Of course I would. And like, look, Lyd, the way you talk about the past all of a sudden, like you're obsessed, well, I just don't feel the need or see the point in all that fault and blame stuff. And if I'm honest, you're not exactly a good advert for it because it sure as shit does *not* seem to be doing you any good. More like it's eating you alive, but if you need us to ... talk, talk about it we can. I'm not going to pick it over and over but one night, *once*, we can talk about it all and then, please, Lydia, if we do that, can we just leave it?'

Lydia imagines the conversation, the messy mud-wrestle between Pan's perception and her own. As that metaphor materialises, it brings with it the thought that it wouldn't be right to haul Pan's affable view of the past into congruence with Lydia's own gloomy assessment. Especially her intention to bring up the green-room incident with the magician, because even if Pan does remember it as an assault, that's for her to approach in her own time, in her own way; to do whatever's helpful or healing for her. Dredging up deleted memories, and recasting an incident now remembered as innocuous as an abusive one, will only serve Lydia's impulse to atone for her.

Some Henry-triggered, half-familiar question about the difference between realisation and revelation resurges: the hunch that one's arrived at from inside, the other externally imposed.

And Lydia has no desire to enforce on anyone else the unsought retrospect Henry obliged her to engage in.

'Pan,' she says, 'you know that day when you called me, and I was upset and you told me to come here?'

'Yes?' Pan kisses the top of Lol's head in a way that makes Lydia somehow feel like the kiss is for her too.

'Why did you call?'

'I just . . . ' Pan looks at Lydia as if she is the stupidest person she's ever had the misfortune to converse with, 'because even though we're both totally dogshit at staying in touch, and a pair of weird, arsey, touchy fuckers, you're my best friend.

'You popped into my head that day and I realised it had been a stupid amount of time since we'd last spoken and I just thought, for whatever reason, this time I'm going to get straight on and call you. Because I miss you. Or I did. Miss you. But now I don't because you're here. And you're staying, aren't you?'

But Lydia still doesn't know and cannot answer.

Chapter 26

When Joyce walked into the hospital ward and saw her mother's vacant bed, her puzzling stoicism had cleared off as violently as a spooked bird.

'She's not dead. Try and take some deep breaths. I know you've had a shock, but she's not dead. We tried to call you, but you must have already been on your way. Do you really not have a mobile? Is that right? Come on, lovely, try to calm down, she's not dead.'

The nurse pats Joyce's arm and speaks to her softly.

But she remains unable to still the flapping and now the nurse is trying to spoon-feed Joyce something she cannot ingest – something about a second stroke, likely more damaging than the first. How could *that* happen here, in hospital, where people are meant to get better, not worse?

Joyce follows the nurse through a maze of corridors, so uniform and endless that Joyce starts to wonder if she has died and gone to purgatory. The nurse makes small talk about the weather and Joyce blurts, 'She was Miss Halcyon Holidays, you know? My mother. A beauty queen – when she was young, she was a beauty queen and on her wedding day, a stranger, a complete stranger to her this was, asked her to wait a moment outside the church so he could get his camera.'

The nurse looks over her shoulder at Joyce and as if humouring a prattling child, says, 'Oh, lovely, interesting.'

They arrive at a smaller ward where fewer patients are attached to more machines, each person's appearance so altered by apparatus that they seem a species apart.

Betty is in the furthest corner, sedated, Joyce is told by a different nurse; the one who led Joyce here seems to have dematerialised.

'Are those her things?' the nurse asks, gesturing to the small red suitcase in Joyce's hand, filled with fatuous dresses and hair curlers and make-up.

'I think I got it wrong. I didn't quite ... they're her going home things, you see.'

Joyce looks down at her shoes, which pinch her feet, while the nurse says gently that Betty might not be going home for a while and Joyce can bring nighties in the morning.

Joyce hovers by her mother's bed, watching the rise and fall of her chest, turquoise waves of her heartbeat gliding steadily across the black screen of the monitor, while the nurse goes to see if Betty's doctor is free to talk to Joyce.

'Mum,' she says, 'I don't know what to do. I can't keep things right in my head.'

Hollow composure has reoccupied Joyce and she finds herself thinking that this is not reason or resilience; that nothing ever is with her. That stillness and frenzy are only two kinds of panic trading places like a train switching tracks to avoid crashing.

For such a long time, years, decades, and especially recently, all Joyce wanted was for her mother to put a sock in it so that she could talk to herself, and now she is discovering that she has nothing to say and that she does not know how to speak to this version of her mother who cannot reply.

So, when the nurse returns and tells Joyce apologetically that no one is available to talk to her, that the doctor will call in a couple of hours should Joyce want to go back home, she kisses her sedated mother and leaves with a briskness which feels unseemly.

Martin is waiting in the car park, jotting numbers onto a Sudoku puzzle propped on the steering wheel with one hand, scrabbling in a bag of toffees with the other.

'How's Mum?' he asks, as Joyce climbs into the car. 'Want a toffee?'

'Oh, awful, she's had another stroke and no one was free to explain . . . what to expect . . . prognosis, you know?'

Martin untwists a wrapper and pops a toffee into his mouth. 'Tricky having no sense of the road ahead,' he muses, words misshapen by the sweet smacking wetly round his mouth. 'Not knowing's more difficult than dealing with bad news sometimes, I reckon.'

'You shouldn't talk with your mouth full,' Joyce snaps. 'Not nice, not nice at all.'

Martin looks crestfallen, hamsters the toffee into his cheek. 'Sorry Joyce, you're right.'

'No Martin, sorry, I don't know what's got into me, really, I'm sorry. I'll have a toffee too, thanks.'

Joyce shunts the toffee around and spits it discreetly into her hanky as Martin turns the engine on and starts to drive.

As the coast road carries them into town, the Ferris wheel and the rollercoaster appear, contours black against a sunset which is all the plastic colours of childhood toys.

Joyce thinks she has never really been an adult, that it is as if her whole life has been practice for a game that never got going, pocking tennis balls round a dusty court on her own as she'd once done to pass the summers, or sending back the serves her mother spat out like a machine.

Of course, there's someone to play with now. Joyce looks at Martin but the thought rolls through her skull without bouncing, like a ball stranded in the corner of an empty court, then exhaustion overcomes her and she nods off.

Martin wakes her up outside the flat and because she can't imagine what she'll do alone, Joyce invites him in.

Inside, he potters a shallow circle around Betty and Joyce's living room.

His presence makes the massed trinkets appear tawdry to Joyce, their insane abundance sets her tummy tweaking.

'What a collection,' Martin's eyes swivel across the dolls and ornaments; he rubs his big square hand onto the bald spot that makes Joyce feel painfully tender towards him. 'It's like a little museum in here, Joyce.'

'Martin?' Joyce inflects his name with a question.

'Joyce?' he smiles shyly and bites down on his plump bottom lip with teeth the colour of old dominos.

'I hate them, Martin. I absolutely *hate* them. They're Mum's thing, and, you know, I thought they were my thing too but— Now ... what with Mum not being here, I realise that I hate every last one of these dolls and I'd like to open the window and throw them all out. And I hate these stupid dogs.' Joyce points to a pack of china puppies and begins to giggle. 'And those kittens, and I hate doilies and Roman blinds and I hate this little ... *idiot*,' she gestures to Joey, frenetically working the bars with his beak, and Martin laughs too.

'He's a bit, well, not to be rude, Joyce, but I never like caged birds, they make me sad actually. Being frankly honest with you, this chap here is a bit depressing.'

247

'Oh, Martin, thank goodness, honestly, it feels so nice to tell someone. I never have you know, I couldn't say these things to Mum.'

'Course not, Joycey, you're a nice person, and they like their little things, don't they? Got to let people have their little things, enjoy their little things. Gran's got all these what-do-you-call-thems? Brasses, horse brasses, not that they've been near a horse, and all thimbles and bells and that carry on. And it's a bit – I'm not sure what the word is – a bit much being surrounded by someone else's stuff, tastes so to speak, but, yeah, I mean, Gran's life hasn't got loads of pleasure left in it now and she won't be around forever, will she? And you've got to let people have their little things that they enjoy. No point spoiling them.'

'What do you enjoy, Martin?' Joyce asks.

Martin's sweetness, his right-here-now-ness, has sent a smudgy, honey sensation hazing through Joyce's body.

'Birdwatching,' Martin replies, still distracted by the budgie. 'Not very rock and roll, it won't surprise you to find, Joycey. A bit square, nerdy or what have you, but it's just peaceful. You don't think much at all. I just sit with my binocs, looking, and my head gets all nice and empty-like. Nothing in there, just watching for a bit of movement. Not worrying about Gran or the future or regretting anything in the past – just totally right in the minute, so to speak. Not very macho I'm afraid, Joyce, not very sexy.'

Martin looks a bit bilious, but his openness is seductive to Joyce.

'That's lovely, Martin, but I was trying to be ... sort of a bit saucy. Sorry, I'm not very good at this you see.'

Martin blinks and swallows rapidly.

'Oh Joyce, I haven't ... it's been so long. I mean, I'd be

embarrassed to tell you how long and I already feel like I might . . . you know. Oh, bloody hell,' Martin's eyes flit about fish-like, evading Joyce's. 'Like, not remember how to do anything and finish off really quickly. What a brass neck, Joyce, I'm mortified.'

Joyce thinks Martin might cry. His face red and sweaty as hers when she's having one of her *spells*. She laughs, and Martin's skin turns almost purple.

'Oh *Martin*,' she says, 'when exactly do you think I last? You know . . . I mean, look at this place, my life – Mum and I living on top of each other. I couldn't even make a date with you, remember?'

Martin's cheeks pale.

'I've hardly ever anyway,' Joyce continues, 'you know, *done* . . . *it*. In my whole life, I've hardly. I'm not, um, experienced.'

Martin steps towards Joyce and kisses her close-mouthed but ardently and afterwards says, 'Phew, Joyce, you might as well know, there was one, my . . . only person. I had a wife, see? Eons ago and briefly. Childhood sweethearts you might call it. Her parents were very religious, so we rushed . . . far too young. We were hasty and, well, being a young man, brains in the trousers and all that, you don't really know what's love and what's lust. Anyway, disaster would be putting it mildly. She went off with an older man. Very painful that, and then, well . . . 'sakes, look at me, Joyce, I'm not exactly male-model material and I wasn't back then either. Nothing ever really got going and after a while, you get used to living without and you stop putting yourself through it. You have to, otherwise it gets you down. It was getting *me* down anyway, feeling like my whole life consisted of waiting. Cheery stuff this eh, Joycey?'

Martin puts his hands over his face. Joyce pulls them away.

'Martin ... There was this man, long ago, my only, and I can't really keep it right in my head. When I try and remember how it was at the time, it's all scrambled?

'He worked with my dad, business partners sort of. It was complicated between them, messy money stuff, dodgy I think, maybe not very ... legal, but business matters, anyway, that I didn't get. Still don't, truth be told, and I was brought into it ... like a playing piece in a board game. He didn't want me, not really, this man, he just wanted to win against my dad – the money situation – and when he eventually did, that was ... it. Afterwards, well it's all been sort of the same thing, life, a little life, just going along. We've always had our routine, me and Mum; it was what it was. Until now.'

Joyce hears her own account of the past as if it is a radio broadcast, like the Shipping Forecast, a stranger serenely describing weather elsewhere.

'Shabby,' Martin says, shaking his head. 'Makes me cross, the thought of you being mistreated, Joycey, a lovely girl like you.'

His sympathy makes Joyce feel tearful. Kindness can be the most wounding thing of all, she thinks. It confirms you're injured.

'It was just ... oh, I don't know,' Joyce sighs. 'I don't suppose I let myself have my feelings about it. I don't know how to explain, Martin. Just, one minute we had this big house and The Palace, swish cars, fancy togs and the next, it was all gone. Daddy was gone and poor Mummy. Oh, Martin, she was a beauty queen, you know? Miss Halcyon Holidays, someone really special. I've never seen a photo, I'd love to. Love to be able to show Mum now she's ... not herself. I'm afraid she never will be again. It was one thing losing our house, it was one thing losing Daddy, but—'

A sob wavers out of Joyce and Martin clutches her tightly, 'I'll look after you, Joyce. And your mum if needs be. I wasn't kidding when I said I've got a tidy sum saved.'

'You shouldn't tell me about your money, Martin.'

Joyce's previous calculations confront her. She hangs her head, 'You shouldn't have told me you're well off.'

'Bit flash Harry, show off, that. Sorry. I wanted you to know I'd look after you.'

'No, it's just,' Joyce sinks her face into Martin's bobbly pullover, 'I'm penniless, me and Mum are flat broke, so how will you ever know it's not, what do you call it? Cupboard love.'

Martin strokes Joyce's hair, sounding shocked, 'You're not like that, Joyce, I know you're not.'

'How do you know?' she asks, sitting up, scrutinising Martin's pale grey eyes.

'You just see something. You get a glimpse of something about someone that feels so true that you can't help but believe it.'

'Will you make love to me, Martin?' Joyce asks.

'I've never wanted anything more, but it might not be any good.'

'Maybe it's like the first pancake. The first pancake's always rubbish, but you've got to get it out the way.'

Joyce starts peeling Martin's jumper off over his head.

Across the room, the old-style rotary phone on its doily begins to mewl.

The sound plucks Joyce out of Martin's lap, she picks up the receiver and, just like that, the moment is lost. A doctor whose name evaporates from Joyce's brain as soon as he says it is talking about potential cognitive impairments, probable mobility issues, long roads and waiting, assessments, scans and physiotherapy.

Dirty, Joyce's head says, *selfish, dirty, acting like a tramp, like a hussy when your poor mother is sick, terribly sick, not nice, Joyce. Filthy, disgusting. What sort of person lets a man have it off, get his leg over with her in the middle of a crisis? What kind of animal would even entertain the thought? Unbelievable, Joyce, vile, simply vile.*

On the other side of the room, Martin pulls his jumper back on and looks at Joyce with concern.

What sort of a man tries to get his end away with someone like you, Joyce?

What sort of . . . beast . . . would take advantage?

What sort of grubby little man?

Joyce tries to concentrate on what the doctor is saying but she can't stop thinking of how, when she'd got into Martin's car outside the hospital, she'd noticed it smelled and then become aware of the way his nose whistled while he hummed that inane little ditty of his all the way home.

Now Martin sits in Betty's chair and Joyce can see how their life together might be.

And even though Doctor what's-his-name speaks very clearly, scrupulously employing layman's terms that an intelligent child could probably comprehend to explain her mother's prognosis, Joyce feels the old psychological sea fret rolling in and the struggle begins anew to try and keep things right in her head.

Chapter 27

Lydia leaves for London on the first train out of town. Low sun, slow rising, bronzes and liquefies the view from the window, as the starkly black overhead lines merge and part, slicing and sliding through the frail but strengthening light.

The train canters along the tracks beside the coast road, which curlicues around the headland like an unspooled C-90, curving towards town, the hotel.

The thought of Lol and Pan, warm in their beds and fast asleep, creates a cosy sensation.

Lydia fixes her eyes onto the sea, which is yolk yellow, smeared with reflected sun climbing into the navy sky, beginning to bleach it, giving soft shape to the edges of the world, revealing buildings and boats, birds and trees.

Lydia leans against her own reflection, head-to-head, like lying in bed with a love; the gentle doting expressed by converging with another, at some still steady point when the rest of the world spins and spirals.

Sun flames across Lydia's profile, deleting her features and she thinks, *I could be anyone.*

For the first time, that thought is beautiful rather than brutalising; liberating rather than lonely.

An unaccountable surge of something almost like optimism.

When she arrives in London, Lydia is swamped by the vast, undulating eddy of commuters; swallowed into the crowd. Automatically, she begins moving with a hectic vigilance which for so many years appeared the only way to navigate the world, and which she has not missed.

Behind her someone tuts, she turns: an impatient wideboy smelling noisily of aftershave and hangover, jockeying to get past her. The kind of swaggering fuck she's met a million times. Yet something about his apparent lack of singularity overwhelms Lydia with the knowledge that he is just as human as her; that this man and all these strangers in the station are filled with the same immense complexity and history and emotion as Lydia herself. They are all so alive to her and the London-centric sensation of smallness, which for so long felt like painful irrelevance, now feels consoling.

Lydia is glad to merge with the traffic of strangers, each freighted with the cargo of things they have done and that have been done to them. To feel she is part of a vast human tide, rather than all of herself – a pebble being tumbled along in its waves.

She goes to Catford and pauses on the street to listen to the squeaky rubber novelty noise of the parakeets, on the doorstep of the terraced house which she never once called home in all the months she lived there. Lingering to drink in the very London-ness of the sound before she lets herself in.

Katya, the curator who owns the house, is having one of those knee-trembler quickie coffees, gulping it over the sink, wearing a bandage-coloured cocoon dress that looks like some kind of giant collapsed lung.

She barely looks up, bossy nostrils flaring, tugging at the

statement necklace she is wearing, a sort of expensive, chunky geometry set on a cord. 'So then.'

'So.'

It is as though Katya and Lydia never lived together: such close quarters, no intimacy, living the same days in the same rooms without listening to each other or looking at each other properly, neither really hearing nor seeing, occupying a shared space without being present.

It makes Lydia think of Pan's offer to discuss the past despite being reticent to, which seems more generous to her now, even though she's starting to think it's best left alone. Maybe her desire to reach an accord about what she and Pan did and what was done to them isn't a world away from Henry's self-justifying dragging up of old events in the coffee shop.

She and Pan were once two halves of The Lollies: they stood beside each other and did the same things at the same moments, but that doesn't mean they experienced them together, since the same scene viewed from separate angles, even inches apart, can create a mutually exclusive perception of what transpired. So Lydia is truly certain now that the most conciliatory act is to respect Pan's version of events instead of trying to conscript her into Lydia's.

Maybe in memories, people are not taxidermised birds under bell jars, but living ones, migrating, with whole wide skies and separate habitats that they fly away from and return to, flitting from the centre to the edge and back again.

It feels freeing to Lydia: allowing that everyone is an unreliable narrator of their own experiences.

'I'll just pop up and pack then,' Lydia says.

Katya runs her coffee cup under the tap and upends it on the draining board, 'Cool, post your keys back through the letterbox.'

Dithering uneasy silence: Lydia almost says, 'Thank you for having me.'

Then she almost says, 'Fuck you for always making me feel like a guest here while I was paying your mortgage.'

Instead, she wishes Katya all the best, as if signing off a neutral email to a colleague she has literally no opinion of.

Upstairs, in the room, which felt no more like Lydia's than the Flamingo Suite, less so even, there is still a vodka bottle on the bed, blister packs and a note addressed to no one.

The bedclothes cradled the shape of Lydia's body all these weeks. A spectral splat as if she had fallen onto it from a height.

Something about looking into the hollow of her own form makes Lydia realise that she's always imagined living to be like writing a life as if it's a book – the days and years advancing a linear narrative like pages in steady sequence – when now, she's starting to think it's more like making an action painting: everything she ever ran towards and retreated from, every dance step and stumble, every flight and every fall, contained in the map of marks left behind, drawn but not designed, and that if only she can step back far enough in the months ahead, she will be able to really see it, in all its ugliness and beauty, clarity and confusion.

Tugging briskly on the corner of the duvet, Lydia expunges her outline.

Over the next two hours, she folds the clothes that fit her into checked laundrette bags and bins the ones she has relinquished all intentions of fitting back into, alongside ornaments she has no attachment to – bought to personalise rooms which would always feel impersonal.

She takes down her battered box of photographs and clippings, keeps the ones of her and Pan from when The Lollies were starting out. The two of them on stage in the grotty basement pub in the small cathedral city where Lydia's parents still live. When the music belonged to them and they were just teenagers with something to say, songs to sing, and no real desire for stardom. Just best friends improvising a joyous racket.

The press shots and headlines, Lydia tips into the bin: they are out there on the internet, growing ever further from the truth of who Pan and Lydia were then and who they are now.

She labels the bags 'Charity Shop' and 'Rubbish' and leaves them for Katya to dispose of. She'll be livid, Lydia knows, but they are unlikely ever to meet again.

Blundering and burdened, Lydia hefts her remaining belongings to the station. Bulky as the bags are, she recognises that most middle-aged lives need a moving van to be transplanted from one location to the next. The thought is charged, yet mostly she feels a pleasant, empty numbness as she rides the train, as she changes from train to Tube. She is only a faceless body traversing space as she makes her way . . . home?

Yes.

The hotel is home for now. Lydia has chosen it. A family?

Yes.

With Pan and Lol. If family is the daily practice of trying to limit the harms and foster the goods in as many little actions and efforts as possible.

And Lydia does intend that.

She thinks of this as she angles and arches her body away from the man beside her in the cramped carriage, who is determinedly looking away, tensing his own body in a futile attempt not to make contact.

He is one of those studiedly normcore middle-aged boy-men, whose unbothered aesthetic implies effortful insouciance. The thick-framed specs of a *Wire* reader. Artfully unkempt beard, threaded with silvering streaks. Chore coat and beat-up New Balance Expensive earbuds and shit phone. A lot like Henry.

There are so many men who look like Henry in this world: seeing them used to be overwhelming, allostatic overload, a full fight-or-flight experience.

This man makes Lydia feel nothing.

Lydia stares at his hands. Thick fingers and hairy knuckles, the silver peep of his old-school digital watch from beneath the coat cuff.

They are just like Henry's hands, the ones he violated Lydia with even though she said no, and said stop, and then said nothing more, since *it* was already happening.

The same hands which once pulled Lydia back onto the pavement as a car sped towards her when she inattentively stepped into the road while flirting with Henry.

Henry's hands did both of those things.

And both of those things were just as real as each other and both those things are in the past.

Pan was right, Lydia thinks, about fault and blame. They are not doing Lydia any good.

You cannot give someone guilt: you can only hope they take responsibility.

All that baggage Henry had tried to hand to Lydia. Baggage mislabelled with her name that belonged to him. And maybe he will walk away, unburdened by it. But what matters now is that Lydia is finally starting to feel capable of putting down a load that was never hers to carry.

Furtively, she steals a glance at the man's face, which he is trying to turtle into the neck of his hoodie.

Lydia always believed she would know Henry anywhere.

That she'd be able to pick him out of any crowd, no matter how large; that she would always recognise him and experience the survival kick inside, that pounding, palpitating sensation of her self-worth depending on being able to make him *see* her, on being able to make him feel something, anything, because she loved him or because she hated him, because she wanted him to fuck her or because she wanted him to get the fuck away from her.

Except that she did not.

The identikit, Henry-esque man's face resolves into Henry's face as Lydia watches him try to conceal it from her. It *is* Henry, squirming like a maggot on a hook.

And it seems insane, the way only a fortnight ago Henry and Lydia had sat together in The Hotel Duchesse Royale, so recently they were communicating, and now they are standing next to one another, as close together as the few times they shared a bed and—

And there is nothing. Nothing to save. No redemption, no revenge, no reconciliation. Just two people, trying not to look at each other or make physical contact like everyone else in the carriage.

Lydia stands very poised, very erect, flourishing her brittle new dignity like a forged document. Almost believable to herself.

And at the next stop, Henry steps off the train and the doors close. He crumples onto the first bench on the platform.

Henry takes off his glasses.

Henry takes off his hat.

Now he is as blank as a Mr. Potato Head with all the features removed. And as the Tube pulls away, Lydia sees Henry put his face in his shaking hands and understands that this time *he* is frightened and that she is not.

What just happened is almost unfathomable to Lydia. That in all of London – where she doesn't even live any more, having never in all the sixteen years of their intimacy bumped into Henry anywhere – this was the day when they both got onto not just the same train, not just the same carriage, but stood right next to each other. But more than any of that, that Lydia just saw him as a man. Just like all the others, the good ones, the bad, the mediocre and indifferent.

And it doesn't actually need to be divided down lines of gender, she reckons, only by the sort of person who hurts others and the sort of person who does not. People who walk in the world wounds first, inflicting pain on others in the vain hope of lessening their own, and those who choose to heal and to use their most painful experiences to ensure they avoid injuring anyone else.

Enough, thinks Lydia. *Enough.*

And this time it feels as if she really, really means it.

The comma she usually perceives after *enough*, which turns it into *until next time*, shrinks back like a tadpole shedding its tail, finally becoming a full stop, on a sentence in a story, the rest of which is still being written.

Chapter 28

In the hospital, Betty's right eye rolls around in the socket like a marble and on that side of her face, her mouth is down-turned and wet. Her right arm is laid across her lap, heavy and unmoving as a roasting joint, the fingers stuck shut over the palm like the flap on an unopened envelope.

The nurses have put Betty's long hair into a pigtail. She looks unbearably childish.

Joyce starts to remove the elastic but Betty slurs, 'I don't want it,' and pulls her head away.

'You don't like your hair like this,' Joyce tells her. 'You don't look like us, I mean, you don't look like yourself.'

Sometimes Betty knows who Joyce is; sometimes Betty has little spells of herself like sun suddenly burning off fog, and she complains about the food and the nurses, asks when she's going home. Sometimes she even reminds Joyce that Joyce can't keep things right in her head, which is true. Maybe truer than ever.

But often she slips away, stumbles through time, right eye perambulating aimlessly, and asks when Chickie is coming, or even worse smiles brightly and asks Joyce if she is one of the nurses. 'You're doing a lovely job,' she says and smiles with half her face. 'You remind me of someone.'

'Do you remember,' Joyce asks Betty, 'when you were Miss Halcyon?'

'Who's this?' Betty replies. 'Who's Miss Halcyon?'

'You, Mumma.'

Joyce takes her mother's left hand and grips it tightly, she has heard her mother tell this story so many times, she knows it off by heart.

'It was a wonderful summer. Perfect sun, every single day. The days were so long, so warm. You and your mummy and daddy went on a trip to the Halcyon Holiday Camp. Your daddy had such a time keeping the boys away from you. Your daddy was such a smart man, such a rugged man, a real, proper man; you always said, don't get men like your daddy any more. Ties. Hats. Decent. Always wore ties and hats, your daddy. And all the boys. He used to terrorise those boys, such a big man.'

Betty looks like a scared little girl. Her teeth come out and chew at her lip. 'No,' she says, 'I don't like this.'

But Joyce goes on, 'There were flowers everywhere. And the smell of flowers. Roses. It was everywhere. The smell of boys and roses. It was a lovely summer and, of course, they had a Miss Halcyon Holidays competition and, well, from the moment you arrived practically, they were begging you to enter.'

'I don't want this,' Betty shouts. 'I don't want this.'

'Try to remember, Mumma, please,' Joyce clutches Betty's hand, which is trying to worm free.

Sister Kate comes over, 'Everything all right?' she inquires, lightly but with something stern behind it.

'I was just trying to help her remember,' Joyce says, a needy wheedle.

Sister Kate shakes her head, 'Just *be* with her,' she says

262

firmly. 'I know it's hard to accept, but it'll be better for you if you learn to just *be with her*, the version of her in front of you now. It's much more upsetting for both of you if you try to force her to remember things that she, well,' Sister Kate shrugs, 'can't.'

Joyce sits for a while, watches her mother blink and sigh into a drowse, thinking that Sister Kate was pert, rude actually, a rude madam, they seem to let all sorts be nurses these days. And those shapeless uniforms they wear, not nice, not nice at all, not like the little white hats and aprons, the smart dresses they used to have, less professional actually.

Then she catches herself and feels as though Betty is talking to her, or through her, and it is as if her mother's spirit has possessed her, which chills Joyce to her marrow.

'I think I'll pop off, Mumma, leave you to your rest.'

Joyce doesn't risk a kiss in case it wakes Betty. She walks out into the lift, which carries her to the ground floor, where she walks out into a vague afternoon, cars and buildings pearled round the edges with white winter sun, descending towards the sea.

When Joyce reaches the town, she walks by the statue of the Come On In Girl. As she passes it, she wonders what it would be like to have been someone special, someone who strangers might recognise. Then she wonders, only idly and for a second, if The Come On In girl was a real person or just some man's perfect ideal of a girl.

Joyce walks away. She crosses the road and waves to Shandy, who is standing behind the counter of Beauty Box next to a vase of fatigued-looking lilies, with her pen poised over a form of some kind. She is gazing out of the window, across the prom, out to sea where, in the distance, wind turbines perform their smooth, ceaseless semaphore.

Shandy sees Joyce. She waves and smiles, beckons to Joyce and comes out from behind the counter.

'Hi Joyce!'

'Hi,' Joyce says shyly. 'Oh, Shandy, what happened?'

Under thick make-up, a grape-hued shiner refuses to remain concealed. Shandy tries to cover it with her hand. 'Nothing really, clumsy me,' she says. 'Fell over my own feet and banged my face.'

Joyce knows it is a lie.

'You all right, Joyce?' Shandy asks. 'I heard your mum took poorly.'

Joyce is about to ask Shandy how she heard but decides it doesn't matter.

She's learning nothing's private in this town, especially not her family's business. That in spite of Joyce and Betty's circumstances, or in fact because of them, they are still, in a certain way, *somebodies* around here.

'Do you want to come in for a cuppa? I was doing some paperwork, making a few plans.'

'Something nice?'

'Well I'm thinking of ... next year, March,' Shandy's fingers flutter to her bruised face. 'This is just between you, me and the gatepost, Joyce, haven't told my boys yet ... I'm going to be heading off for a while. You can keep a secret, can't you?'

'Of course, where are you going?'

'Working in a salon on one of the cruise ships, with Scotty.'

'Your husband?' Joyce winks at Shandy and Shandy roars with laughter.

'That's the one. You know, Joyce, if you want to go out for a fizz sometime, you could come by at closing time one evening.'

'I will, Shandy,' Joyce beams. 'I'd really like that and, Shandy?'

'Yes, m'love?'

'Do you think maybe you could, maybe soon, if you're not too busy, do you think you could . . . ' Joyce catches up her crispy black curls into her fist, the words won't come and her lower lip has started to tremble.

Shandy puts a hand gently on Joyce's arm, 'Time for a change?'

Joyce looks down at her shoes and nods. She feels a tear bead up and tip over.

'Whenever you're ready, sweetheart,' Shandy tells her, 'there's no rush, I'm not very busy at the mo. As long as it's before next March.'

Joyce nods, surprises herself by reaching out to Shandy for a hug.

Shandy holds Joyce reassuringly, bundled inside her arms like a child. Joyce realises that Betty never held her quite that way.

Betty had her own ways of expressing love and even if it was not always easy, even if it often manifested as criticism or punishment, Joyce will miss it. She already does.

But, she thinks, perhaps the time for mothers is over. Perhaps all children have to become their own parents eventually.

'You take care of yourself,' Shandy says before Joyce walks away.

She is meeting Martin for a meal later, a curry in the Sish Mahal restaurant that her mother always crossed the prom to avoid, wrinkling her nose and wafting her hand in front of her face.

Afterwards, Martin will tell Joyce that he's got a little

surprise for her. He's done a bit of detective work and discovered that the little museum above WHSmith has all the old papers and photographs from the Halcyon Holiday Camp, including every girl who won Miss Halcyon.

The woman who runs the place had only once looked through those all those pictures of all those girls – each of them old women now, the ideas they must have had about themselves back then long ago put to bed.

Certainly, she had long ceased to think about the day, decades before, when she was a girl sitting astride a giant beach-ball, dressed in her new red bathing suit, unaware that a man designing an advertisement for train trips to this town was watching her shift her weight back and forth on top of the ball, opening and closing her legs.

Once Martin tells Joyce, she will well up and dab her eyes with the corner of her napkin. It's so important, somehow, to see her mother in her youth, now she's slipping away. Photographs tell you who people were, and who they are. They always tell the truth.

It will occur to Joyce that no one has taken her photograph for years, and that if anything happened to her, if she walked out onto the prom and got run over by those cars that tear up and down all night, blaring horrid music, the last photograph of her would be from decades ago, in The Palace with Mummy and Daddy. No evidence of the version of her who lived through all the years spent with just her mother in the flat full of dolls. And Joyce will start to cry in earnest.

Martin will promise to take her in the morning.

Snuggling down in his own bed, still smiling at the memory of Joyce's gratitude, he thinks he'll just have a little look on the local Facey B. Maybe he'll watch one of the sexy videos on his phone before he nods off, thinking of Joyce of course, imaging her face over the ones on screen.

On Facebook, he'll see a new post – URGENT JOURNO REQUEST, WHO IS SHE??? – written by a woman who lives in Brixton, who edits a women's magazine and until this week, had never heard of the small seaside town.

He'll see that the photo below the post is of a woman, taken from behind, who very much appears to be Joyce. And he will read the text of the post, over and over, which makes it seem like Joyce is some kind of celebrity on the internet, even though he can't quite make head nor tail of what it's all about.

He'll ask her tomorrow, he supposes, depending on how her mum is.

And for the first time, Martin will realise that he doesn't know the first thing about Joyce, except that he really loves her. Of course, darling Joycey, sweetheart. But he will struggle to go to sleep, wariness gnawing in the pit of his stomach like worry, watching a little bit of every hour tick by on the radio alarm.

On her way to the restaurant, Joyce won't notice Lydia, standing on the opposite side of the prom from the restaurant watching a murmuration of starlings moving as a single body above the water, as the last of the winter sun goes.

When Lydia had dropped her bags at the hotel, she'd gone up to the apartment to find a hand-drawn banner that read 'Welcome Home Lydia'. There was a note on the table: *We've gone to the supermarket to get some food, we're gonna make you a welcome home dinner.*

Lydia pressed the letter to her chest and cried with a ferocity that felt final, like maybe, just maybe, she will never have to cry in quite this way ever again.

Lydia had no idea that at the same moment in the massive Tesco on the outskirts of town, Lol was also crying. Pan had told her off for putting too much chocolate in the trolley and made a point of calling her *Laurence* while chiding her. Now Lol is storming out of the shop while Pan fills it with wine instead.

When the tears dried up, Lydia had gone out for a walk, to see how this small seaside town feels, now that she calls it home.

She'd passed by the statue of the Come On In Girl and had not experienced her customary hatred of it; she simply hoped the girl it was based on never had any idea that it was her.

As she walks away, Lydia thinks of the photograph she took of the woman.

There isn't, Lydia reckons, anything she can do about her, she will probably never see her again and is glad.

That photograph has become something so divorced from Lydia, from the magical moment captured on film, from the poor woman in the hospital.

She can only hope it sinks, the way that things on the internet do, replaced by the image of some other person employed the same way; to symbolise something that bears little or no relation to the way the person lives their days or the way they love their friends, or families or themselves.

She understands however old we grow to be, the past versions of us will always shock us with more youth than we'd understood we still possessed. Our seventy-eight-year-old selves will look back on the forty-eight-year-old version, who already felt so tired, so aged and afraid that the best part of life was beginning to be over, and with a great intensity of treasuring think: if only you had known you were really still only a girl.

She can only hope that something in the spirit of it, the Zero F G, really does reside somewhere inside Joyce, whose name Lydia still doesn't know. That the resilience and self-possession that appear in the photograph are somewhere at the core of her, waiting to spring into life, to take the air.

Now, Lydia is no longer thinking, she is looking to the beauty: watching a vast murmuration of starlings clustering and bunching across a sunset that blushes and blazes.

The birds spread and shimmer, they swirl like a bolt of lace unravelling, they blossom into a single black chrysanthemum of motion that sheds its petals, shattering into individual birds which skim the surface of the sea and curve back into the sky.

Lydia has read that they gather and travel this way to defend themselves against predators. That each small group joins the larger flock and they move together that way, as one large dancing mass, because together they are safer, together they're more forbidding, less vulnerable to attack.

Lydia thinks of Henry. She will never really know what it was that kept her returning to him for so many years, since limerence feels the same as love the way a panic attack and a heart attack share almost identical symptoms.

And although Lydia is starting to disentangle herself from him, she could still vomit on the spot each time she remembers that in April, Henry's play, his comedy, based on his perception of what happened between them, will be open. And every night for weeks, hundreds of people at a time, probably a few of them people Lydia knows, will be packed into the theatre together, filling the darkened air with uproarious laughter, wide mouths and wet eyes Lydia can almost visualise.

But when she tries to summon Henry's face there is only

a palimpsest: an older man, who Lydia believed was capable of better things than the younger incarnation. The younger beset by unhappiness which mistakes carelessness as its right. The older just as negligent; he allowed another error of perception to violate Lydia's consent.

Some men, Lydia realises now, are more skilled in gaining forgiveness than permission.

Some, not all.

Not all men.

Not all people.

Henry cannot rejoin their number. Without telling himself Lydia wanted it. No one ends up splayed without inviting it.

But, Lydia tells herself, *it is no longer your job to try and make Henry understand.*

You never could, and you never will, make Henry understand what he did to you, how he harmed you.

You cannot tell Henry who he is.

You cannot tell him who he is not.

You can no more do those things than you can help a bird to comprehend that it is a bird, if it lacks the apparatus to understand.

Lydia does not know if they can understand but she has seen them peck at their own reflections in mirrors as if they are trying to.

Then she shrugs the thought of Henry off, and amazed and almost unbearably moved, Lydia marvels at the acrobatic loops and curlicues the starlings perform as the light falters, thinking that the birds will never know they are a metaphor or comprehend that they are poetry to her: the birds are simply bodies moving through space, answering the call inside themselves to survive.

And in a few short weeks, it will be 2020, a year that sounds so much like the future, like after and better and forwards and freedom, that Lydia almost thrums with its boundless electric possibilities.

She smiles to herself. This one will be beautiful, this one's for the birds.

Acknowledgements

I have been thinking about how best to use these pages to really *acknowledge* in a meaningful way, so first of all I want to say that a book like this is very much a collaborative endeavour despite only having my name on the cover.

Some of the greatest strengths and best parts of *Birding* are due to the involvement of other brilliant, beautiful people: I'm a good writer and I'm proud of this book, but others are equally due a debt of thanks for improving it enormously.

I would like to thank my amazing agent, Jo Unwin, who is unfailingly warm and wise, fabulously forthright and endlessly encouraging; that dream reader who is able to see all the positives and pitfalls of a book in the becoming and to help it reach its potential.

Infinite love and gratitude are due to my incredible editor, Sarah Castleton, whose editorial eye always places a prism over my writing, lending such light and clarity to every part of the process of bringing a book into being. The kindest caretaker of words and author equally, so many of the best parts of this work only exist because of her – both because of her immense professional skill and her profoundly appreciated friendship.

Many aspects of the creation of this book were difficult. While it is entirely fictional, its taproot is in truth and trauma and some unrelated awful things happened in my life during the editing process, which Sarah made safe, supporting me with a patience and kindness that I will never forget.

Such immense appreciation to Hannah Boursnell, who understood exactly what this book needed and whose generous, clever copyedit was so invigorating and exciting, really reigniting my love and pride in the work with her witty, astute notes and shrewd, sensitive suggestions.

Thank you to all at Corsair and Little, Brown – some of my gratitude is pre-emptive and anticipatory, because there are people there who will be due such huge appreciation for their work in helping this book into the world who I have not yet met, but who will be instrumental to it reaching readers. You will know who you are by then, and I hope I will have told you in every email and interaction how much I appreciate your efforts.

I am choosing not to acknowledge my friends and family individually by name in this book because I have a mortal dread of missing someone out, which makes me feel deeply fortunate that the list of those I feel grateful to is so long.

From every fellow artist and writer who commiserates and stimulates by teasing out the text and dispelling doubt, sharing the strange job of having very real problems with imaginary friends, to every dear person in my life who supports me by letting me rattle on when I'm feeling enthusiastic and consoling me when I'm feeling down, who asks how the book is going, in an already caring act, also validating the still amazing fact that writing is my job and that sometimes it is as difficult and depressing and doubt-inducing as it is easy, exciting and confidence-inspiring: I love, treasure and appreciate you all for the people you are and your presence in my life. Jack most of all — you get a namecheck because without you, my very dearest one of all, none of this would be possible. Thank you for everything, especially all the excellent coffees.

All of which draws attention to the absence in my life which arrived suddenly and shockingly during the editing process. I am sad to say that if I was naming all those precious to me, as I did in the acknowledgements of my last novel, someone who I assumed would always be there no longer is. Ralph Mackenzie, you really were the best of us, and everyone misses you so much. Thank you, Ralph. Thalph.

And since these *are* acknowledgements, and many readers are also writers themselves, I think it is important to say that much of what allows me to create is unearned privilege. I have many layers of privilege: whiteness, cisness, middle-classness, no caring responsibilities. I have secure housing and relative financial stability, right now anyway, and a supportive network of friends and family who help me with my ongoing chronic illnesses. I have enough money to manage my long-term mental health issues through private therapy, which I would often be unable to write without, and I am aware that all of this eases my path through life and work, allowing me time and space to do so, which is not the case for many other people who are equally talented and skilled and I hope maybe there is something useful in declaring it here as a reminder that what lets us bring books into the world is mostly located so far outside of the writing itself.

Last of all I'd like to thank my cats Dennis and Carwash, who are frequently either annoying or absent while I'm writing, but who are also a balm and blessing, and a wonderful, welcome distraction from hurt and human things, as cats generally are.